She reached for the Saint Christopher's medal around his neck. Eliza was about to read the inscription but dropped the medal instead.

Dario undid the silver chain. "I shouldn't be wearing this, Liza. It appears to have upset you."

She looked away from him, unnerved by the intensity in his eyes. "No, it doesn't bother me. You didn't have to do that. I—"

"Shush, baby. We'll talk about it later, okay? I want to make you very happy right now. Nothing else is important to me."

"I am happy, Dario." *Because something is happening to me that hasn't happened since I was a girl,* she reflected. *I'm falling in love.* The sensation was just as exhilarating as it had been before, but she felt a small stab of pain in her midriff when she thought of the reverse process, of falling out of love. No, she wouldn't think about that. Not now.

ABOUT THE AUTHOR

Katherine Coffaro lives in San Francisco with her husband and two children. She holds a Ph.D in biology and has done research in invertebrate immunology. Currently she devotes herself fulltime to her writing career.

Books by Katherine Coffaro

No Other Love

KATHERINE COFFARO

Harlequin Books

TORONTO • NEW YORK • LONDON
AMSTERDAM • PARIS • SYDNEY • HAMBURG
STOCKHOLM • ATHENS • TOKYO • MILAN

Published September 1984

ISBN 0-373-16070-4

Printed in Canada

Chapter One

As in the tricks the mind often plays upon one, the split second it took Eliza Rothcart to recognize the man directing her actors on set three seemed like an eternity. It was Dario Napoli, all right, and he had aged more in the nearly fifteen years than she would have supposed. The ebony hair, the darkest she had ever seen in a person of Italian descent, was now a variegated mixture of black and white with the opposing shades blended evenly except in the long sideburns, which were predominately silver-gray. The bright studio lights lent an unearthly quality to the hair, transmuting it to the colors of a midnight bay reflecting the brilliance of a full moon. Yes, he had aged somewhat prematurely, but well.

As she saw him glance from the script toward her, Eliza stepped into the shadows of a potted dogwood tree that would be used later in the afternoon to film an "outdoor" scene on the daily soap opera. A scarlet branch scraped against the side of her face, and she impatiently brushed it away. It was early fall in the fictitious town of Beacon Heights, just as it was fall in the real city of New York, where they worked in a spacious studio that had once been a factory in Brooklyn. The irony of hiding in the studio that housed her own production company wasn't lost to Eliza, but she didn't want Dario Napoli to see her, not until she had some time to recover from the shock of encountering the man she had loved so intensely and wed so briefly fifteen years ago.

For a period of two or three years after the divorce, she had often fantasized various scenarios in which they would meet again, but such daydreaming had long since been abandoned, and the life that seemed prematurely doomed by early tragedy in the overly romantic imagination of an eighteen-year-old woman had marched quite successfully onward. Eliza hadn't thought about Dario Napoli for a long time, but if she were to weave a scene in which they met again, it would be here, in her domain, on set with Rothcart Productions, Incorporated. Eliza felt safe there.

He stared off into the shadowed regions beyond set three for a few seconds and then turned his attention back to the group on stage. There was a frown on his face, and the members of her company didn't look very happy either. A surge of almost maternal protectiveness toward the cast swept through her. When she had known Dario, he was the most critical and demanding of directors. Of course, that was years ago, but the reports she'd heard about him since then had followed suit. She knew he'd directed several films in Europe before returning to California to work in television, and as far as she knew, he lacked experience in daytime. She instinctively felt he was wrong for a daily drama where perfection was an unattainable goal, and Dario was known for never settling for less than perfection. There simply wasn't enough time or money for the way he wanted to see things done, though what her ensemble did, they did damn well.

Secretly she watched him for a while longer. Casually dressed in navy-blue cords and a gray pullover sweater, he fit in well with the rest of the equally informally attired cast and crew. They didn't do dress rehearsals, and her "doctors" and "lawyers," whether they be male or female, would remain in blue jeans or sweatpants until they took the only taping, one that would have to suffice even if someone forgot a line or the microphone boom was visible on screen. Eliza continued to appraise him silently with great curiosity though with dispassion, almost as if he were an art object in a genre she admired but had never appreciated on a personal level. He presented quite a contrast to the young man she had known so long ago, the one who dressed in three-piece suits and smoked a pipe he didn't like in order to look older.

Dario had been a type of genius in his field, making his own movies at the age of thirteen and starting college a year or so later. At the time she hadn't understood the pressures of such talent and success at an early age, but as the years passed, she'd come to not only understand but to forgive the sins he'd committed against her, to see his behavior from a perspective that can be learned by maturity alone.

It was time to stop playing the part of a fugitive on her own set and find out what Dario was doing there. His back was toward Eliza as she passed by on her way to the office in the rear of the studio, and she concentrated on staring straight ahead. But she couldn't resist looking over her shoulder just as she passed the set. It was a mistake. Dario had turned away from the cast, and his eyes were monitoring her progress to the office.

She wanted to ignore him, not to acknowledge his presence until she knew exactly what he was doing there, but the intensity of his stare held hers. It was impossible to proceed straight ahead without looking back. She saw the confusion in his eyes and nodded, waiting for the inevitable flicker of recognition that was certain to follow. But he neither returned her greeting nor appeared to remember her at all, looking away and then standing to demonstrate a gesture he wanted one of the actors to use in the next scene.

It didn't seem possible that he had forgotten her, but nothing in his gaze indicated otherwise. Mutely she pulled herself from the magnetic force of his presence and continued on her way. Eliza stared at her reflection in the glass door to the office, while pressing her hand against the bronze handle. Had she changed past the point of recognition in fifteen years? Her hair was the same shade of dark brunette it was then, almost black in some lighting; her skin that never needed sun to stay the color of dark honey was unchanged; the eyes, as sparkling and black as ever; her weight nearly the same. Considering everything, she had made the transition from late adolescence to full maturity at the age of thirty-three with only the most rudimentary signs of aging. Still, the image she saw on the glass was not that of the girl Dario had married fifteen years ago. That Eliza seldom wore anything more elaborate than a cotton skirt with a wild geometric print in bold shades of purple and red, topped by a simple white blouse rescued from a local thrift shop, while this Eliza was an executive from head to toe with her upswept hairstyle done by the set stylist and her tailored suit purchased from one of Manhattan's finest shops. No wonder Dario failed to recognize her.

"Good morning," her secretary said when she entered the outer office. "May I get you a cup of coffee, Miss Rothcart?"

Eliza shook her head and smiled. If she had told Beverly Sampson once it was Eliza or Ms. Rothcart, she had told her a hundred times, but apparently old habits are difficult to break, and the middle-aged woman continued to address her in the same way. "Beverly, where is Jared?" She wanted to talk to her producer, and she wanted to do so at once.

"I'm not certain. Somewhere around the studio. Shall I page him?"

"Please do. I want him in my office on the double, if not sooner." She heard the door to the inner office open and pivoted to see Jared Vernon.

"Is this soon enough?" he asked with a blatantly flirtatious wink before stepping over the threshold to kiss Eliza's cheek.

Beverly frowned her disapproval, coughing to make certain anyone who didn't see it heard something from her.

"I need to talk to you, Jared." Eliza grabbed his elbow and propelled him toward her desk in the next room, closing the door behind them.

"All right." He pulled up a chair. "Eliza, why do you keep that stuffed shirt of a secretary of yours around? Did you see the way she looked at us a few minutes ago?"

"How could I miss it? I have a sneaking feeling you deliberately kissed my cheek to provoke her. You know how straight she is. Can't you find some way of amusing yourself besides raising the poor lady's blood pressure?" she reprimanded lightly.

"No, she bugs the hell out of me. Besides that, she hates our soap. Says there's too much sex and violence in it. The old bat watches the competing shows on a portable television during her lunch hour. You should fire her for disloyalty."

"Each to her own, I always say. And Beverly's a damn good secretary."

"Yeah, I suppose," Jared conceded with a frown. He brightened immediately, smiling broadly and sweeping his hand through his long blond hair with a triumphant wave. "By the way, have you seen our new director? I really outdid myself this time in getting him to work with us for a while, if I do say so myself. The man is brilliant! Those films he made in Italy have become classics. I never did understand why he left film to do television, but the cinema's loss may prove to be our gain," he enthused. "I've wanted to work with Dario Napoli ever since I was a kid. I tried to get him to take me on one summer after my first year in college, but he couldn't. I never dreamed I'd be the one to ask him to work for me someday, much less that he would accept!"

"Yes, I saw him," she said, dismayed by her producer's bad case of hero worship. Jared seemed as starstruck as the women ranging in ages from ten to one hundred who frequently waited outside the studio to catch a glimpse of her leading men. "That's exactly what I wanted to speak to you about. Where did he come from?"

Jared was confused by Eliza's failure to share his enthusiasm. "What do you mean, where did he come from? I hired him while you were in Hollywood. You asked me to give top priority to finding a new senior director, remember?"

"Yes, I know that, Jared. What I want to know is why you hired a man with his background. Dario Napoli is all wrong for the job." Jared had been with Eliza for nearly five years, since the beginning of the half-hour daily drama she had created, packaged, and sold to Home Entertainment, Incorporated, a nationwide cable television network. As her producer, he was fully empowered to make hiring decisions that were not legally binding until she signed the contracts, and in the past they had never disagreed on any personnel matters. She had fully expected him to find a new director while she was in Hollywood discussing the creation of another daily drama with ABC, because the former director had left the company on very short notice when she received a higher-paying job offer from NBC.

"Wrong for the job? Why do you say that, Eliza? The man's clearly a genius! Everything he touches turns to gold. I thought you'd be pleased. The HEI people are ecstatic. They're trying to talk him into directing some of their own productions right now. If you can help persuade Napoli to do it, I'm sure we can count on HEI to do something for us."

His final statement made Eliza stop and think. She certainly needed all the goodwill she could build up with HEI. They had been at odds for nearly a year now, fighting over creative control of her show. HEI wanted to put some of their own people in key positions in her company as a step toward that control, and she had adamantly opposed them. It wasn't in the contract and she wasn't about to hire their people. In the original agreement, which still stood, Rothcart Productions owned and packaged *Beyond Tomorrow* and had complete control over what was known as above-line elements or the "talent," the producers, the production assistants, the directors, the actors, and the writers. HEI supplied the below-line facilities, the studio, the sets, cameras, grips, set designers, and costume people, all of whom worked under the auspices of Rothcart Productions.

Since HEI did not have to abide by major network censorship standards as an independent subscription broadcasting company, its representatives had been after Eliza to make the show more sensational, especially in the love scenes. They wanted *Beyond Tomorrow* to begin where the other soaps left off, with the camera fading away as a pair of lovers approached the bed, depicting instead the preliminaries of lovemaking with two barely clothed people. Eliza strongly opposed such a format for her show and hadn't budged an inch, though she had been forced to make other concessions to HEI. Several of her storylines had to be changed to suit the HEI people, and it seemed as if they were never satisfied that enough change had been made. The network people always wanted more, and Eliza dreaded the monthly meetings when they argued over plot and characters in the show. The bottom line was that they controlled the show's yearly budget, and whenever Eliza chose to oppose the HEI executives too much, she was subtly reminded that the purse strings would be drawn tighter the following year if need be.

"He's never done daytime before, Jared, not as far as I know," she said in defense of her position, not adding that the prospect of working with her ex-husband made her slightly uncomfortable, though she couldn't say why at this point in time. She certainly bore him no resentment because of the past, and she certainly wasn't still in love with Dario. Eliza thought only a fool would carry a torch for fifteen years after the way he had betrayed her love, and she was anything but a fool.

"So he's not the first person we've had in here who hasn't worked on a soap. A man with his ability can master anything, Eliza. You know that. I'm surprised you're so negative about having him." Jaret paused and snapped his fingers together, his eyes narrowing with a sudden insight as though he'd just seen the light. "If you're worried that he's a company man for HEI, forget it. No one can tell Dario Napoli what to do. He's his own man and will do what's best for the show."

She shook her head to discount his suspicion. "No, I don't think Dario's a plant for HEI. He has too much class for that. In fact, I'm surprised he'd want to work here at all. I'm more worried about his independence. I need a director who will do what I tell him to do, not follow his artistic impulses. It's going to take some convincing to get me to sign his contract."

Jared frowned and left the seat near her desk. It wasn't like Eliza to be so closed-minded about anything. As long as he had known her, he always found she was willing to give anyone with potential a chance, and if anyone had potential as a director for a daytime drama, it was Dario Napoli. He suspected there was more to her opposition than what she had verbalized, and Jared knew her well enough to call Eliza on it. "It sounds to me like the two of you have met before," he said after a brief pause. "What is he, Eliza? A former lover or perhaps someone who crossed you on a business deal in Hollywood? Both maybe?"

His perceptiveness never ceased to amaze her, but this was one time when Eliza wished her good friend and right-hand man were far less insightful than he was. She could do with more of an insensitive clod at the present. Eliza toyed with the ever mounting pile of papers on her desk and decided to tell him the truth about Dario and herself. He'd find out anyway. Like any other ensemble company, theirs was a closely knit group that enjoyed gossip about other members. Eliza knew they would all find out one way or the other she and Dario were once married, and she didn't even know why making that information public should bother her so much, but it did.

Although she had several friends around the studio besides Jared, Eliza tended to be highly reserved when discussing her personal life. She had never mentioned her disastrous marriage to any of them except one, her best friend and leading lady, Barbara Hesse. But it was time to tell Jared the truth. Chances were excellent someone on the set already knew and would convey the juicy tidbit to him within an hour anyway. Several of her actors had worked in films abroad as well as on nighttime television, and it was likely a few knew Dario personally.

She took a deep breath and stared directly into Jared's eyes. "We were married once, Jared, a long time ago. I don't know if I can work with him."

"You and Dario Napoli? You're kidding! I can't imagine it!" For some reason that struck Jared as highly amusing. He shook his head and laughed, rubbing his beard with one hand.

"Apparently Dario couldn't imagine it either. We were together all of a week." Jared was making her extremely uncomfortable. Eliza stood and poured a cup of coffee. "Want one?" she asked.

"No, thanks. I'm coffeed out. I didn't realize you were ever married, Eliza. I know you considered it with that doctor several times, but you never took the final step. When were you and Napoli married?"

"My first year of college, back in Los Angeles. Dario was a graduate student. He was just finishing up on his master's in film. I took a class he taught, and one thing led to the next, as they say." What she didn't say was that a cup of coffee in Dario's office had led to a romantic dinner in his shabby studio apartment, which eventually took them to his bed, climaxing in a month's whirlwind courtship that ended in a marriage proposal. Eliza was only seventeen when they first met, and her parents adamantly refused to sign the papers necessary for them to marry, but it was only a short wait until her eighteenth birthday when they could marry without parental consent.

"And it only lasted a week? I've heard about things like that happening, but I've always found them rather difficult to believe. You could have at least given it a month," he commented without so much as a faint smile.

Eliza found the statement mildly amusing and grinned.

"Dario received an unexpected offer to direct a film in Italy. It was too good an opportunity to reject, and I was on a scholarship that I'd lose if I didn't complete the semester. I was going to join him as soon as possible, but..." Her voice trailed off in an effort to conceal her tumultuous emotions from Jared. He had always known her as the well-poised executive, and Eliza didn't want to dispel that image now.

Jared sat down and scratched his short amber beard again. "So which one of you met someone else?" he asked bluntly, cutting to the heart of the matter.

"Dario," Eliza said without further explanation. It seemed so far away now that when she thought about the marriage, it was almost as though she were recalling a scene she had written for one of the characters on *Beyond Tomorrow*, rather than an event in her own past. The discovery of his infidelity had once shook her to the roots of her being, but now and for a long time before, Eliza viewed it with the emotional detachment generated by the passage of years that had erased the pain.

Jared took her hand. "I'm sorry, Eliza."

She laughed. "Don't be silly. It happened a long time ago."

"Geez, you haven't had much luck with men, have you? Your husband runs off with someone else when he should be on his honeymoon, and then you and old Leonard never could work things out," Jared said. "You haven't seen him for several months, have you?"

"No, we broke up." She didn't bother to say she was the one who terminated what she saw as a stagnating affair over Leonard James's strong protests.

"That's too bad," he commiserated. "Breakups hurt."

"It could have been worse for both of us," she remarked philosophically. "Let's get back to business here. How is it that Dario came to apply for this job? A man with his credentials must have better offers coming in from everywhere. Those miniseries he wrote and directed for ABC last year broke all viewing records."

"He didn't apply, Eliza. Dario came to New York to teach a course at Columbia. I was on the committee that hired him. When he mentioned he was working on a book about the history of television in America, I persuaded him to get some firsthand experience in daytime. He agreed to do it until we can hire someone more permanently. Of course, my hopes are that he'll get hooked on doing a soap, like you and I are, and stay forever. He never mentioned the two of you had been married or that he knew you at all. Eliza, if you'd just as soon not have him around, I can understand." He winked and made a motion to raise her hand to his lips. "As a matter of fact, it's a delight to see my all-business boss admit to honest, plain old human emotions. I was beginning to think you were an android there for a while."

She snatched her hand from his grasp. "Oh, stow it, Jared! That's what you say about every woman who doesn't fall down at your feet within five minutes! My major objection to Dario's employment here is strictly professional, not personal. The personal aspect is a very minor component."

Jared grinned. "Sure it is. Shall I give him the heave-ho, or do you want to have the satisfaction of doing it? They say revenge is sweet. This would be the perfect opportunity to get back at the infidel."

She rapped her fingers on the desk top in an uneven rhythm and considered the situation. Eliza had gone too far in life to be unsettled by the unexpected appearance of one Dario Napoli. Although she didn't, as of yet anyway, fully understand the ambivalent emotions he engendered, she could handle things. She needed every ace in the hole she could get in dealing with HEI, and the high ratings on her show had recently dropped a few points. Dario's talent was indisputable. He might be the shot in the arm the show needed, and she wouldn't really have to deal directly with him that much. She had trained Jared herself to handle all aspects of production so he could take over at times such as the present when she was concentrating on other projects. "No, don't ask him to leave now. Let's see how he works with the rest of the company."

Jared seemed relieved by her acceptance of his mentor. "I've learned everything I know about directing from his movies and books, Eliza. I'm glad you're willing to give him a chance. What was he like when you knew him?"

She wasn't inclined to discuss the past. "Oh, I don't know," she said evasively. "It was so long ago. He was very young and very ambitious. Everyone's golden boy at the university." And she had loved him with all her heart and soul, and he had betrayed that love.

Jared extended his hands and counted on his fingers. "Let's see, if you were eighteen, he was only twenty-one, wasn't he? I read somewhere he started college at the age of fifteen and left with a master's degree six years later."

"That's right." It was hard to believe they had ever been so young.

"Tell me more about what he was like," Jared persisted.

"I'd prefer not to, Jared. If you have any questions, go ask him. Dario Napoli was always his favorite subject. Right now, I'm far more concerned with how he'll be on the set than what he was like as a budding prodigy fifteen years ago."

He knew he'd be fighting a losing battle to get her to

say anything else about their new director. "Do you really think he's going to be that difficult to work with?" Jared asked instead.

Eliza felt he would be if he was the same Dario Napoli she knew fifteen years ago and had later read about in the trade journals. The man was temperamental and convinced there were only two ways to do something, his way and the wrong way. "Yes, first he's used to film. Most of the things he's done on television have been movies or miniseries, nothing like daytime. And secondly he can be a bastard to work with. I've met a few people over the years who worked with him in Italy. He demands perfection in everything and has his own ideas on what perfection is. He's going to give the actors nervous breakdowns, unless he's changed that is, especially if we go to an hour."

Jared groaned, but she could tell he didn't really mean it. "That bad, huh? I haven't had much opportunity to observe him on the set. Hopefully he's changed since you knew him."

"We'll see," she said. The intercom buzzed and she depressed the button. "What is it?"

"Mr. Napoli to see Miss Rothcart."

Jared stood and excused himself. "I'll let this be a private reunion, okay?"

"It's not necessary." She told Beverly to send him in.

"I have work to do anyway. We're going on location this afternoon to shoot a few scenes in Central Park. Are you coming? The little kids in the cast will be there, and I know how much you love working with them."

"I don't know yet," she said calmly, trying to keep the mounting anxiety from creeping into her voice. Why should she be so nervous? Dario was nothing to her now, a part of her past that had long been forgotten, yet she experienced something strangely akin to panic in the pit of her stomach, now that she was about to confront him directly.

"Well, I'll buy you a hot dog in the park if you decide to go. Please try to make it, will you? A few of our kids, Laura and Joanie mainly, have been difficult to coach lately. They always respond best to you, Eliza. We could really use you."

Their cast included five children, ranging from ages six months to twelve years. Eliza loved each and every one and had willingly spent hours rearranging scenes to accommodate their best interests. Three of the children had been with her for five years and frequently visited her home. She had hoped to be in a position by the time she was thirty to cut back on her professional activities and have a family of her own, but it had never worked out due to the lack of one essential ingredient: the right man to share her life and dreams.

"I'll do my best to be there, and if I'm not, take good care of my kids, okay? I think I'll invite Laura and Joanie out to the house sometime soon and see if I can sort out the problem between them. I'm sure it's just a little professional rivalry. Both of them have pushy mothers," Eliza replied as he left the office, closing the door behind him.

She heard Jared and Dario talking in the next room and returned to her desk. Eliza sat down, folded her hands, and took a few deep breaths to compose herself, to keep the rising anxiety in check. From what she could hear of the conversation outside, Jared was telling Dario she had approved the contract. Since Dario had obviously failed to recognize her, Eliza wondered if Jared would tell Dario who she was. No, that was an absurd thought. How could her close friend possibly say something like, "By the way, did you know Eliza Rothcart is your ex-wife?" No, Jared wouldn't say anything to Dario other than to congratulate him on the contract.

Eliza almost wished Jared would tell him and spare her that split second when Dario would remember who she was. Eliza knew the instant he saw her face to face Dario would know. She wondered what his first words would be and ran a few sample scenarios through her head, smiling wistfully as she realized each was more melodramatic than the previous. You've been writing for soaps too long, old girl, she told herself, closing her eyes and taking another deep breath. This is the *real* world.

Eliza's eyes jerked open when Dario stormed into the room and slammed a script onto her desk.

He sat down on the edge. "Liza, who writes this garbage?" he demanded.

Dario was the only person who had ever called her Liza, dropping the first letter of her name. "I do, and please don't sit on my desk, and please don't call me Liza. The name is Eliza, got it?"

"Sorry on both accounts. May I pull up a chair? Incidentally, Eliza, I'd also like to apologize for not taking time to talk to you earlier when you passed through the set. I was trying to salvage this miserable scene." He found a chair, moved it in close, and straddled it with the back facing Eliza's desk. "Read this dialogue. It's unbelievable."

"I don't have to read it, Dario. I wrote most of it."

"I don't believe it." Dario shook his head, continuing to scan through the script. "You used to write such good stuff when you were in my class at UCLA. This is the worst tripe I've ever encountered in my life, barring none."

"You'll get used to it. Don't forget, Dario, you're taking that scene out of context. Given the long history of the characters, it will seem quite plausible to the viewers." Eliza watched him as he read. If anything, Dario was even more attractive than he'd been when she'd seen him last. Fifteen years ago, he was almost unbecomingly slender. He had since added several pounds to his frame of slightly over six feet, all in the form of lean trim muscle that added girth to the shoulders that weren't nearly so broad when he was younger. She had already noticed how the color of his hair had changed, but it was as unruly then as now, hanging over his collar in back and across his forehead in front as he bent over the pages in his hands.

"You mean this show has an audience?" he asked flatly, still reading the script. "I assumed the network was using it as a tax write-off." He skipped two pages ahead. "Oh, for heaven's sake. No wonder these clowns you call actors out there are so lousy. No half-way self-respecting performer would ever do this."

"Is that what you came in here to tell me, Dario?" she asked dryly. "I don't think we're going to get along very well."

"That remains to be seen." He slid the chair from the front of her desk around to the side. His knees were inches from her lap.

Eliza stood abruptly and, walking backward with her eyes fixated upon his enigmatic expression, came to rest against the wall. She had a very strong intuition that he was going to say something personal now, that he would no longer be content to play the role of a cocky stranger meeting his employer for the first time.

He looked into her eyes for a fraction of a second that seemed interminably long to Eliza before speaking. "When did you find out I'd been hired by your boy wonder Gerald, or whatever his name is?" he asked quietly. His tone was as intimate as though they were old friends who had never fallen upon bad times.

"It's Jared," she corrected brusquely, trying to lend an impersonal air to conversation that was anything but. "I found out when I saw you on the set this morning. When did you realize I was your boss?"

"As soon as I heard your name from Gene Stone." Meeting her again at HEI was not the result of coincidence. He knew where she was in Manhattan and planned to visit her. Dario was overjoyed when Jared had approached him on the subject of working with Eliza's company. The book be damned, he only wanted to see her again after all the years. Maybe this way he could get her out of his system once and for all, prove to himself she was just another woman, that his remembrances of her as the embodiment of total sensuality were only so much romantic nonsense that a man might associate with the first and lost love of his bygone youth.

"So you knew before today? I didn't even think you had recognized me when I walked by the set earlier," she admitted candidly.

Dario looked up from the script. His eyes were still the warmest shade of brown Eliza had ever seen in her life, smooth and rich like good milk chocolate, with the most delightful tiny gold flecks around the pupils. "Forget you? Never, Eliza," he said simply, as though she'd asked him if he remembered the color of grass. "Besides, I knew you had your own company and did daytime."

The honest but rather cryptic response unnerved her, and Eliza glanced away from his pensive stare. "How did you know that?"

"Oh, someone I met a few years ago in Paris mentioned you one night. A guy by the name of Peter Mendoza. Do you remember him?"

"Very well. He was the male lead on the show here three years ago. Pete left more than one broken heart in his wake when he left us to go to Hollywood after a few seasons."

"Did he? Was yours among them, Liza, I mean Eliza?" he asked with a smile in his eyes.

It seemed as if Dario wanted to turn back the clock, to assume a note of easy familiarity with her, and Eliza wasn't ready for it. In many respects he stood before her as a stranger, though they shared a common past, and she didn't relate well to strangers. It took a long time for her to make new friends, and that was with people who had never injured her previously. She honestly didn't know if she and Dario could ever be friends, but if they could, it would take time.

"I was speaking about the fans. Pete had quite a following then. Now, can you get to the point, Dario? You'll find that people around here don't have much time for off-camera chitchat," she remarked coolly, smoothing down the front of her tapered A-line skirt with outstretched palms. When she met Dario's eyes once more, she found his gaze had followed the path of her hands. Eliza turned and looked out the window, affording Dario a rear view of what he had been admiring.

"You look good, Eliza," he murmured in the soft tones a lover would use. "Damn good. If anything, you're even more attractive now than when you were a girl."

She lost her temper and whirled toward him. "Is that what you came to say?" He was straddling the chair again as though it were a mechanical bull, smiling up at her.

"No. I wanted to talk about the teleprompters you have on the sets. They're encouraging shoddy acting techniques, especially for that Dawson fellow. He can't remember two lines without reading them off the prompter. I need eye contact between the characters, especially for the graveyard scene. I can't do a damn thing with that guy staring off into space ninety percent of the time."

Eliza welcomed the fact he'd shifted the conversation back to the show. "If you review the final tapings, Dario, you'll see things appear differently. Rob Dawson only reads from the prompter when the camera is on the other actor in the scene."

"I noticed he tries to do that, but he doesn't always succeed. He was terrible today, Eliza. I say get him to learn his lines or get someone else to play the part," he said flatly.

She was appalled by his regal declaration and complete lack of insight into the mechanics of producing a daily drama. Eliza shook her head in disgust. "You certainly have a lot to learn, Dario! Your statements are so ignorant that I don't know where to begin with you!"

Instead of taking offense at her outburst, Dario smiled and gracefully eased himself from the chair. "Well, I came to learn. Teach me everything you know about daytime drama."

She found herself imprisoned between the window and his body, and involuntarily stepped back toward the sill that was inches behind her. "That would be a formidable effort. I understand you don't plan to be with us very long," Eliza replied. She felt the warmth of his breath on her forehead, and her own body temperature seemed to rise precipitously as the fresh male scent of him drifted to her nostrils. Eliza wanted to fling open the window, but there wasn't enough room to turn without coming into direct physical contact with Dario.

"I wouldn't be so sure about that. This job looks more interesting by the moment." He edged in closer and was about to place his arms on her shoulders when Eliza slid sideways away from the window.

"Then I suggest you go and do it. Did you want to discuss anything other than the teleprompters?" Maintaining her composure under the circumstances presented an ultimate challenge to the cool, poised executive she had learned to be. Eliza had thought countless thoughts about him over the years, but never had she anticipated the possibility of finding him so attractive after all the years and all that had transpired between the two of them.

"Yes. Dinner might be nice. Are you available tonight? We can talk over the good old days."

"Good old days?" she repeated. The precariously balanced control was beginning to break. "I would prefer to forget our old times, Dario." It was all resurfacing, the bitterness, the hurt, the anger, coming to life once more when Eliza thought all was dead and buried, put behind her forever. Perhaps it was simply the shock of seeing Dario on the set that kept her emotions bottled up at first. Then he had seemed more like a dream figure, a character she had created for a scene in a show who didn't actually exist in reality. Now the man stood before her as a flesh and blood memory of the most painful days of her life. And of the most joyous. She didn't care to think about either, not just now. She needed more time to assimilate the events of the morning, and her body had yet to adjust from the coast-to-coast flights to and from Hollywood.

"All of them?" he asked quietly. Dario crossed over to where she stood and tilted her face toward his.

Unwilling to look into his eyes, Eliza stared down at his feet. He was wearing the same kind of high-topped tennis shoes he would have worn years ago on a day when he wasn't trying to impress people with his maturity. "No, but I remember the bad more easily than the good."

The laughter in his eyes dimmed, and he suddenly became very serious. "The human mind does have a tendency to work that way sometimes," Dario conceded in a reflective tone. He let his hand drop from the sides of her face. "Eliza, look, perhaps we had better reconsider this arrangement. I took the job because

I needed the background in daytime for my new book, and because..." God, he hated lying to her.

"Because why?" she urged, driven by an uncontainable curiosity to know all of the reasons why he chose to work with her company.

He walked to the window and stared out at the Brooklyn Bridge. "Because I don't think nearly a day went by in the last fifteen years that I didn't think about you, wonder how you were, what you were doing, if you remarried, had any children. You know, that sort of thing. Perhaps I was wrong. Maybe there's too much bad blood between us and it won't work out. Why don't we tear up the contract and forget it?"

"Why would you say a thing like that, Dario? The past is entirely behind me. I don't mind working with you as long as you can do the job and not upset the flow of things around here. You have to realize this is a closely knit ensemble company. We have our set ways of working together, and a newcomer has to enter cautiously at first."

"Especially a newcomer with a past," he interjected.

"Don't be ridiculous! It was a long time ago, and I don't hold any grudges about the past. I simply don't care to discuss it either. Let's pretend it never happened, okay?" she suggested, wondering if she could indeed put the past aside.

"I can't do that, Eliza. Forget it, I mean. But I can avoid discussing it." He paused briefly. "Can I ask you just one question about what happened? There's something I've never been able to understand."

She hesitated, torn between curiosity and a fear he would ask about something she preferred not to remember. "All right, Dario, just one question. I don't promise to answer it, either."

"Why didn't you answer any of the letters I mailed from Italy?"

She knew he meant the letters he had written after she made the surprise trip to Rome at Christmastime three months after their wedding in Los Angeles. Instead of finding her husband at the hotel where he claimed to reside, she learned he had moved into a posh villa on the outskirts of town with an older woman, the star of the picture he was directing. "I did answer some."

"Stop playing games with me, Eliza. You know I'm referring to the letters I wrote later."

She heard the sharp inhalation of her own breath in the still room. "Because I didn't read them until nearly six years after they were written. My parents kept them from me. When my mother died, my father asked me to go through her things. I came across them then."

His face tightened and paled. "They did what?" he demanded harshly.

"You heard me. They kept the letters."

"Well, my only hope now is that my anguish and intimate thoughts provided your parents with ample thrills," he said bitterly, sitting down on her desk. Those letters contained the most erotic thoughts he'd ever put down on paper.

"They were unopened, Dario, all of them." All twenty-five that made her cry even though they had been written years before and another man had since entered her life.

"Why in the hell did they do it?"

"To protect me. You know they never approved of you and of our marriage. When I told them where you were living in Rome, they were convinced it wouldn't work."

"I wonder why they didn't just throw the damn letters away."

"Good question. I never figured that out either. I think my mother meant to give them to me at some time, but never did." She lapsed into silence, having already told him far more than she ever intended. "Anyway," Eliza continued, "I think they both forgot the letters were in an old, unused desk in the garage." Her hands strayed to the loose bun on her head, and she unnecessarily replaced a few hairpins, nearly dropping one as his gaze cut through her attempts to maintain her composure. This whole thing was going to be far more difficult than she'd ever thought. Before now, it had been relatively easy to play the part of an aloof professional whenever need be. She could do it with men whose attention she didn't wish to encourage, and she could do it in the context of her career. But it was different with Dario.

"Would you have forgiven me had the letters not been kept from you, Liza?"

The urgency in his question surprised Eliza. The man had asked it as though the answer were intensely important to him. "I can't answer that question. I couldn't do it then, and I can't do it now. Dario, all of this is making me uncomfortable. Let's just forget it and talk about the job at hand. You criticized our scripts a while ago. Do you have any better ideas?" she asked politely. "Many of the storylines come from the people who work on the show."

"I really can't concentrate on it now, Eliza. I never was as good as you in concealing my emotions. Even as a kid, you were able to hide your vulnerability from the world. Somehow, meeting you again wasn't the way I had expected it to be," he admitted. "I'd better get back to work. I'll talk to you later." He left the room without saying good-bye.

Chapter Two

As the morning hours dwindled toward noon, Eliza began to regret mentioning the letters to Dario, to regret allowing him to bring up the past at all. She should have been cooler, more aloof, the composed professional woman she had been for a long time. Perhaps she should have taken him up on his offer to resign the position. It was only temporary anyway, and there was no doubt in her mind that any of the Manhattan-based daily dramas would love to have Dario acting as director on their shows.

The man unnerved her to no small degree, and it wasn't solely due to the unpleasant memories dredged from years long gone by. He was evocative of everything she identified as sensuous, from the way he walked with an unconscious swagger and ever so slightly hunched shoulders, both hands in his pockets, to the way he sat on the wrong side of a chair with his long legs extended in front. And his eyes. She had never forgotten their golden brown color, and though the brows were coarser now, grizzled evenly with silver-gray, they didn't begin to diminish the youthful fire in his eyes. Dario still had that devil-may-care spark in his gaze, and Eliza had a premonition he'd grown older without aging in so many ways. He fascinated her just as he had years ago, only as an innocent girl she'd never felt threatened by the allure he held for her.

Until the very moment when he walked into her office and spoke to her for the first time in fifteen years, Eliza considered Dario to have been relegated to the realm of old memories, too old to hurt and haunt any more, spent and exhausted in a surfeit of youthful emotionalism that could never upset the equanimity of her present life. She was wrong, and didn't know what she found so disconcerting, the recollection of the passion she had known for him before, or the fact that she still found him to be a powerfully attractive man, a man for whom she would have felt an instant affinity had he just walked into her office as a total stranger and they had met for the first time. But it wasn't the first time, and she didn't know if she could ever forget the past.

Eliza looked at the stacks of papers on her desk and sighed. It was a day when she wanted to go home and put her head under the covers until dinnertime but knew she couldn't. The trip to Hollywood had run two days overtime, and there was a lot of catching up to do here. Fortunately Rothcart Productions had been entrusted to capable hands, but Eliza liked to keep a tight rein on her operation and began to carefully review the budgetary decisions made by Jared during the previous week. Eliza vetoed his intentions to expand the dressing rooms. There simply wasn't enough money to do that now, and though she desperately wanted to please the cast, she had other priorities. They had to go on location more. The outdoor scenes were highly costly, but Eliza felt they were necessary to keep up the show's high ratings, providing the viewers with a welcome change from the four indoor stage sets that were used most of the time, redone daily so that a hospital lobby on Monday became a shabby hotel room on Tuesday.

Eliza turned her attention to the script for the following month after going over the budget. Although she had written the story outline herself, the dialogue had been filled in by her two cowriters. She was dismayed to see one of the writers had taken such liberties with the long-term story projection as to render the scene unrecognizable from her outline. Eliza picked up her red pen and began to make changes, pausing when there was a knock at the door.

"Come in," she said, wondering why Beverly hadn't buzzed her first on the intercom.

It was Barbara Hesse, one of the show's most popular leading ladies and Eliza's close friend. Although she was on good terms with most of her actors, Eliza frequently found that day-to-day conflicts between her role as executive producer and the desires of the actors impeded deeper friendships in many cases. All too often the cast wanted more than she could give them in the best long-term interests of the show, and this led to problems on a personal level. Barbara had proved to be a delightful exception, and Eliza treasured her.

"Hi. Beverly wasn't at her desk. I hope you don't mind my coming in like this."

Her friend seemed mildly agitated by something, and she picked up on it immediately. "Of course not, you know better than that, Barbara. Have a seat. How are things on set this morning?"

"A hell of a lot better than they were at the line rehearsal this morning. Dario kept trying to make a life's work out of a single scene earlier. We would have been here either until midnight or until everyone deserted the ship, if he hadn't wised up some. Did you give him hell when he came in here to talk to you, Eliza? Fortunately for us, he's been sitting there, hardly saying a word and letting the cast play the scene." Barbara sat down and began to unwind the foam hair curlers to see if her hair was dry. It was still wet. "Damn! It's getting too long to air dry by tape time! What am I going to do?"

Eliza's thoughts were a hundred miles away. The Dario she had known so long ago was far too headstrong and set in his own ways to have been persuaded by their brief conversation to change his directing techniques. The only thing that would make him a more effective director for daytime drama would be time, time to learn for himself that traditional methods simply didn't work because of time and budgetary considerations. He was too upset to concentrate on his job, and Eliza knew that only something of considerable magnitude could take his mind from his work. He had to be thinking about the letters that were kept from her. Eliza wondered if Dario had any intimation whatsoever that she had lied to him, that she would have taken him back had she read those letters when they were written. In some intangible and inexplicable way they had made her understand the incomprehensible, begin to forgive the unforgivable, but she had stumbled upon them too late.

She let her thoughts travel back over the years while Barbara rambled on about her hair. Eliza had never confronted Dario directly in Rome when she went there to surprise him. She had found a mutual friend of theirs from Los Angeles living in the room Dario occupied upon his arrival from California. Nothing of his was there except for a few of her unopened letters on the desk, and she knew from the way their friend told her Dario was living in a villa outside of the city that he wasn't living alone. So she had fled back to her parents' home in Santa Monica, filing for divorce the following week, secretly praying Dario would contact her with some kind of explanation. When she never heard from him, Eliza interpreted his silence to mean Dario was glad she had filed for a divorce, glad to be so easily rid of his young, inexperienced wife.

Six years later, when her mother passed away, Eliza learned of the hell he had gone through, learned of it too late. She was already discussing marriage with Leonard then, and although it wasn't the passionate love affair of the century and they were never to marry, each too intensely involved with his own career, she just couldn't walk out of his life into the past, and of course, the letters were as old to Dario as they were new to her. For all she knew, he could have had a wife and half a dozen kids by then.

"Eliza? Are you okay? I swear you're as spaced out as that new director of yours. What do you think?" Barbara said, waving her hands in front of Eliza's face.

"Think? About what?"

"My hair. It's still wet, and I don't have time to sit under a hair dryer in the morning. What shall I do?"

"Oh, I don't know, Barbara. I guess you can sleep in curlers if you want to."

"I hate to sleep in curlers."

Eliza laughed. "So do I. Why don't you have Gloria restyle your hair. You can always wear it up. Is this what you came to discuss with me, your hair?" Barbara still seemed upset by something, and Eliza knew her hairstyle wasn't capable of inspiring such anxiety in the beautiful woman.

"Oh, no. I just mentioned it. I've been asked to do a promotional tour for the show. I'll be making guest appearances with people from other soaps. We're touring sixteen cities nationwide. *Beyond Tomorrow* is the only cable network show that will be represented, and I think the press will do us good. The only thing is, I need two weeks off," she explained.

Eliza was overjoyed. "Barbara! Congratulations! That's wonderful! I've been after the people in public relations to get our cast into something like that for the last few years, but so far, no go. It's going to take some fancy shifting to rewrite your scenes, but we can do it. When do you have to leave?''

"In February."

"February, huh?" Eliza ran the six-month story projection through her mind, trying to recall what "Sabra Boshe," the character Barbara played, was supposed to be involved in four months down the line. "That's actually a good time, Barbara," she said, recalling Sabra was to marry a character who hadn't even been introduced on the show yet. Good leading men were hard to hang on to, and Eliza and Jared were constantly on the lookout for new ones.

"Really? Am I going to be in the hospital dying from something again?" Barbara asked, unwinding a few more curlers and checking her hair for dampness.

Following the tradition set in major network daytime dramas, the actors didn't know the fates of their characters until they got the scripts, a week or so in advance of taping the show. It was easier for everyone that way and freed the cast and crew from questions by loyal and highly curious fans. "No. Whatever gave you that idea?" Eliza asked.

"Oh, these symptoms I've been having. Am I pregnant?"

"Not unless it's an immaculate conception. Sabra hasn't had a lover on the show for a year, not since Ted died."

"I've known of stranger things to happen on the show. Well, I won't press you any further as to the trials and tribulations of Sabra Boshe. Thanks for the time off. I'm looking forward to the trip."

"Thank you. I'm sure you'll attract even more fans to our show." Eliza hesitated. "Barbara, are you sure that's all you wanted to talk about? You seem kind of on edge." She recalled a phone call from Barbara while she was in Hollywood. Her friend had met the latest in her long line of suitors and was so excited that she'd phoned Eliza in the middle of the night. "What ever happened to the man you mentioned? Still seeing him?"

"Off and on," she said vaguely. "I was worried about approaching you for more time off. I know how you hate to give people time off, and everyone's been asking for it lately," she said unconvincingly.

Eliza was quick to realize her friend was keeping something from her but respected her privacy and dropped the subject. "I'm more than pleased to give you time off to promote the show, Barbara. When most people around here want off, it's to promote their own careers by working on another show. I understand their motivations, of course, but it's hard on *Beyond Tomorrow*." She was compelled to change the topic back to Dario, driven by more than a professional interest in his performance on the set. "You mentioned something about the new director, Dario Napoli. Is he doing better now?"

"Much better, like I said. This morning he was a real bear, but now he seems more laid back. Did you give him hell?" she asked once more.

"Not exactly," Eliza replied evasively, "but I'm glad to hear he's easier to live with now." Eliza's private line rang. "Excuse me," she said to Barbara, reaching for the receiver.

It was Jared, calling from the set. "Eliza, get down here right away. Napoli and Rob Dawson are really getting into it. If you don't do something soon, it wouldn't surprise me a bit to see Dawson break contract and walk off the set by noon."

"Can't you handle this, Jared? I'm busy up here."

"No, short of lowering the boom and hitting Napoli over the head with it, I don't know what to do."

Ordinarily Jared had no difficulty in handling such problems, and Eliza correctly surmised he was too awed by Dario to properly handle the situation. "Okay, I'm on my way."

"Troubles on the set?" Barbara asked.

"Yes, it looks like we spoke too soon about our new director. That was Jared. He said Dario and Rob are on the verge of homicide."

Barbara stood and followed Eliza out the door. "That doesn't surprise me. They were at each other's throats all morning. Dario can't stand the teleprompters. He wants them off set. I heard him tell Rob he was having the stage managers remove them before the final taping."

Eliza arrived on the scene to find her cast sitting around the set in despair while Dario and Rob battled it out off stage near one of the cameras.

When Rob saw her, he rushed to Eliza's side. "Either he goes or I go! That fool not only had the nerve to remove the teleprompter, he's complaining because I left parts of the script lying around the set."

She glanced at Dario who eyed her with interest, no doubt wondering whose side she would take. Eliza knew if she overrode him too much in front of the cast, they'd lose respect for the new director; yet on the other hand, she couldn't have him walking into the studio and upsetting an already hectic schedule his very first day on the job.

"Rob, how much longer are you going to be in that off-Broadway play?" He was currently starring in an evening performance of a play written by one of New York's most promising playwrights, and as a result he had not been able to give sufficient time to memorizing his parts for *Beyond Tomorrow*. Eliza and Jared had allowed him to slide somewhat, to rely too much on either the teleprompter or notes that he scattered around the set in various places because he was too popular with the viewers to write off the show for a month.

"I'm not sure. It's getting such good reviews that we might run twice as long as we originally thought," he said. Rob fiddled with the stethoscope required for his part and glared at Dario. "What in the hell does he think he's doing?" he demanded.

Eliza turned toward the set. It appeared as though Dario had directed the cast to do the scene without Rob, substituting an actor with a walk-on part to ad lib the lines. "I think that orderly has just been promoted to surgeon, Rob," she commented and then grabbed Rob's arm when he made a motion to return to the set. "Leave it be for now. I'll talk to Dario. So you're saying the play might run for another month? I don't know if we can let you coast that long, Rob. You're still getting more fan mail than anyone else here, but a few of our viewers are starting to wonder about you. Did you see the letter from the lady who thinks Dr. Willensky must have a brain tumor? She's trying to explain to herself why you keep blowing the lines and staring helplessly off camera or down at your feet. Either find a way to get your job done here, or we'll have to send the good doctor off to a medical convention somewhere."

"I need the money from both jobs," he grumbled. "I'm almost afraid to leave my wife home at nights in our crumby place." Rob removed the stethoscope from around his neck and slammed it into the palm of his hand.

"Then do the job," Eliza said, "and easy on our props, will you?"

"Am I excused for today?" he asked.

"Yes, see you tomorrow. Go home and learn the part, okay, Rob?"

After he left, Eliza took a seat behind Dario's and watched him direct the scene. His abilities as a director were indisputable, as well as his instinct in selecting a talented extra who replaced his white lab coat with a green surgical gown and finished the scene flawlessly. The lines he used were his own, but they flowed naturally and retained the content of the scene. Of course, he had help from the other members of the ensemble who were used to covering for one another when someone flubbed a line.

"Good work," Dario said, shaking the man's hand when the scene was over.

Eliza shuddered to think of the expense Dario had incurred by his refusal to work with Rob. "Dario, get the assistant director to take over. I have to talk to you."

"All right," he agreed easily. "We were just getting ready to break for the morning and go on location. I'm looking forward to it, Li... Eliza. I've been in Manhattan nearly three weeks and haven't had time to visit Central Park. I'm glad the children in the cast will be in the scene. I love directing little kids. They're great to work with, so spontaneous and full of life. I've always regretted never settling down and raising a brood of my own."

Her head jerked up in response to his last comment, but Eliza forced it from her mind. Now wasn't the time to think of what might have been. She ushered him to a quiet corner of the studio where they stored props. "Dario, I don't want you to go on set to Central Park. You've cost me enough money already this morning, and it costs at least five times as much to work outside the studio. We can't afford any added expenses for a while. You can go and observe if you want, but that's it."

Eliza knew from gossip in the film community that

Dario was used to total control of the films he directed and wouldn't take kindly to her directive. His reputation as a chauvinist who didn't work well with female producers had also preceded him, but then she already knew about that. Dario had always thought women were fine in front of the camera, but the behind-the-scenes intricacies of filmmaking were best left to the men in the profession. She prepared herself to be the brunt of his quick temper.

Instead he seemed very calm, taking her comments in stride. They were standing next to a half set used in restaurant scenes, and Dario motioned for her to sit down. "I'm awfully sorry. What did I do wrong, Eliza?"

She slid into the leather-lined booth, all too aware of the ability he had to make her feel like a visitor in the familiar surroundings, to feel ill at ease as though the sexual attraction he held for her was constantly undermining her role as his employer. No one had ever made her feel quite that way before, though she had dated several of the actors and production people over the years.

"You had that extra take over the extended part. It wasn't in his contract, and now we're going to have to pay him. Rob has already been paid to do the scene, and according to his contract, he continues to get paid whether or not he does anything," she explained, still waiting for Dario to blow up.

He remained calm, smiling his apology. "I knew about that, Eliza, but it can't be more than a few hundred, can it? What's that?"

"On our budget, plenty. Look, Dario, you'll get used to things around here after a while. We just don't have the time and money that add up to the kind of perfection you're demanding of the cast."

"I'm not demanding perfection. Just plain old competency." Dario stretched his long legs under the table, brushing them against hers. "Sorry," he said, seeing how Eliza flinched and pulled herself upright at his accidental touch. Dario sat erect in the booth and folded both arms behind his head.

Her eyes followed the movements of his hands, straying to the unbuttoned shirt where the hair was as speckled with gray as that on his head. "It's okay," she muttered, beginning to feel like a fool for reacting as she had to an inadvertent touch. She forced herself to concentrate on the problems on the set. "Generally Rob is quite competent, more than competent I would say. We've been allowing him to slip a bit because he's doing something off-Broadway and doesn't have enough time for his role."

"Off-Broadway?" Dario repeated. "How far off-Broadway? Across the Hudson River to Hoboken, New Jersey?"

Eliza couldn't help laughing. Dario had always had this way of making her laugh, even in situations that wouldn't have amused anyone else. "No, not quite that far off, but I can see how you may have gotten the impression. He's doing *Harrison's Company*."

"The play by Joyce Ashley?" he asked. "I've heard well of it," he added when Eliza nodded.

"So have I."

"I find it hard to believe Rob Dawson can actually act, though. Gibson is directing, isn't he?"

"Yes, and from what I hear, Rob is doing quite well. So well as a matter of fact that I don't think we'll have him with us anymore once his contract runs out. Why don't you go see for yourself sometime?" she suggested.

Dario removed his hands from behind his head and folded them on the table between them. "Will you go with me?"

It was the second time he had asked her to see him outside the studio, and something kept her from accepting his invitation. Eliza didn't think she was ready to resume a personal relationship with Dario again. "No, I have a great deal of work to catch up with, Dario. I've been out of town for a few weeks, I'm behind here, and I'm negotiating several deals for new shows. The ratings for *Beyond Tomorrow* are slipping just a little, and I have to work on getting them back up a few points."

"My God, Eliza, you sound just like one of those company men we always used to hate. Don't you ever think about anything besides work and ratings?" he asked flatly, staring into her eyes.

She had the definite impression he was criticizing her, teasing her, and flirting with her, all simultaneously. "I happen to enjoy my work very much."

"And what do you do for fun?" he asked, looking deeper into her eyes with a warm humor shining in his own.

She averted her gaze, unnerved by a stare that seemed to see right through her, as though he could read her thoughts. She was fully aware how ridiculous that was. It had been a very long time since she and Dario were the most intimate of friends and lovers. Then, they really could almost read each other's mind, and Eliza chastised herself now for her failure to distinguish between the past and present with him. "None of your business," she snapped. "Dario, as you saw, I had a discussion with Rob. My original understanding was that he wouldn't be involved with the play for more than a month, but it looks as if he may be doing it longer. He has two weeks to go on his contract."

"Two weeks? And you haven't renegotiated?"

"It's a standard daytime contract that allows us to terminate every thirteen weeks, but the actor is under obligation for years, three in Rob's case. Usually the

renewal is routine in his case, but not necessarily this
time around. If his performance doesn't shape up during that time, I'll rewrite his part, or give him a month
off. Meanwhile I'd appreciate it if you could do your
best to get along with the company and keep our budgetary considerations in mind."

"I'll do my best. Does the director have any role in
reshaping the storylines around here?"

"Do you think you can do better?"

"Yes."

"Then write up a few proposals and I'll read them."

"I'll do that." He stood when Eliza did. "I find some
of your storylines so outrageously melodramatic and
otherwise unbelievable."

A few technicians approached the booth, pushing a
backdrop from the hospital scene between them. Dario
grabbed Eliza when she made a motion to step into
their path. "Careful, Liza."

She came to rest against his chest, two things above all
registering upon her senses. Dario had addressed her by
the old familiar term of endearment once more, and she
was crushed against his body, the lean length of it contacting hers nearly from head to foot. Instinctively her
eyes closed briefly, and when she opened them a second
later, she saw around his neck the silver chain of the
Saint Christopher medal she'd given him less than a
week after their marriage, just before he left for Rome.
Had Dario actually worn it all those years? A feeling of
déjà vu besieged her senses, only she knew it was real;
she had been here before, in Dario's arms, and it felt
good. Eliza raised her hand to touch the chain where it
lay over a tanned neck flanked by black-white hair, but
as she did so, Dario freed her from his embrace.

"Careful, Eliza," he repeated, grasping her shoulders
and pushing her gently so that she came to be an arm's
length from his body.

For some reason she had expected him to be as moved as she from the momentary embrace, but clearly Dario was unfazed by it, politely dropping his hands from her shoulders and stepping back as though he had simply performed a courtesy for a stranger who happened to be nearby. He wasn't even looking at her, staring instead at the stage crew who were hastily rearranging the sets required for tomorrow's show.

There was an introspective smile on his face, and Eliza couldn't refrain from asking him what he was thinking. She did so in an oblique manner. "Still worried about the problems with Rob?"

"Rob?" he asked as though he'd never heard the name before. "No, something else."

Eliza was about to ask him what when he volunteered the information.

"I was thinking about some of my criticisms of your storylines for *Beyond Tomorrow*. You know, about when I said how unrealistic and contrived they all seem, and well..." Dario paused and sat back down in the red leather booth.

"Yes," Eliza said quietly, sliding into the seat next to him.

Dario chuckled. "Oh, nothing. It was a silly thought."

"Tell me. Maybe I can use it on the show. We do our best to interject frivolity whenever possible into the script," she said lightly, but it was no joking matter to her. This man and what he thought had suddenly become very important to Eliza.

"Do you? So far, all I've seen is the weeping and wailing and people tearing out their hair at the roots."

"Well, stay tuned."

"I intend to." Dario removed a small cigar from the shirt he wore under his sweater and stood to search for a lighter in his back pocket.

"Dario, please, we have a 'no smoking' rule in the

studio. There's a balcony on the south exit you can use or the lounge.''

"Sorry." Dario sat down again, sitting closer to her than he was before he stood. "Anyway, about the script. You know, now that I think about it, half of it isn't as preposterous as it seems upon first glance."

"How so?"

"I mean look at us. Our whole damn marriage was something straight out of one of your soap operas. The concealed letters, the damn stupid thing I did in Rome, the way we came to meet again, everything."

Eliza was unprepared for his candor, for the intimate sway in the conversation, and attempted to alter the tone, though she had to agree with Dario in his assessment of their relationship. "I see your point, Dario, but it's not quite like a soap opera. You see if it were, you'd find out next week that we had a baby who was sold into slavery, or perhaps put up for adoption, but otherwise alive and well and ready to reenter your life at any time, or that our divorce was never finalized and we're still married."

Dario shook his head and laughed. "You know, that wouldn't be half-bad. I wouldn't mind a child, though I'd prefer one younger than ours would be now, and as far as finding myself still married to a lovely lady like you...hm. That might have definite advantages." There was a smile in his eyes when he looked into hers, and Eliza wished she hadn't said what she did.

"Unless there's anything else we have to discuss, I'd like to get back to work now," she said, standing to leave.

"I have one other question. What's the payoff for a lady hiring an ex-husband she hates?"

The question took her by surprise, and Eliza struggled to maintain a calm exterior. "Dario, I don't hate you. Not anymore. I did for a while, but that was a long time ago. My major concern about hiring you is your lack of experience in daytime," she said slowly.

"Well, I learn fast and I don't like to stay in one place very long," he reassured her.

"You never have," she retorted quickly, wishing they could keep the past from creeping into their conversations.

"No, I suppose not. And you still haven't told me what's in this for you yet. A second intuition about this business tells me you hope for something from HEI by keeping me around."

"It's not just for me. It's for the company," she began. "I hope to get an hour out of this, among other things."

"An hour?" he asked with a pleasant laugh. "An hour of what? Whatever it is, it must be pretty good stuff from the hostility level I sense from you, Eliza."

"I want to expand the show to an hour format," she said impatiently. "And I'm not hostile. You artist types have the biggest imaginations."

"You're the one who writes the soaps, not me," he reminded her gently. "Look, Liza, I mean Eliza, I'm not saying you don't have a right to be hostile. I deserve it."

"No, you don't. Everything happened a long time ago, and I've come to understand your behavior over the years. Let's not talk about it now, please?"

"Some other time?"

Eliza didn't fully understand his need to rehash the past, but she sensed he was asking for her forgiveness. "Perhaps."

"Can I walk you to your office?"

"Yes."

As they walked silently down the corridor, Eliza felt

a nervous need to say something. It wasn't a pleasant silence. "Have you been watching our show?" she asked.

"No, I haven't," he admitted.

"Well, do it. You can take home one of the video recorders and watch it there if you don't have time to do it here. The more you know about the show, the better for everyone. Where are you staying by the way?"

"At a friend's place in the East Village," he replied. It was one of Manhattan's more bohemian areas. "Sean neglected to tell me he passed out keys to every other transient person in the world of film and television. There are actors, dancers, people like me, coming and going at all hours of the day and night."

"It sounds like the kind of life you used to lead fifteen years ago," she said.

"I suppose. Where do you live, Eliza?"

"Gramercy Park."

"Federal facade and all?"

She smiled. "Federal facade and bright red bricks."

"You've done well," he said politely, turning to leave. "I'm happy for you. Success always did mean a great deal to you. I can't tell you how good it makes me feel to see you with everything you ever wanted from life." His tone was stilted, but she knew he had spoken sincerely.

"Thank you," she replied in an equally formal tone, not feeling half as satisfied with her life as she had before Dario reentered it.

"Well, I'd better get back to work now. If I'm going to do this job for a while, I might as well do it properly and try not to break the bank. See you later, and thank you for allowing me to stay on with your company."

"It's my pleasure," she said automatically, without attaching any particular significance to the words.

"Not from what I've seen so far, but maybe there's hope for us yet, Eliza," he said enigmatically, leaving her to wonder at his words as he walked away.

Chapter Three

The two weeks after her return from the West Coast were busy ones for Eliza. The negotiations to create a new daytime drama for a major television network came through, and she had less than a month to write ten one-hour scripts. So far she'd presented the network executives with what is frequently known as the "Bible" in the business, a lengthy character sketch of each person to be in the proposed show, describing enough of their pasts to give the reader an insight into their motivations and goals in life, along with general information about the fictitious town where the drama was to take place. Now she had to come up with the dialogue to flesh out those characters, to translate them from paper to believable people the viewers would want to cheer and jeer, to love and hate.

As a result of her preoccupation with the new show, Eliza had once again entrusted *Beyond Tomorrow* to the very capable hands of her producer Jared. There were times when she wondered if she was secretly relieved to have a sideline role in the drama now. It kept her away from Dario and all the confusion he induced within her with that indolent smile of his that rose ever so subtly from his lips to the golden brown eyes. She spent most of her time working in her home office now, so the lazy grin was out of sight but never very far removed from her conscious thoughts.

After the brief moments of intimacy at the studio when Eliza had told Dario about the concealed letters and had allowed the old bitterness that she hadn't even been aware of harboring to resurface, she hadn't seen much of him during the following two weeks. And when they did encounter one another around the studio, he treated her with detached professional courtesy, acknowledging neither their past nor the conversation on the first day they had met after nearly fifteen years. Eliza supposed it was better that way, though she found herself curiously drawn to Dario and keenly aware of his presence. The more she avoided him physically, the more he came to pervade her thoughts, and she had to force herself not to watch him so closely while she visited either the control room or the sets on the days when she found it necessary to leave home and monitor the production of the show. They seldom spoke to each other; she let Jared indoctrinate Dario to the art of directing the daily drama and was surprised to hear that despite his inauspicious beginnings, he caught on rapidly and did the job well. A few of the cast members even liked Dario, though most found him intimidating and difficult to approach.

At eleven Eliza's secretary phoned her home to remind her of the monthly meeting with the HEI executives at the 21 Club. The reminder was entirely unnecessary, but Eliza thanked Beverly anyway. Eliza never forgot an important meeting, and today's had special significance for her. She and Dario would be sharing lunch together for the first time in nearly fifteen years.

Eliza had been working at her typewriter all morning in flannel pajamas and a pair of tennis shoes. She took a quick shower and dressed in something more appropriate for a business lunch at 21, a teal-blue linen suit and a cream-colored silk blouse that complimented both her olive complexion and the brisk fall air. Her naturally deep bronze skin came from her mother, a woman of Mexican descent. Eliza's other parent was of English descent, and she resembled him so little that people were often surprised to learn they were father and daughter.

Her cab was on Madison Avenue crossing East Thirty-eighth Street when she saw Dario, walking against the breeze with both hands in the pockets of his maroon alpaca sweater and a dark attaché case under his arm. He had fourteen more blocks to go to reach Fifty-second Street and would never make it on foot. Eliza asked the driver to pull over.

She rolled down the window and shouted. "Dario!" He couldn't hear her over the noise of the traffic and Eliza repeated herself.

Dario turned around, smiled, and walked to the cab. "Thanks, Eliza. I'd forgotten how long Manhattan is, especially when one's in a hurry." He opened the door and slid into the seat next to her.

"Surely you didn't walk all the way from your place in the East Village. That's pretty far!" The fresh male scent of him managed to override the stale odor of tobacco in the cab, and she noticed how the brisk air had whipped a ruddy rose color into his dark complected cheekbones. Dario's skin was darker than that of most people of Italian descent, and when Eliza had first met him, she'd assumed him to be of the same Mexican lineage she was.

"No, I never made it home last night. So how have you been, Eliza? I've barely seen you in the last few weeks," he said.

Eliza wondered where and with whom he had spent the night but didn't dream of asking him. It was none of her business, and the fact that Dario might have already found a female companion after less than a month in the city shouldn't have bothered her. But it did. "I've been working at home."

"I heard your proposal to create the new soap came through. Congratulations. You must be very excited about it."

"Yes and no." Dario's hair was still wet from the shower, waving and tumbling riotously over the collar of the blue shirt he wore under his sweater. Again she wondered whose shower he'd stepped from a little while ago.

"How so? I should think doing a show for a major network would be a dream come true to a lady with your talent and ambition."

She picked up on the sarcastic inflection in his voice and frowned, deciding not to call him on it. She wasn't about to let Dario provoke her once more into unleashing hostilities she didn't know were there. "This isn't the first time I've created a new show, Dario. I've done three others."

"Really? You must be raking in royalties hand over foot."

"Hardly. You see, they all flopped. Getting a new daytime drama going is probably the most difficult thing to do in television. Viewers who watch the soaps are already loyal to one in the same time slot. It takes quite a while to build up a following, and meanwhile the network loses money hand over foot, as you would put it," she explained.

"I suppose that makes sense," he agreed. "Well, I certainly wish you success, Eliza."

Perhaps she'd misread sarcasm into his earlier statement. "Thank you."

Eliza found her attention drawn to his hands which were folded on the briefcase on his lap. There were two fine scars between his thumb and forefinger from an accident with an electric jigsaw when Dario had tried to build some bookcases for their bedroom in Los Angeles a few days after their marriage. Eliza had completely forgotten the incident until now. Later that same day, he had received the offer to direct the film in Italy, and she gave him the Saint Christopher medal the following evening, the one she had noticed around his neck the first time she saw him two weeks ago. Unconsciously, her eyes strayed to his neck.

"What's the matter, Eliza?" Dario asked. "Do I have ring around the collar?" he teased lightly, drawing her gaze up to his.

Eliza laughed. "Not so far as I can tell."

Dario pulled the medal from under his collar. "Is this what you're looking for then?"

She didn't deny it. "Yes, you're very perceptive, Dario. How did you know?"

"I saw you staring at it before. Does it bother you that I still wear it?"

"No, it simply surprises me." She felt uncomfortable about the personal turn in the conversation and changed the subject. "All ready for your first meeting with the people from HEI?"

Dario was relieved himself she had moved from the potentially volatile topic. He wasn't certain what was going on between Eliza and himself yet, but whatever it was, it was something powerful and seething beneath the veneer of their attempts to behave as disinterested parties toward one another, and it was something that could erupt at any minute if they didn't keep tight reins on their emotions. Regardless of what she said, Dario felt Eliza hated him, and he agreed with her right to hate him. She had every right to do so, and in a sense he'd never entirely forgiven her for not giving him a second chance to make things right after her trip to Rome. Of course, he knew now why she hadn't responded to his letters, but that did little to salve the old wounds. Dario was beginning to think it would be best all around if he got out of New York as soon as possible. He'd been a fool to think he could touch bases with her after all the years as though the past were entirely behind them, to meet again as a pair of childhood friends who'd shared the good and bad, but recalled all with fondness. It was obvious to him she hadn't forgiven him, and that pained Dario to no small degree because he found himself on the threshold of falling in love with her all over again. It was something he hadn't bargained for when he decided to see her again. He was supposed to convince himself she was just another woman, not fall in love with her for the second time.

He ignored her question about the upcoming meeting. "Eliza, did you hear a job offer came through from Hollywood for me? My lecture series at Columbia only lasts another month, so I really don't have any ties here. I'm relatively confident I've learned all I need to know about daytime from the month I've spent with your company, so I'm seriously considering this offer."

Her heart stopped dead in its tracks. Although she sincerely wished Dario had never reentered her life, now that he was there, she didn't want him to go, not just yet. "No, I hadn't heard. What kind of offer is it?" They were nearing their destination. The cab passed by the Helmsley Palace, turning west on Fifty-first Street to Sixth Avenue.

"Tell you in a minute," Dario said. As the cab turned onto Fifty-second Street, he put his hand over hers when she made a motion to open her purse. "I'll pay the driver." He did so and then stepped from the cab, smiling to himself as her skirt rode past her knees when he helped her from the rear seat. Damn, if they weren't the best legs he'd ever seen in his life.

"Be sure to put it down as a business expense," Eliza said, pulling the skirt below her knees.

"I planned to."

Eliza realized she was still holding on to his hand and jerked hers away.

"Why do you do that every time I touch you, Eliza?"

"Obviously because I don't want you to touch me, Dario," she said crossly, unable to handle the flood of emotions that overtook her whenever he touched her.

"Well, remind me not to ask you to sit on my lap during the meeting, okay?" he said dryly. Dario was more and more convinced that for whatever the reasons might be, he and Eliza couldn't work together. The past was still there between them like an impassable bridge, and the waters ran too swiftly beneath for them to ever journey across.

"I'll do that," she remarked. Her hand was still tingling from the warmth of his, and it made her senses reel to think she could have just as easily kept his hand in hers as they walked along instead of dropping it as though it were a forbidden object.

Dario nodded without saying anything as they walked into the restaurant where Eliza was addressed by name and shown to a table. They were a bit early, and none of the three people from HEI was present.

Eliza looked around for Jared, but he wasn't there either. She was alone with Dario. She ordered a glass of wine and asked Dario about his offer from Hollywood.

Dario took a few sips of his water before answering. "It's to direct a picture with Antonio Fanucchi," he said, referring to a producer of several recent box office hits.

"I'm impressed," she replied.

"Well, that makes one of us, because I'm sure as hell not impressed."

"But I thought it was the offer you were waiting for." She had intentionally left an empty seat between the two of them and had to pivot sideways in her chair to see Dario while they spoke.

"No, I wanted another one to come through, not Fanucchi's. I've never had any particular respect for his films. Most of them are unadulterated commercial crap from beginning to end, but I've been known to do pictures I don't particularly care for just to work."

"At least it would pay well. Fanucchi never works with anything less than a twenty-five-million-dollar budget."

Dario shook his head and laughed. "Is that all you ever think about, Eliza? Big budgets and money?"

Dario was accusing her of far more materialism than she possessed, but she forced herself to take his comment with a grain of salt, to remain calm. She found the monthly conferences with the HEI executives tense enough without having to lead into one after an altercation with Dario. "Money helps the world go around. It's pretty difficult to get along without it."

"Well, I learned a long time ago it takes more than money and commercial successes to make my world go around."

She wished he'd stop staring at her with that accusatory look of his as though she would sell her best friend to the highest bidder. She wasn't like that. Eliza had never gone after success and wealth as ends in themselves, though she greatly enjoyed both. They were simply the by-products of doing the job she loved and doing it well. "Good for you, Dario. Wherever would the world be without such great, self-sacrificing artists as yourself?"

"Eliza," he began, "don't be so defensive. I certainly didn't mean to be critical of your successes. I admire you for them." He halted abruptly when she raised her fingers to her lips.

"Shush!" she whispered, waving one hand in the air at the approaching man. "There's Gene Stone and Donald Kennedy."

The people from HEI greeted Eliza and Dario and sat down at the table, after explaining that Bud Talbort, the executive vice-president, wouldn't be able to make it due to an unexpected problem in the network's home office.

"I'm sorry to hear that," Eliza murmured politely, secretly relieved Bud Talbort wasn't coming. He was a lecherous, patronizing fool who taxed her patience almost to the breaking point every time they were in the same room for more than sixty seconds.

As usual, Gene and Donald made small talk after ordering lunch and during most of the first course. They always did that, and Eliza resented their perennial tendency to beat around the bush for nearly an hour before getting down to business. Jared didn't like it either and had been showing up late for the last three months, leaving her with the task of putting up with the two of them. It was a little easier this time because of Dario, who didn't seem to be bothered by their mindless banter.

Finally after his second drink, Gene Stone mentioned the show. With perfect timing Jared arrived a fraction of a minute later, taking the empty seat between Dario and Eliza.

"I'm sorry about being late," he said. "There was a screw up with some of our audio equipment. It took me all morning to iron it out in time for the taping. Did I miss anything important?" he asked, knowing very well he hadn't.

Gene told him no and produced a computer printout from his briefcase. "Look at these ratings. They've dropped a point since our last meeting, but we're still flying high with the show. Eliza, what do you think about doing a spinoff from *Beyond Tomorrow* instead of expanding the show to an hour format?"

"Not much," she said bluntly. "I'd far prefer to add

more characters to the present show and develop the storylines."

"So would I," Jared said in support of Eliza.

Donald Kennedy turned to Dario. "What about you, Dario? A man with your experience in film and television should have some kind of an opinion on this."

Eliza watched Dario while he took another sip of mineral water before answering. Donald Kennedy had an annoying way of speaking to everyone as though they were about five years old, and she wondered how a man like Dario would take to his air of patronization.

"I don't know this show well enough to give a damn one way or the other, Don," he replied calmly enough, although Eliza could tell by the line of his jaw and the single quirked eyebrow that Dario knew the other man was talking down to him.

Donald seemed relieved to have found a possible ally in Dario. "Then let me explain why a spinoff would be better than a longer show, Dario. I'm sure you'll agree with me."

"I'm listening," Dario said.

He began his proposal, saying exactly what Eliza had feared. A spinoff without her control of production would be one way HEI could capitalize on the audience *Beyond Tomorrow* had acquired in the last five years and come up with a show that promised more sensationalism than her company had ever offered.

Gene took over after Donald finished, talking more to Dario than to either Eliza or Jared.

Since it was Eliza's program, she had full rights to the creation of spinoffs and didn't know why they were courting Dario's approval. Perhaps they felt he had more influence with her than he actually did, or perhaps they were priming him to come up with an entirely new show if they couldn't persuade her to go along with their plans.

"So you can see our point, can't you, Dario? HEI needs to reach out to a younger audience who wants to see the same kind of exciting entertainment they get from watching the uncut movies on HEI. What do you think?" Gene asked, leaning over the table toward Dario.

"I think the whole thing stinks, Gene," he replied.

Eliza and Jared looked at each other and smiled.

"And may I ask why?" Donald Kennedy demanded gruffly.

"Certainly. The viewers who watch *Beyond Tomorrow* do so because they like what they see. Any drastic change is apt to alienate your present following. It would be better all around to simply create an entirely new show," he explained, downing his third glass of mineral water.

"Maybe you have a point there," Gene Stone interjected. "We do have another soap under consideration now, but I don't want to go ahead with it right now. I've been hoping Eliza will change her position on creative control of *Beyond Tomorrow*. I think there's room for improvement." He turned to Eliza. "Have you had a chance to go over the ideas we sent by last week?"

She hadn't cared for any of their suggestions. "Yes, and I don't see how I can fit them into the present scheme of things, but I'll give your proposal more thought."

"Like hell you will," Donald Kennedy said in a loud voice that jerked more than one head toward their table. "I'm getting tired of your stonewalling, Eliza. Admit it, you have no intention of accepting any of our ideas."

"But, Donald, I think the record indicates otherwise. If you review each of the long-term storylines for the last five years, you'll see that several changes have been made in accordance with the wishes of HEI," she countered in a calm tone. Eliza found herself unable to eat because of the high tension level and set her plate aside. She felt Dario's eyes on her and glanced in his direction. The kindness and sympathy she saw there relaxed the furrowed lines on her forehead and brought a smile to her lips. It faded quickly when Donald Kennedy renewed his attack. He'd been drinking heavily since his arrival nearly an hour ago, and Eliza knew it would be futile to attempt to reason with him at this point.

"Bull! You've made only the most minor concessions on every front, Eliza, and you know it!" he said in a tone audible to nearly half the people in the restaurant. "What's wrong with more sex on the show? What are you, some kind of an old maid Puritan or something? Come to think of it, you never have been married, have you?"

The headwaiter was casting anxious looks in their direction, and Eliza knew she had to act quickly. She prepared to leave. It was the first meeting she'd ever walked out on, but this was the most intoxicated and unruly she'd ever known Donald Kennedy to be in a public place. "If you'll excuse me now, gentlemen, I have another engagement."

Doing *Beyond Tomorrow* with HEI was Jared's first big job, and the twenty-six-year-old man hated any form of direct confrontation with the network people. He reached out to place a cautionary hand on Eliza's knee, moving his palm in the wrong direction.

"Try fondling another knee, Jared," Dario said dryly. "You're not doing anything for me."

Eliza overheard the softly spoken comment and felt like laughing in spite of the seriousness of the conversation. She looked at Jared, whose face was a bright crimson and wanted to laugh even more.

"What would it take to get you to sell out entirely,

Eliza?'' Gene Stone asked quietly. ''I understand you have something going with ABC now. Maybe this would be a good time to move to Hollywood and leave *Beyond Tomorrow* behind,'' he suggested. Fortunately for all at the table, Donald Kennedy had left for the bar.

Dario jerked his head toward Eliza. The prospect of Eliza and him winding up in the same place after encountering each other in New York had never crossed his mind until now, but then she had always been with him over the years, in spirit if not in the flesh. Only he didn't know what he was drawn to at the present, the memory of a girl barely eighteen that he had loved more than life itself but betrayed anyway, or to the mature, dynamic woman who sat a place away from him at the table, holding her own in competitive bargaining that would have made him tense for days.

''If I ever leave the show behind me, Gene, I'm afraid it won't be in your hands,'' she said resolutely.

''You'd let it die out completely? That would disappoint a great many people, wouldn't it?'' he said.

''No, I wouldn't have to do that. I had an offer on it while I was in Hollywood. ABC wants it when the contract with HEI expires.''

There was complete silence at the table for a few minutes. ''What did you tell them?'' he asked.

''I told them I wasn't interested at the present, but I may be in the future.''

''You'd have to give up control with them, too, Eliza,'' Gene reminded her.

''True, but they wouldn't change the show into the kind of thing you want, Gene,'' she contended.

''I think we'd better talk about this at the next meeting,'' the senior executive suggested. ''Here comes Don. I'd better give him a cup of coffee and take him home. Will you accept my apology for the things he said to you, Eliza?''

"Of course," she replied graciously.

As Eliza expected, Jared wanted to stay around and have another drink with the HEI people to make amends on his behalf. Eliza knew he saw his future more with the cable network than with her, and she understood it.

"I think I'm ready to call it a day, too," Dario said. He stood and pulled out Eliza's chair for her.

She said good-bye to Jared and the other two men once more and followed Dario out to the street, not paying any attention to him until he spoke again. "What did you say?" she asked. The midafternoon sun was bright in a cloudless sky, and Eliza removed a pair of dark glasses from her sleek blue leather purse.

"I asked if I can get a cab for you, Eliza," Dario repeated.

Her thoughts were elsewhere, on the meeting with the men from HEI and the eventual fate of *Beyond Tomorrow*, but when she turned to Dario, he was all she could think about. They passed through the wrought iron gate as they exited the restaurant and she saw the shadows on his face where the sun cut through the grille. "A cab?" she said vaguely, thinking of how handsome he looked with the play of light on his cheekbones and the wind whipping through his black-and-white hair. The breeze carried the fragrance of the shampoo he used to her nostrils, and she marveled more that she had remembered the scent over all these years than that he still favored the same brand.

Dario smiled. "Yes, Eliza, a cab. You know, the yellow-and-black things with four wheels and a meter. Do you want one?"

"No, I think I'm going to take a walk. Forty characters have been running around inside my head day and night now for the last month, and I need a bit of fresh air." Not to mention the need to walk off some of the nervous energy from her most trying meeting with HEI to date, she thought to herself.

"Would you like some company?" he asked.

Eliza hesitated, pulled in opposite directions by her mixed emotions. On one level she was afraid of resurrecting a past between them that was best forgotten, yet in the two weeks that had followed their initial encounter at the studio, she'd come to the conclusion she bore Dario no ill will because of their history years ago. Some immature component of her psyche had prompted her to lash out, and she didn't think it would happen again. But it might. She had told herself the past was dead the first time she saw him on set, yet within five minutes of his entry into her office, there it was, alive and hurtful once more. Perhaps it would be best if she avoided him as much as possible until she sorted out her feelings, put everything into perspective, but the man who stood before her was too damn attractive, and Eliza didn't want to send him away.

Dario sensed her ambivalence to his suggestion. He reached into his pocket and removed a watch. "It's later than I thought, Eliza. I should probably get back to work myself. I'm working on a few new storylines for your show. With a little luck I may be able to take some of those forty people out of your head."

She smiled. "I'd like that. I'd also like some company on my walk."

His frown rose and blossomed into a contented grin. "You've got it, come on. Would you like me to carry your briefcase?"

Eliza shook her head and smiled. "No, I think I can manage. Would you like me to carry yours?" she teased gently. Coming from any other man, the comment would probably have been a snide one, but she knew that wasn't so with Dario. Raised in a closely knit

Italian section of San Francisco, he was the son of immigrants from Sicily who didn't speak more than a few words of English the time she had met them, though all five of their children were born in California. There was a great deal of old-world charm about Dario that had always appealed to her, stopping short of the point when she found his treatment of women to be chauvinistic or out and out patronizing.

"No, I think I can manage also. So, how often do you have to put up with those jerks from HEI, Eliza?" Dario asked. A car sped across the intersection at Fifth Avenue and Fifty-third as they stepped from the curb, and he swore under his breath, grabbing onto Eliza's arm at the same time. "This Manhattan traffic is the only thing I've ever seen that's worse than Rome," he muttered.

"You'll get used to it," she said. Dario's hand remained on her elbow. She was disappointed when he let it drop after they crossed the street.

"I sincerely doubt that."

"You never have been much of a New Yorkophile, have you, Dario?"

"No, I can't say I am. You always..." On the verge of reminding her of one of the many conversations they had nearly fifteen years ago about her desire to live in New York, Dario didn't complete the sentence. Now wasn't the time for sharing memories. "How long have you lived here?" he asked instead.

"Nearly ten years. I love it."

"I can't stand it."

"Then why did you come here?"

"I came here because of the class at Columbia," he explained, taking her arm again as they crossed Fifty-fourth Street and dropping it as he had the last time when they reached the other side.

"That's right. Jared told me about the class and you mentioned it earlier. What are you teaching?"

"I'm giving a series of lectures on a variety of topics. It's only a one-semester course, part of an Artist in Residence program in the drama department. I've wanted to teach for a long time but never got back to it after graduate school. Now seemed like a good time."

"That sounds like quite an honor. Congratulations."

"You're welcome to come by and sit in on a few of my lectures if you wish."

Eliza thought of the last time she'd attended a class taught by Dario and laughed. It seemed impossible that that starstruck teenager and she were one and the same person. She was still smiling when Dario glanced at her sideways.

"I'm glad you find the prospect of attending one of the classes so amusing. I assure you, I'm a hell of a better lecturer now than I was the last time you saw me," he said, nearly shouting over the roar of traffic and people surging down Fifth Avenue.

"Oh, you were good then too, Dario. I was thinking of something else."

"You're very kind, Eliza. I was awful and scared half to death every time I walked into that lecture hall at UCLA," he admitted. Dario put his arm around her shoulders when the crowd threatened to separate them then dropped his hand to his side when she stiffened against his body.

"Really? You never told me that."

"That's not the kind of thing a young man usually confesses to a girl he's trying to impress," Dario replied, annoyed by both his constant inability to keep his hands away from her and Eliza's repeated rejections of his affection.

"But you did a fine job," she reassured him. "No one ever knew you were nervous."

"Well, I was. Except for you and a few others, most of the students in that class were older than I was. Remember? I was only twenty-one when the semester began.''

"Yeah, I remember," she said commiseratingly. She almost felt like crying at the poignant memory.

Dario whirled her toward him on the pavement, taking her face in his hands. They stood motionless for a few brief seconds before the sea of people propelled them onward. "Eliza, I'm sorrier than I can ever say for what I did."

"I know. It's over and done with now, so let's forget it, okay?"

Dario lapsed into silence, not answering her question. Eliza followed suit, and they didn't say anything to each other as they walked along. She turned to him when they reached the corner of Fifty-seventh Street.

Dario was staring into the window of Bergdorf Goodman and didn't hear her when she addressed him by name. Eliza tugged on his arm, and he turned to her. "Thanks for being at the meeting. It helped," she said.

"It did?" he asked in amazement. "How?"

"Just having you there."

"You'll never know how tempted I was to put my fist through Donald Kennedy's face when he made that crack about you."

She giggled. "Well, I'm glad you didn't. It would have done more harm than good."

"I know," he said with a disarming grin. Dario placed his hand to his eyes to shield them from the low-angle late-afternoon sun and peered up at the green copper and slate roof of the Plaza Hotel. "That thing still there?" he asked.

"You bet. When's the last time you were in New York, Dario?"

"About ten years ago. We filmed a few scenes here for a film I did with a studio from Rome."

Eliza saw an empty seat around the Pulitzer Fountain and suggested they sit down. "What film was that?"

"It was called *Per Unpelo.*"

"What does that mean?"

Dario's arm came to rest near hers as they sat down. "By a hairbreadth."

"Never heard of it," she said.

Dario chuckled. "Few people have. It was never released in this country."

"Was it any good?"

"Not bad, considering the budget we had to work with."

"Sounds familiar. What kind of a movie was it?"

"A suspense thriller. I don't think you would have cared for it. I'll never forget how you once fell asleep during that Hitchcock film festival." He thought of how that was more because of the way her warm breath felt on his neck than anything else.

Eliza giggled. "Neither will I. That was during finals, wasn't it? I don't think I got any sleep at all that week."

"Yeah, it was. I didn't get much sleep either that week. I had so many final exams to grade. Did I ever tell you how it nearly broke my heart to give you a D on yours?" Dario's hand moved to her neck, lightly caressing the smooth skin exposed by the upswept hairstyle. Without saying a word, she'd given him permission to touch her now, and he seized the opportunity like a drowning man surfacing from the sea.

She laughed again. "Yes, many times. I should have just taken an incomplete in the class or dropped it. It was too hard to concentrate," she admitted, recalling her emotions every time she walked into the class he taught. Eliza had been too madly in love with the young instructor to do anything more than sit there with a starstruck expression on her face and had daydreamed through the final examination, thinking about the elopement she and Dario had planned for the following weekend.

"I know," he replied with a wistful smile. "I had trouble concentrating then for the same reasons."

"Well, at least you weren't too distracted to see a bad paper for what it was," she remarked. Eliza leaned her head against his arm. "Oh, Dario, we were such kids then, weren't we?"

"Yes, we were."

"I thought you were so much more grown up and mature than I, but you were only twenty-one yourself, just a kid, too."

"Yes, I sure did some stupid things then," he said sadly. "Liza, you were so beautiful. I've never loved another woman the way I loved you then. I've regretted—"

Eliza turned to him, placing her forefinger over his mouth. "Shush, now, I don't want to hear any more apologies." In that instant she knew for certain she'd forgiven him completely.

Dario kissed the tip of her finger. "There's nothing I'd like better."

When he looked up, his brown eyes were warm with desire and Eliza knew he wanted to kiss her. "What are you thinking?" she asked.

"I think you know. May I?"

"I guess that depends on who you want to kiss, me or the girl you knew fifteen years ago. You were always so romantic on the topic of one's first love, remember?" she reminded him. Eliza was beginning to dwell more on the good than the bad in their former relationship, and it was a wonderful feeling.

"Guilty as charged, but I know one thing. I want to kiss you, Eliza."

"Then, yes, you may."

He moved his hand from her neck to the side of her

face, tilting her head back ever so slightly as his lips descended to hers.

All of the noise of the heart of the big city was drowned out as Eliza opened her mouth in response to his gentle persuasion. She placed both hands on his shoulders, drawing him nearer to her.

Dario cupped his other hand to her face briefly and then let it drop to her shoulder, stopping himself when his palm strayed toward her breast.

The prolonged kiss continued amidst the roar of activity in midtown Manhattan, and Eliza moved her hands to his shirt collar, inserting a few fingers beneath to where she touched the silver chain around his neck.

Dario sighed and sat up, withdrawing from their kiss. "This is about all I can take of you in a public place, baby."

Eliza laughed, the laughter husky and deep in her throat. "Come on, Dario. We used to kiss for hours on public benches back in L.A."

"Maybe so, but that park wasn't smack in the middle of the city that never sleeps, and I was too shy to ask you to come to my apartment then," he said, lifting her hand from his chest and kissing the palm. "I'm not now. Do you want to come to my apartment, Liza?"

She shook her head. Dario was moving too fast for her, and Eliza needed more time to sort out her own emotions. The fact that she'd forgiven him didn't necessarily mean she wanted to have an affair with him now. "No, Dario, I don't. I have to think about this more."

"Think? About what? We've been apart for nearly fifteen years, Liza, and the last time I saw you, not counting here in New York, you were my wife. Isn't that time enough to know what you want?"

She reached for his face, running her fingers over the silvery sideburns while her thumb caressed the angular slope of his jawline. "You were always such a hopeless romantic, Dario! The fact that we've been apart so long doesn't really mean anything now. One can't take an old memory to bed, especially when it's not an altogether happy one. Tell me one thing, Dario. Who do you want to go to bed with? Me or the girl you knew a long time ago, or maybe neither, something you've created in your own mind over the years?"

"You," he said without hesitation.

"Me now or then?" she persisted.

"You, now and then. Certain aspects are inseparable in my mind, Liza."

"Well perhaps you'd better work on sorting some things out, Dario. Or you just might find yourself in the position of waking up in bed in the morning with a stranger you don't particularly like. I've changed over the years, you know."

"I'll take that chance. Go to my apartment with me now, Liza. I've wanted to make love to you since the very moment I saw you again."

"You've barely talked to me the last two weeks," she reminded him. The sun was beginning to set and Eliza shivered.

Dario drew her closer to his body, wrapping both arms around her waist. "I know, Liza. I had a few things to think about. I never expected to be so attracted to you again."

"I know. I felt the same way," she admitted without hesitation.

Dario brushed his finger across her lips and kissed her briefly.

When Eliza opened her eyes afterward, she looked over Dario's shoulder to where the setting sun reflected off the bronze statue in the top basin of the fountain. She told Dario how beautiful she thought it was.

Dario turned around. "Yes, it's lovely. It reminds me of a fountain in Milan. Have you ever been there, Liza?"

"No, I've never been there. Dario, it's getting too cold to sit here. Let's take a walk."

He stood and pulled Eliza to her feet. "Lead on."

Eliza smiled and linked her arm through his. "Care to go in any particular direction?"

"The one you take," he said.

"Fine with me. Let's go across Central Park South toward Broadway, okay?"

Dario nodded. "Do you want to stop and get something to eat? I noticed you barely touched your lunch."

"Yes, I would. The people from HEI seldom stimulate my appetite. How well do you know Gene Stone, Dario?"

"I knew him fairly well several years back in Rome. I ran into him again shortly after I accepted the teaching position at Columbia."

"Was that here or in Rome?"

"London."

"That's right. I remember he went there in May. Did you know of the affiliation between my company and his station?"

"Not at first. Where would you like to eat?"

Eliza sniffed the air. "I smell barbecued lamb."

"So do I. Is that what you want?"

"Please."

Dario purchased a shish kebab from a street vendor and gave it to Eliza. "Would you like anything else?"

"No, this is fine. Thank you." She ate as they walked, moving quickly with Dario's arm resting lightly on her shoulder as they merged with the swarm of other pedestrians on the wide sidewalk. Eliza wondered if Dario would ask her to go to his apartment again, and as they made their way through the crowd, she became progressively less certain her response would be in the negative. His hand on her shoulder was an inviting caress, and when their thighs happened to brush together as they walked, Eliza felt the warmth throughout her entire body. Yes, she wanted Dario, wanted the fulfillment promised by his kiss, wanted to spend the night in his arms.

Dario and Eliza didn't speak as they walked the long crosstown blocks leading to Columbus Circle, but occasionally they exchanged intimate smiles, and Eliza felt full and content, more carefree than she had for quite a while.

When they rounded the corner to Broadway, Dario asked Eliza how much farther she wanted to go.

Her cheeks were a deep pink from the wind and physical exertion, and her upswept hair was beginning to fall to her shoulders. "Oh, I don't know. Want to walk to Times Square?"

Dario groaned. "Eliza, do you know how far that is?"

She laughed. "It's not that far. They're all short blocks."

"Not short enough, but let's go."

"Well, where do you want to go?" she asked, grinning up at him.

"I've already told you that, Liza." He tugged at a loose strand of dark brown hair that flew around her face. "Why any woman would want to stroll to a sleazy street lined with porno theaters and other disgusting things when she could be in my bed is beyond me, Eliza," he said wryly. "I must be losing my touch with women."

Eliza giggled again. "From what you've told me about your apartment, Dario, it sounds like Grand Central Station. I don't know if I can take that after a long, hard day. I mean, even if I wanted to," she added hastily.

"Then let's go to your house. You live alone, didn't you say?"

Eliza hesitated briefly, holding one hand to her hair that was coming loose, flying freely in the brisk autumn breeze. "Dario, all I'm offering is a glass of wine and a little hospitality."

"That's all I'm asking for at the present, Eliza."

"Okay, then as long as that's understood, let's go and I'll introduce you to Tim and Eli."

"My only hope is that Tim and Eli have four legs, Liza," he remarked, propelling her forward as a crowd of people swept into a theater lobby.

"They do."

"Cats or dogs?"

"A rabbit and a dog. Dario, get that cab over there and I'll take you home to meet them."

Chapter Four

Dario began to have second thoughts about his suggestion that he accompany Eliza to her home as the cab drew nearer to Gramercy Park. As much as he wanted her to be a part of his life again, he was afraid of pressuring her into something she wasn't ready for, and Eliza had been right about the possibility of his waking up in the morning with someone he didn't like. But it wasn't what she thought. Though he pleaded guilty to a certain amount of sentimentality on the subject of one's first love, Dario didn't want to go back in time, to relive when he had become the first lover of a seventeen-year-old woman. He knew Eliza had changed, and he liked what he saw, but he feared her recrimination and couldn't bear the thought of waking up with all the old resentments, full blown through the years, though she protested that was over now. Dario didn't believe her. A part of her would always hate him, just as a part of him would always love her.

"Why so quiet?" Eliza asked. She rested her palm on his leg.

Desire coursed through his loins at her light touch, and he placed his hand over hers. "Oh, I was just thinking I can't stay at your house very long, Eliza. I have a lecture to prepare for tomorrow's class. Where about in Gramercy Park are you located?"

"East Nineteenth." She sensed he was fabricating an excuse to run away from her and understood. Eliza shared his ambivalence about the relationship.

"Block Beautiful?" he said with a slow smile.

"Yes, that's what they call it. It is very beautiful, Dario. Well, maybe you can stay longer some other time. I have a lot of work to do myself this evening. The studio in Hollywood would like to put the new show on the air in early January," she told him, following Dario's tactics of leaving an easy exit should the evening become too tense.

Dario whistled softly. "That doesn't give you much time. Why do they want to do it so soon?" He rotated her hand, linking his fingers through hers.

"A competing network is taking all their soaps off the air that week for some kind of a special sporting event, and they figure all the regular viewers who don't like sports might give our show a try." The cab halted in front of her house, and Eliza paid the driver over Dario's protests.

"You really should have let me do that," he complained, helping her from the rear seat.

"Why?"

"Common courtesy, Eliza."

"Oh, Dario, you're so old-fashioned! I bet you'd pass out if I picked up a check at a restaurant," she teased, laughing into his eyes. In the dim street lighting, her own deep brown eyes appeared as dark as midnight on a starless evening.

"Probably," he agreed, resting his hand on her raven-black hair. Eliza had always insisted to him the color of her hair was brunette, not black, but he'd never accepted that. To Dario it was the color of ebony, especially on a moonlit night. "Want to try me? How about dinner tomorrow?"

Eliza hesitated. It would be so easy for their lives to

merge together once more. "I don't know. Let me check my schedule, okay? Besides, I thought you had a class tomorrow," she reminded him.

"It doesn't last all night." Dario gazed up at the red brick building as they passed through the wrought iron gate. "It is lovely, Eliza. This part of New York has always reminded me of London."

She inserted her key into the lock. The dog barked, and Eliza instructed it to quiet down. "I know. We did some London scenes on location right here for the show once."

"Easy, boy," Dario said when Eliza's sheepdog bared its fangs at him. "I didn't come for the family heirlooms."

Eliza laughed. "He'd probably give them to you for a hot dog, Dario. Come on in." Her house was four stories tall, and Eliza led Dario to the skylit room on the third floor. It was where she worked and spent most of her time. The dog followed at their heels. "Can I get you anything, Dario?" she offered.

"No, not now. I'm fine." He walked to the window and drew back the drapes. "I can see why you'd film the London scenes here. Did it fly with the viewers?"

"More or less. We got a few letters from some local viewers who knew what we did, but we anticipated that. It was the best we could do on our budget. I'd love to actually film on location in Europe someday, but I don't think HEI would ever spring for it. There's some possibility we may tape a few shows on an island down in the Caribbean, though."

"Really? I did a film there two years back on a privately owned island near the Lesser Antilles. The owner is a close business associate of mine. I bet I could get use of the facilities there for you without charge," he remarked.

"Dario, that would be wonderful!"

"Maybe we can fly down there some weekend and check things out," he suggested casually without turning from the window. "It's a lovely place. I think you'd appreciate it. The colors of the sea are unlike anything I've seen on either coast here, and the temperature is so mild one could run around stark naked in the middle of December."

Eliza didn't know what to make of his comment, and the thought of running around nude on a tropical island with Dario was enough to bring a hot flush to her cheeks. She wondered if he had meant to suggest more of a personal sojourn than a business trip to inspect a set. "Perhaps," she replied evasively. "Jared usually does things like that for me."

"Well, I don't know if I want to camp out with him for a weekend," Dario replied.

She ignored his innuendo. "There are no housing facilities?"

"No, just a few primitive huts."

"What did you film there? A Tarzan movie?" she asked with a giggle.

"Not quite. It was a spy film."

"You and your spy films! Haven't you ever worked with anything outside of the suspense thriller area?"

"Yes, I wrote another type of screenplay once. It's never been produced." He didn't tell her it was an autobiographical film inspired by their former relationship.

"Tell me about it," she urged.

"Some other time, okay?" Dario didn't say anything else for a while and continued to stare out the window. Eliza sat down on the small loveseat and watched him, wondering what was going through his head. "On second thought, I think I'd like a drink, Eliza."

She stood. "What would you like?"

"What do you have?"

"You name it and I have it, Dario," she replied.
"My home doubles as the corporate headquarters for
my company. I do a fair amount of entertaining at
home and conduct business meetings here as well. The
bar's on the first level."

"I'll walk down with you."

"Okay, just a minute." Eliza's feet were sore from
their long walk, and she sat back down and removed
her shoes and then took off her jacket. When she
looked up, she saw Dario staring at her with an amused
expression on his face, the lines at either side of his
mouth drawn into an easy grin. She didn't dare ask him
what he was thinking.

"More comfortable?" he asked. His mind was on
those nights he had watched her undress in his shabby
room in Los Angeles.

"Much."

"Mind if I kick off my shoes?"

"Be my guest." The dog grabbed one of his shoes
the second he placed it under the coffee table, and
Eliza retrieved it from the animal's mouth.

"Eli! Bad boy!" she reprimanded. The dog wagged
his tail with pride and accompanied them to the lower
level.

"Does he follow you everywhere?" Dario asked.

"Whenever possible." She flicked on the light.

Dario looked around the room. A twenty-foot oak
bar flanked the left wall, and the shelves behind were
stocked with every conceivable type of alcoholic bever-
age. "Wow, when you said the bar was downstairs, you
really meant it, didn't you?"

Eliza glanced over at his amazed expression and
laughed. "I sure did. What will you have?" She
stepped behind the bar.

Dario straddled a stool on the other side. "Given the
surroundings, I feel I should order something very

elaborate, but a glass of dry red wine will do." He
continued to stare around the room in bewilderment.
He'd never seen anything like this in a private home
before. The walls opposite the bar area were lined with
rich brown leather upholstered booths, and there was a
large banquet table in the center of the room. "This
place is incredible, Eliza, but somehow it doesn't strike
me as something you would own. It looks like a public
bar room, and you always preferred warmer, more intimate surroundings." He took the stemmed glass from
her hand, tracing his fingers across her wrist. "But then
that was a long time ago." Dario released her hand and
raised the glass to his lips.

"Yes, it was," she said quietly, "but not all of my
tastes have changed that much, Dario. I didn't have
this room done. It was here when I moved in. Originally I planned to redo it when I had the time and
money, but I've never gotten around to it, and it has
been useful for the business meetings. Maybe I'll keep
it the way it is." She sat down on a stool, resting her
hands on the bar between them.

"Aren't you having anything?" he asked, taking
another sip of wine.

"No, I still have work to do. That stuff makes me
sleepy."

"Mind if we go back upstairs? I didn't invite myself
to your house so I could feel I was sitting around at the
local pub, Liza."

She heard his use of the diminutive form of her
name and didn't bother to correct him. "I was just
about to make the same suggestion, but I'd like to
show you something else first. Come here." She
stepped from behind the bar and led him to a heavy
oak-paneled door that opened onto her garden. "Oh,
damn, I forgot the keys. I keep this door locked on both
sides. Hang on a second." She returned to the bar and

removed a set of keys from under the counter. "There." She flung open the door, and they were enveloped by the heavy perfume of rose blossoms.

Eliza and Dario stepped into the garden. "Those are my favorite," she said, pointing out a bush with deep lavender flowers. The color was so dark it appeared nearly black in the dusk.

Dario shifted so the light from the room could filter through the open door. "They are lovely, Eliza. I don't think I've ever seen purple roses before. And look at those." He reached out to touch a bright yellow rose tipped with crimson at the ends of the petals. "I had a rose garden in Rome, too. I wrote an entire screenplay in that garden once."

"Oh? The one you mentioned inside? Have you written any other screenplays?"

"No, just that one. It was never produced. Fanucchi was interested, but he wanted to make too many changes I couldn't agree to. Someone from MGM is reading it now."

"What type of changes couldn't you agree to?"

"They wanted to give it a happy ending for one."

"A happy ending? I've never been opposed to happy endings myself," she said wistfully. "Tell me more about it."

Dario didn't want to ruin a good evening by dredging up the past, so he evaded her question. "It's a movie about two people."

She laughed. "Well, that certainly tells me a lot."

He wrapped a strand of her hair around his finger. The strong afternoon wind had blown most of it free from the coil on her head, and Dario wanted to remove the final pins. "At least it tells you it won't have a cast of thousands if it's ever produced, Liza."

"Okay, so I'll rule out historicals with big battle scenes. Is it another one of your suspense thrillers?

You always did go for those kinds of films, Dario," she said, forgetting she'd asked him the same question less than fifteen minutes ago. Dario's hand so close to her face that she could feel the warmth wasn't at all conducive to clear thinking.

"No, it's not." His thumb stroked the length of her neck, and he set his glass down on a marble birdbath and placed his other hand around her waist.

"Is it set in the present?"

"No, and is this Twenty Questions?"

Eliza wondered why he didn't want to talk about his screenplay. "If that's what it takes to find out about your movie. I have a producer friend in Hollywood who may be able to help you," she said jokingly.

Dario lowered his head and kissed the top of her head. "You do, huh?" he whispered. "Well, put in a good word for me the next time you see this producer friend of yours."

She placed her hands on his chest. His heartbeat was strong and rhythmical beneath her fingertips. "How can I if I don't know what it's about?"

"Just tell him it's good."

"Her."

"Then tell her."

"Why are you being so difficult, Dario?"

His hands moved down her back, pressing her into his body. "A natural disposition, I suppose."

Eliza closed her eyes and inhaled the fragrance of her garden and the man in her arms. "I suppose," she repeated.

"Liza?" Dario kissed her tousled head again.

"Uh-huh?" she asked contentedly.

"Baby, I could stay here forever, holding you in my arms in this lovely yard of yours, except for one thing."

"Mmm, and what's that?"

"My feet are so damn cold." They were both in their stocking feet and the stone path in the garden was damp.

She giggled against his chest. Now that she thought of it, her feet were freezing, too, but it had failed to register on her senses. "And thus passes another great romantic moment. Let's go, Dario."

He released her from his embrace and took her hand. "Well, it could have been worse."

"How so?"

"One of us could have tripped and fallen down in that mud puddle," he said, pointing to an area she'd dug up over the weekend in preparation for planting spring bulbs.

Eliza laughed. "You're right, it rained here last night. Wait a minute, you forgot your wine." She returned to the fountain and gave him the glass.

Dario thanked her, and held open the door.

"Can I refill your glass?" she offered inside.

"I'll get it. Eliza, you didn't lock the door. Go do it right now before you forget, okay? Doesn't it worry you to live alone in a city like this?" he asked when she joined him at the bar.

"No. I'm pretty careful most of the time. Where did you say you lived again?"

"Not very far away. In the East Village by Tompkins Square on Tenth Street."

"That's right, now I remember." They returned to the third floor.

Dario snapped his fingers together. "May I use your phone, please? I just remembered I was supposed to be somewhere else for dinner tonight."

"Of course. I hope I wasn't keeping you from an important engagement," she said. Eliza recalled for the first time that evening that Dario hadn't spent the night at his apartment and wondered if he had a dinner date with the same person. She experienced a dull pain in the pit of her stomach.

"No, it wasn't important." Dario dialed the number. He addressed the person at the other end of the line in Italian, and Eliza didn't learn anything about where he had been or where he meant to be this evening.

"Speaking of dinner, Dario, are you hungry? I'd be happy to fix something for you," she offered. Her mind was still on the telephone conversation and the prospect of his involvement with another woman.

"I wouldn't want to put you to the trouble. I'll grab a bite on the way home."

"It wouldn't be any trouble. I'm starting to get hungry, too. I can reheat something in the microwave oven in a few minutes."

"Thank you, I'd like that. Where's the kitchen?"

"On the floor right below us." Downstairs, she surveyed the contents of the refrigerator.

Dario bent over her shoulder, his hand resting on her back. "Can I do anything to help?"

"Why don't you make a salad?" she suggested, handing him a head of lettuce and a few tomatoes. "What would you like, Dario? I have leftover roast beef and some lasagna."

"Anything but the lasagna, Eliza. I've had enough Italian food in the last two weeks to last a lifetime."

She removed the roast from the refrigerator and put it in the microwave. "Do you have an Italian friend here in New York?" she asked cautiously.

"Yes, several of them. Manhattan probably has more Napolis than skyscrapers."

Eliza smiled brightly. "Is that where you were last night?"

"Yes. Why? Did you try to get in touch with me at my place?"

"No, just wondering." Relief swept over her like a

welcoming breeze on a muggy night. Dario hadn't spent the night in another woman's bed!

He removed the outside leaves from the lettuce. "Where's the trash?" he asked.

"Next to the pantry, but don't throw the lettuce away. Give it to Tim."

Dario smiled. "The rabbit? Where is it?"

"On the fourth story balcony. He has the run of the entire floor. He's box-trained and I should tell you now he's very nervous and has a tendency to bite strangers. He's quite territorial."

"I see. Well, maybe you'd better feed him then."

"My hero!" she quipped with a contented grin.

Dario laughed softly. "All right, Eliza, if it takes handling a killer rabbit to impress you, I'll do it. Does he ever come downstairs?"

"No, he can't climb up or down stairs."

"That's very reassuring. At least I'm safe for as long as it takes to eat dinner."

The meal was ready in less than twenty minutes, and Eliza suggested they eat in her combination study/living room on the third floor. The phone rang as they sat down, and she motioned for Dario to begin without her.

"I don't mind waiting for you, Liza. If dinner cools off, we can always zap the plate with thirty seconds worth of microwaves."

"No, go ahead. I don't mind." she said with her hand over the receiver.

The caller was Jared and he seemed extremely upset. "Eliza, what are you doing?" he asked tersely.

"Just sitting down to dinner. What's up?"

"I have to talk to you right away. May I come over?"

"Jared, I have a dinner guest. What's so important?"

"I'd prefer to speak to you in person," he insisted.

"You can come by in the morning."

"I don't want to wait until morning on this. When's your dinner guest leaving?"

Eliza looked at Dario and smiled. It could be in fifteen minutes or tomorrow for all she knew now. "I don't know. Stop playing games, Jared. What's up?"

He was unwilling to give her more information and hemmed and hawed until Eliza cut him off.

She had surmised the reason for his agitation herself. "HEI offered you a better job and you're leaving me, right, Jared?" It was something she had expected for a long time and considered herself lucky to have had Jared with her for so many years.

"How did you know?"

"I knew HEI was interested in you, and I figured now that the differences over creative control of *Beyond Tomorrow* were escalating, they'd make some kind of move to get you. Don't feel bad about it. You've made a wise career decision, and I would have done the same thing were I in your place. You've advanced as far as you can go with my company. The potential to move upward in a nationwide network like HEI is far better than anything I could ever offer you."

"I'll stay if you tell me to," he replied sadly.

"No, I can't do that, Jared. You have to make your own decisions, and as I've said, you've made a good one. Do you know who else they're going to try to get?"

"Everyone, as soon as their contracts are up. They're out to pressure you into selling the show, and they mean to play dirty. Eliza, HEI is coming up with a soap that's a direct rip-off of *Beyond Tomorrow* with different names for the characters, but it's the same damn thing. It's still not too late for you to sell it to them. No one else is going to want it after they take your cast and duplicate the themes."

"Never," she said firmly. "Most of the good people have a long time to go on their contracts, Jared, and if HEI is going to take their show in the same direction they wanted to go with my program, it will bear little resemblance to the original before very long. What did they offer you?"

"I'm head of daytime programming now," he replied without any enthusiasm.

"Congratulations," Eliza answered. "You deserve it. Look, Jared, we'll talk tomorrow. My dinner is getting cold." She said good-bye and hung up the phone, slamming it into the cradle. "The bastards," she muttered. Eliza returned to the couch and sat down. "Did you hear all that?" she asked Dario.

He patted her shoulder. "Yes, I did. I'm sorry, Liza. Don't worry, you'll find another producer."

"This comes at such a bad time. Jared's the only person I know who is capable of running the entire show without me. I have one month to come up with the scripts for the new show, and now I'll have to spend more time with the old one until I find another producer. Damn!"

"Can't you get Jared to stay another month?"

"I'm sure he can't. Leaving now was undoubtedly part of the deal. That's the way HEI works. I've dealt with them for over five years." She played with the roast beef a while before deciding she was too upset to eat.

"Well, this certainly doesn't speak too highly of Jared, does it?"

"Business is business, and Jared is too talented to spend the rest of his life with a small company like mine," she said philosophically. "Running a soap is difficult, even if you're ABC instead of Rothcart Productions, Incorporated. Every talented newcomer from New York to Hollywood wants to work for you, and then as soon as they get a little national exposure and experience, they walk out to try to get into nighttime or the movies. Barbara's the only one I've had stay with me for the whole five years."

"Barbara Hesse?"

"Yes, she's wonderful, isn't she?"

"She certainly is. A beautiful woman and one of the finest actresses you have. Has she ever been tempted to leave the show?"

"At times. Her children are the main reasons why she's stayed with me for so long. She wants them to grow up near her ex-husband who lives here in Manhattan, and she likes the flexible schedule I'm able to provide. I gave her a month off last spring when her ten-year-old was in an automobile accident, and she knows she couldn't expect that type of scheduling if she were doing nighttime or the movies," she explained.

"I've met the little girl," Dario said. "I noticed she walks with a limp. Is it from the accident?"

Eliza was surprised Dario had met the child, since Barbara seldom brought her children on set. "Yes, it is."

"Poor kid. Is it going to get better?"

"There's hope." Eliza left the sofa and began to pace the length of the room like a caged animal. "Damn!" she repeated after a few minutes of mulling over her professional problems.

"Eliza, all that pacing is making me nervous. Come back here and finish your dinner." He left the sofa and gently dragged her back, pushing her downward by the shoulders. "My class at Columbia isn't very demanding. I'd be happy to help you all I can," he offered. When Dario saw that she wasn't going to eat, he pushed both their plates aside and moved closer to her on the couch.

"Thank you. That's very kind of you, Dario, but you don't know much about producing a daily show," she said bluntly, hoping she hadn't offended him.

"I could probably do a better job of producing one than directing it. Some of the films I did in Rome were so low budget they were almost one-man operations. I've even acted in a few pictures to save money."

"Really? What parts did you play?"

"The ones that required the fewest lines. You know, the bum sleeping on a park bench in the snow with a stack of newspapers on top."

Eliza smiled. "Somehow I can't picture you in that role, Dario." The smile was short-lived as she began to consider the fate of her show once more. "I knew HEI would come back with something to pressure me into giving them more creative control, but I never thought they'd sacrifice the ratings on *Beyond Tomorrow*."

"Well, sometimes these decisions aren't prompted by the most intelligent considerations, Eliza. There's a lot of ego involved, and you seemed so inflexible on your position at lunch today. It wouldn't surprise me to see HEI renege on the new show after they shake you up a little."

"Yes, I suppose. But meanwhile I've lost Jared and probably two leading men."

"Who?"

"Sam Norval and Elliot Marath both have contracts that expire at the end of the month. I've done my best to get them to sign for at least another year, but they're holding out on me both as leverage for a salary increase and in hopes of getting something better. I'm sure HEI has offered them a better deal than I can afford to meet," she explained.

"That's too bad. I don't care for Marath; he overacts too much, but Sam is good. Maybe we can get them written off the show with a bang instead of a whimper," he suggested. "One can challenge the other to a duel for sleeping with that woman they're both in love with, and they could wind up killing each other."

Eliza pulled the loose pins from her hair and laughed. "You know, that's not half bad, Dario. I kind of like that idea. The viewers wouldn't expect such an outcome. We've never had a double murder before."

Dario watched her hair tumble past her shoulders. It was windblown and tangled, and she looked as if she had just risen from bed. "I was going to do that," he said slowly.

"Do what? Write a double murder into the script?"

"No, take the pins from your hair."

Eliza caught sight of her reflection in the mirror over the fireplace. "I look like hell," she said, ignoring his comment.

"Just the opposite, Liza." He left the couch and embraced her. "Heavenly is the word."

She rested her head on his chest. "You know, the more I think about your idea, the more I like it. A double murder would be good for the ratings, and Sam's and Elliot's characters have been enemies since the show began. How's this?" she stepped back. Her hands were on his arms, and Dario was smiling down at her. "Sam's character, Sal, challenges Elliot's character to a duel in Central Park. We could film it on location in less than a day."

Dario chuckled. "That's terrible! Are you serious?"

"Yes, I think it's great!"

"How about if Sal and Brad shoot bows and arrows from opposite towers of the World Trade Center?" he asked.

"Oh, Dario, try to be serious! How about if Sal's wife tries to shoot him and winds up shooting Brad instead, and then she shoots Sal because he's a witness?"

"How about if a giant ape carries all three of them to

the top of the Empire State Building and throws them off?" Dario raised one of her hands to his mouth and kissed the upturned palm while she laughed.

"Come on, Dario, try to be serious. How about if Sal poisons Brad and then winds up either accidentally poisoning himself or committing suicide out of guilt?" She paused. It was becoming progressively difficult to think of new storylines with Dario's mouth on her hand. He kissed her palm again and then moved his lips to her inner wrist. "No, your original idea is the best one. We'll have them shoot each other in a duel."

"All right, you do that." He inched in closer to her body, dropped one hand to her lower back, and thrust her gently into his pelvis. "And now I have another fine idea."

She knew what he was going to say and extended her forefinger to his lower lip brushing it over the full underside. "And what's that?"

"How about if Eliza asks Dario to spend the night?" he whispered into her ear.

"It's all so soon, Dario. I don't know. It's such a big decision," she murmured. Eliza realized with a start those were the very words she had said to him fifteen years ago when he'd asked her to make love to him for the first time.

Dario felt the convulsive shudder of her body against his and knew what she had thought. "I know, baby. I know. All night long I kept telling myself to step back and give you space, to go home and write that damn lecture, but every time I look at you, all those resolutions go straight to hell." He released her from his arms. "I think I'd better go now."

Her breaths were short and shallow, and Eliza didn't say anything while Dario looked around for his shoes. She had loved him too much to say no twice fifteen years ago, and though she didn't love Dario anymore, she wanted him more now than she had that first time. Before, she had been shy, frightened of what she might find in his arms. She wasn't timid anymore and knew exactly what would be there for her now.

Dario found one of his shoes under the coffee table but couldn't locate the other. "I can't find my shoe," he said needlessly. "I bet Eli ate it."

"It wouldn't surprise me. Look under the couch; that's his favorite hiding place."

Eliza was mortified when Dario stuck his hand under her sofa and emerged with a man's shoe that wasn't his own. It belonged to Leonard, the man she'd dated for years and stopped seeing several months previously.

Dario's head jerked up sharply. There was an unspoken question in his eyes, and he decided not to ask it. "Wrong size," he quipped, tossing the shoe back under the sofa. He bent down again. "Ah, here we go."

She knew he was curious about the owner of the brown loafer, but Eliza didn't feel she owed Dario any explanations at this point. "I'll walk you to the door."

"Thank you, Eliza. Would you mind if I left through the backyard? There's an alley there that leads out to the street, isn't there?"

His request surprised her. "Yes, there is. Why do you want to leave through the garden?"

"Because it's the most beautiful place I've seen since coming to New York, that's why." He reached for his sweater and slipped it over his head.

Eliza took in the broad suppleness of his chest, sighed, and thought that the life of a successful, single career woman wasn't all it was cracked up to be. This was a moment when she longed for a husband and children to round out her life. "Thank you. You'd be surprised how many people walk through my rose garden and never see it. Dario, I have an idea. Why don't you return in the morning and we'll have breakfast in the yard? I usually don't eat out there this time of the year, but I think we can weather the weather.''

"I should think so. After all, we've weathered some very stormy weather, haven't we? I'll be here. What time would be best?"

"We certainly have," she agreed with a wistful smile. "Can you be here around seven?"

"You bet I can. We should get into work early and sort out this mess with Jared and the two actors leaving," he replied.

"That's exactly what I had in mind." Eliza quickly stepped into her shoes and walked Dario to the garden. The moon was full and bright in the sky but the perfume of her favorite lavender roses seemed less sweet now that the evening with Dario was ending. She knew she had only to speak a single word to keep him there for the night, but Eliza couldn't find it in herself to ask. She held back, not out of timidity, but out of fear she'd be doing the wrong thing by taking him to her bed now. Not wrong strictly in the moral sense, though she'd never before taken a man to her bed on so little provocation, but wrong in the sense someone might get hurt. God only knew how much they'd hurt each other in the past.

He brushed his hand across the side of her face and turned to leave in the moonlit garden. "Good night, Liza."

She had expected Dario to kiss her and was crushed when he didn't.

"What's the matter?" he asked, seeing how unhappy she looked.

"I was hoping for a good night kiss," she admitted with a rueful grin.

She sounded so much like the girl he'd loved when he was a young man of twenty-one that it nearly took his breath away. Dario was too moved to act or speak at first.

Eliza construed his silence to mean he'd just as soon forgo the customary farewell kiss. "I'll see you for breakfast in the morning. Good night, Dario. I'd better get in..."

Before she could finish the sentence, he placed his arms on her shoulders and drew her slightly toward him. They weren't touching, except where his hands rested on her, but she could feel the warmth of his body and smell the male scent of him that was sweeter than any other heady perfume in the garden.

Dario kissed her with a gentleness that made her want to cry. Eliza sensed the restraint in his action, knew of his consuming need for her in every part of her being, and almost hated herself for denying him.

"Will that do?" he asked afterward with his lips buried in the tangles of her unruly hair.

"Yes, quite nicely." She could barely stand it when he dropped his hands from her shoulders and reached for a small cigar in his shirt pocket.

"I'll be seeing you in the morning, Liza. Bright and early."

"I'm looking forward to it. Dario, are you sure it's safe to walk home this time of night?"

"I'll be fine, but don't you ever dream of stepping outside this garden of yours at night, okay?"

"I won't." They said good night to each other one more time, and Eliza lingered in the yard after he left. She knew from the halt of his footsteps and the eerie circle of light on the other side of the gate that he'd stopped to light his cigar, and she watched his struggle against the night breeze as it repeatedly blew out the matches.

When she turned to reenter the house, Eliza found herself face to face with Leonard James, the former man in her life.

Dario had also heard the sounds of a person walking into the garden and quickly ground out his cigar, listening and waiting to see if an intruder had chanced upon her home. His face was frozen in a hard mask, and the adrenaline surged through every nerve in his body as he prepared to come to her defense if need be. He didn't debate endangering his own life to help for even a fraction of a second. There was nothing to debate. He'd rather die himself than have her hurt.

"Leonard! For God's sake! You scared me half to death!" she exclaimed.

Dario continued to listen and wait. Obviously she knew this man, but it was still possible he was either a disgruntled former employee or perhaps someone she'd once dated, and he was aware most of the violent assaults against women were committed by men they had met before.

"I'm sorry, sweetheart. I let myself in with the key when you didn't answer. Eliza, I know I should have called first, but I had to speak to you immediately. I couldn't wait any longer. I've done a great deal of soul-searching during our trial separation, and I've come to a conclusion. I do want to marry you. You name the date, darling. I've even come around to your way of thinking on the subject of children. Oh, Eliza, you'll never know how much I missed you," he said fervently, reaching out for her.

She escaped his embrace and glanced over her shoulder to the wrought iron gate that enclosed the garden. It was overgrown with bushes, and she couldn't see through, but she hadn't heard Dario walk away. She knew he was still there. "We have to talk, Leonard. Let's go inside," she said somberly. Damn! Why did he have to come back now of all times?

"That's what I came to do. By the way, I'm on back-

up call for Dr. Gonzales. I left your number with my
service and may have to rush out in the middle of the
night.''

Dario had heard all he needed to hear and quietly
walked away, leaving before Eliza told Leonard he
couldn't spend the night with her.

Leonard took off his jacket and sat down at the bar
inside. ''What do you mean, I can't stay?'' He poured
himself a double brandy.

''Just that. Leonard, you're assuming a great deal. It
was you, not I, who termed our breakup six months
ago a trial separation. I intended it to be permanent.
We're not getting back together,'' she explained.

They both heard Dario's footsteps in the alley outside the window at the same time.

Leonard jumped from the bar stool. ''What the
hell?'' He made a lunge for the door. ''Eliza, there's a
prowler outside your window.'' As a physician who frequently carried narcotics, Leonard was licensed to carry
a handgun. He whipped it from his shoulder holster.

''Oh, for God's sake, Leonard! Put that damn thing
away!'' Eliza shrieked. ''That is my friend. He was just
leaving from the garden exit when you came in the
house!''

''Your friend?'' he repeated harshly. ''I think I'm beginning to understand your reluctance to resume our
relationship. When did you find a new bed warmer,
Eliza? What is he, one of those young studs who are
always chasing after you to get a part on the show?'' He
downed the remainder of the brandy in one gulp.

Eliza knew how nasty he could get when he drank.
When they'd first met, he was a social drinker, and
she'd never seen him intoxicated except once at a New
Year's Eve party when most of the people there had
also drunk more than they should have. During the last
seven years, however, his consumption of alcohol had

gradually increased until now he treaded the tenuous line between a problem drinker and an out-and-out alcoholic. "Let's go upstairs, Leonard. It's cold down here, and the ground floor is so expensive to heat."

He reached for the brandy bottle. "First tell me about this stud of yours."

"That was my ex-husband, Dario Napoli. Leonard, put that bottle down. You're on call," she warned him.

"I can take care of that," he ground out. He made a phone call and persuaded one of his colleagues to take over for him. "Satisfied?"

"No. Leonard, don't you know your associates aren't buying your stories about migraine headaches and every other excuse you fabricate to get out of work when you want to drink? They're completely losing respect for you," she said, knowing there was no point of reasoning with him now.

"To hell with them. I can't believe this, Eliza. Are you actually saying you're ending our relationship and don't want to marry me because you're getting back with your ex-husband? Some jerk who had an affair with another woman almost immediately after he married you? It beats all I've heard!"

"No, I'm not saying that at all. Come upstairs with me now."

He followed her with the bottle under his arm. "Then what are you saying?" Leonard asked, sitting down on the sofa in the third-floor living room.

Eliza sat on the desk chair opposite him. Looking at Leonard now, it was strange to think she'd been involved with him for nearly eight years and would have married him at one point in their relationship, a long time ago. "The same thing I said six months ago. It's over."

"You've said that before, Eliza."

She had to admit he was right about that. "I know,

but this time I meant it. I wouldn't have gone six months without contacting you had I not been serious. In my mind we were finished long before I met Dario again."

"I don't understand. I thought your major objections were my unwillingness to get married and my feelings about having a family. I'm ready to do what you want now, Eliza. Doesn't that mean anything to you?" he pleaded.

She saw the pain in his eyes and hated to watch him beg. "Not anymore, Leonard, and not for a long time. Can't you see? We just weren't right for each other. I think it's a myth when two people say they aren't getting married because they're so caught up in their careers they can't. No one's that damn busy and career-oriented. If the right person came along, they'd jump at the chance for marriage in a second."

He had already drunk half a liter and was beginning to fall into one of his sentimental drunks as opposed to one of his nasty drunks. "Are you saying you never loved me, Eliza?" Leonard reached into his pocket for a handkerchief and dabbed at his moist eyes.

"I loved you in a way, Leonard," she said softly, thinking she had never loved him in the way a woman truly loves a man she wants to spend the rest of her life with. She might have deluded herself into believing she did at one time, but now Eliza realized just how mistaken she was. She didn't have the heart to tell him he'd never once reached the free-spirited and sensuous aspects of her nature, that a single short-lived kiss from Dario had awakened more slumberous yearnings than all of the nights in Leonard's arms ever had. And she knew what Leonard couldn't give her and Dario could transcended desires for physical fulfillment. It was something that defied definition, but she had experienced it totally with Dario this evening and knew she'd never settle for less with any other man.

"In what way?" Leonard asked. "I thought we were good for each other."

"We were good for each other once, Lenny, but not anymore. You were always so kind and supportive of my career. Whenever the pieces started to fall apart, you were always there to help me put them back together. There were some bad times I never could have gone through without your friendship, like the time one of my shows was canceled and it seemed like I'd never work in the business again. And when my mother died, you were there, too. You even helped me deal with my feelings about Dario when I came across those letters. But..." She stopped, at a loss for words. She suspected they'd be lost on him anyway given the rate he was polishing off the liter of brandy.

"But a woman doesn't marry her best friend, right?" His words were slurred and she could barely understand him.

"Yes. A woman should consider her husband her best friend, but there has to be other things there as well. Leonard, come to the guest room. I think you should go to sleep now," she urged. Eliza stood to help him from the sofa, relieved when he followed her suggestion without protest.

"All right, but I'm not giving up on you yet. Once you get this romantic need for an exciting fling out of your system, you'll come back to me. I know, Eliza, because I always came back to you after I slept with other women," he stammered.

It was all she could do to get him down the stairs to the second-story guest room. His admission of involvement with other women didn't come as a surprise to her; she'd suspected it more than once over the years, though Leonard had always denied it.

"Do you need any help undressing?" she asked.

"I'm not too drunk to take off my damn pants," he said, collapsing on the bed, clothes and all.

He fell asleep almost instantly, leading her to believe he'd been drinking earlier in the day. Eliza removed his shoes and covered him.

She contemplated her dilemma while soaking in the bathtub. She couldn't have Dario over for a romantic early-morning breakfast in the rose garden with Leonard there. As she considered the situation further, Eliza concluded Dario might not show up anyway, since he'd obviously overheard Leonard express his wish to marry her. She put herself in Dario's position, and quickly realized she'd be hesitant to show up at a man's house, knowing his fiancée had probably spent the night there.

Eliza logged onto the computer terminal in her study that tied into a system at the studio and quickly obtained Dario's phone number from her personnel files. "Dario? This is Eliza."

"I didn't expect to hear from you so soon," he said in a tone that was impossible for her to decipher. "But I can guess why you're calling. Breakfast is off for tomorrow, right?" The emotions conveyed by his second statement were as transparent as glass. He sounded bitter and damn annoyed with her at the same time.

"Dario, I know what it must seem like to you, but I can explain," she began, only to be cut off.

"I bet you can," he said dryly. "Just answer me one question. Is your intended spending the night?"

"Dario, it's not what . . ."

He interrupted her a second time. "Yes or no, Eliza."

"Yes."

He laughed to himself, and the ridicule in that laughter cut through her like a sharp knife. "Well, you were right about one thing. Had I gone to bed with you, I would have waked up with something I didn't like."

His hostility and unwillingness to let her explain put

Eliza on the defensive, and she chose not to respond in the most politic of manners. "What's that, Dario? A third party in bed? You needn't worry about it. Leonard's in the guest room."

"No, that's not what I meant. I was referring to a deceitful and revengeful woman. Why in the hell didn't you tell me you were engaged? I think I've made my feelings for you obvious, Eliza," he said coldly.

"Oh, Dario! Are you trying to say I deliberately led you on so I could hurt you? How can you even imagine such a thing?" She was crushed to think he'd accuse her of such mean and petty motives.

"Because that's the way it looks from this end."

"Then you're at the wrong end. Oh, Dario," she repeated. "I'm not engaged to Leonard. I'm not even in love with him. We went together for years, and now he can't get it through his head it's over," she explained quietly.

There was a long pause before he spoke again. "What's he doing in the guest room?"

"He drank a liter of brandy and passed out cold. His twenty-five-year-old daughter and her son are living with him for a while, and I hated the thought of sending him home in his condition."

"Eliza, are you sure about all of this?"

That really got to her and she lost her temper. "Of course I'm sure, dammit!"

"Okay, okay, baby! Calm down!" He made a sound of exasperation, sighing heavily into the receiver. "Look, Liza, I'm sorry as hell for not letting you explain to begin with. I hung around outside your gate for a few minutes when I heard someone enter the yard. I was worried sick there'd been a break-in, and I couldn't leave until I knew you were safe. Even when you identified this person by name, I was still afraid you may have been in danger, and when I heard what he said, about having the key to your house and wanting to get married, I assumed he was your man."

"I can understand why you would have made that assumption. I would probably have done the same thing were our positions reversed," she said soothingly.

"Perhaps, but you would have had the patience to let me explain instead of flying off the handle like I did. Do I get a rain check on breakfast in your garden?"

"You know you do," she reassured him with a sleepy yawn. "Any morning except tomorrow."

"Thank you. Liza, how often does this guy come over to your house and pass out?" he asked with concern.

"Not too often, and it won't happen again. We had a talk, and knowing Leonard, he'll be terribly embarrassed about the whole thing in the morning. I'm going to ask him to return the key, by the way."

"Can I have it?" he was quick to ask.

She giggled into the receiver. "Why?"

"Why in the hell do you think? Can't you see the way I feel about you?"

"Dario, my dear, I don't pass out keys to my house to every man who wants to go to bed with me," she replied, trying to maintain a flippant tone and wondering just how he felt about her.

He lowered his voice to a seductive whisper and told her the way he felt. "Would you do it for a man who's falling in love with you?"

Eliza was unprepared for both his candor and the state of his emotions toward her. "Maybe, if I was falling in love with him, too, and everything else felt right."

"Care to be more specific?" he urged.

"Not now, Dario. I can't."

"Okay, then we'll talk about it some other time,

Liza. Do you need any help with Leonard? You don't
expect any trouble do you?"

"No, he'll sleep it off, then get up and shower and go
to his office around nine. Uh-oh," she said, recalling
that she'd put him to bed with the gun in his shoulder
holster. What if it discharged itself accidentally? "Dario,
can guns go off by themselves?"

There was a sharp intake from his end. "Eliza, what
are you saying? Does this man carry a gun?"

"Yes, when he expects to be out late at night. He was
on call this evening, but he had someone else take
over."

"And you put him to bed with a gun? What is he? A
cop or a gangster?"

"Neither. He's a physician, a psychiatrist who sometimes makes house calls for crisis cases. He was
mugged once when he was carrying a supply of narcotics for his patients and has carried a pistol ever since.
He's never used it..."

"I'll be right there," he cut in.

Eliza was stunned by his words and the way they
were spoken, as though her very life were in danger.
"What on earth are you talking about?"

"Do you think I'd actually let you stay in a house
with an armed drunk? Especially one you just broke up
with? Do you have any idea what could happen if he
wakes up and starts boozing again?"

"Oh, for goodness' sake, Dario! I've known Leonard for years; he's the most gentle, nonviolent person
I've ever met. He'd never harm me. Stay where you
are for the night."

"The hell I will. I have a neighbor with a car. Give
me five or ten minutes to get there."

"Dario! No! It's just not necessary!" The notion of
the man who had been her companion for so many
years as a violent criminal struck Eliza as ludicrous, and

she laughed. Not that she wished to discount Dario's concern, but his speculations were simply so far removed from reality that she couldn't help but giggle. She tried to cajole him from his dark mood to a lighter one. "Listen to me. If the way I handle writing soap opera drama is at all based upon the human predicament, and I believe it is, then the crazed maniac is most apt to go off the deep end when he sees his ex in the arms of another man! What do you think Leonard would think were he to wake in the middle of the night and find us together?"

"Hell, Liza, I don't know. Surely you don't think I planned on making love to you with him in the house, did you?"

She saw there wasn't much hope of reaching his lighter side right now and became more serious herself. "Listen to me," she repeated. "I'll take the gun away from Leonard and hide it somewhere. But, please, don't return tonight. It would complicate things on more than one level," she said in reference to her own tumultuous emotions.

There was another long pause, and she waited for him to speak. "Okay, Liza. Just promise me a few things. I noticed most of the rooms in your home have locks. Does your bedroom?"

"Yes. When I bought the house, I tried to restore all of the original fixtures to working order. I do have a lock and key, but I've never used it in my room."

"Use it for me tonight, please? And sleep with the dog, okay?"

"I will."

"Promise?"

"I do."

"Thank you. Promise to call me if you need anything, if anything happens?"

"Yes, of course. Dario, I have an idea," she began.

He chuckled. "I'm almost afraid to ask what, but go ahead."

"Can I come to your house for breakfast tomorrow morning?"

"Are you serious?" he asked.

"Sure, why not?"

"Be here whenever the mood possesses you," he murmured in a gentle tone.

"Dario, the mood possessed me a long time ago, but unfortunately, time, circumstance, and a multitude of other factors have kept me away. I'll see you at seven thirty. Good night, and sleep well."

"Good night, love, and you sleep well."

Neither of the two slept very much that night.

Chapter Five

Dario was standing on the curb in front of the Italian restaurant when Eliza's cab pulled up the following morning. Although they had agreed to meet at his apartment for breakfast, he'd called at the last minute to say one of his roommates had an opening night party the previous evening, and the place was a disaster area. The change in plans was slightly disappointing to Eliza who found herself more and more drawn to this charismatic man she had once married. She wanted to drink in the place where he lived, meet his friends, see the room where he slept. Some other time, she promised herself, waving brightly to Dario.

The restaurant looked familiar, and she recognized it as one Barbara had taken her to a few times. It was a charming place on Mulberry in Little Italy where the two women had shared long, lazy dinners over rich Italian food and full-bodied red wine, but as far as Eliza knew, the restaurant was closed for breakfast.

"Good morning, Liza," he said, rushing toward the street. "How did everything go last night?" He swept her into his arms like a soldier greeting his long lost love and kissed both her cheeks with resounding smacks.

The early morning passion of his action took Eliza by surprise. "Fine, Dario. There was nothing to worry about." She remained imprisoned by his embrace as they walked inside. Had she fainted at the present moment, she would have maintained an upright position from the way he held onto her.

With a dramatic flourish Dario whipped a white apron from a table near the entrance and tied it around his waist. "What do you think?"

She wrinkled her nose and laughed. "I think I've just walked onto the set of a pizza commercial, that's what I think." The decor was precisely what one would expect of a restaurant in Little Italy. Each dark wood table was covered with a red-and-white checkered cloth, topped by a candle holder made from a wine bottle. Eliza noticed a candle was lit at the table nearest to the kitchen. "I didn't realize you were in the restaurant business, Dario."

He offered her his elbow. "You've barely scratched the surface of my talents, Liza dear."

She took his arm and allowed Dario to lead her to the table. "You know, I'm beginning to realize that. Can I give you a hand with breakfast?"

"No, everything's under control. Sit down and I'll serve you." Dario held back her chair. He kissed the smooth column of her neck, exposed by the loose chignon she wore, as she sat down.

It wasn't a prolonged kiss, but the warmth it engendered radiated throughout her entire body. "I've had dinner here a few times, Dario," she murmured in a dreamy tone. "And I don't recall the waiters as being a fraction so charming."

"Good, and it had damn well better stay that way. If any of those cousins of mine ever do what I just did, I'll get the Mafia side of the family after them!"

"So this restaurant is owned by your family?"

Dario nodded as he passed through to the kitchen. He returned shortly with the breakfast he'd prepared earlier. "I hope you like cheese omelets."

"I adore them."

"Good. Dive in." They spent the next fifteen minutes eating, staring into each other's eyes, and exchanging lighthearted banter until Dario abruptly changed the subject. "Tell me about this psychiatrist of yours, Liza." He watched the smile fade from her face. That hadn't been his intention in posing the question, but Dario needed to know more about the man, and her well-being was only a single issue on his mind. He had to determine if Leonard meant more to her than she was willing to admit to herself.

She set her fork aside. "That's a broad subject. Where do you want me to begin?"

"With last night. Did he give you any trouble? You'll never know how tempted I was to ignore your request to stay home. I felt I should be there in case you needed me."

She saw the tension reflected in his clenched fist that rested on the table between them. "Oh, Dario. I've known this man for years. I wasn't the least bit worried, and you had nothing to worry about either," she reassured him. Eliza reached for his hand and, one by one, loosened the fingers to fit between her own.

He wasn't convinced by her attempts to assuage his fears for her safety. "Maybe so, Liza, but I don't like drunks, especially ones who carry handguns around. Did he wake up at all last night?"

"No, he was out like a light all night long."

The tight line of his mouth drew thinner at her words. "Was he?"

She knew what he was thinking. "I mean I assumed as much."

He seemed content with her simple denial. "How did you ever get involved with this guy in the first place?"

"How does one get involved with anyone?" she

asked rhetorically. "We had similar interests, we enjoyed each other's company. The impression you have of Leonard is a biased one. He's usually not like that. I think had you met him under different circumstances, you'd like him."

"I sincerely doubt that, Liza. Over the years, I've found myself hating every man you were ever involved with after me, even when I knew the two of you may have shared nothing more intimate than a meal or two. I knew about Leonard before last night," he finally admitted to her.

"You did? How?"

"Oh, I've met several people over the years who knew you or heard of you. When you get right down to it sometimes, it really is a small world. There were people from New York or Hollywood working in Rome when I was, and, of course, I met actors on the West Coast who'd worked with you. It never took more than five minutes for me to subtly turn a conversation around to your personal life."

Eliza squeezed his hand tighter. "I did the same with you," she confided. "If you're curious as to why I haven't asked you anything about your personal life in the years since our marriage, Dario, it's because I pretty much knew what you were doing. I was always surprised that you never remarried."

"And I was always surprised you never remarried, too. From what someone told me three years ago, I was certain you'd marry the physician you were seeing. That must have been Leonard James, right?"

She nodded. "I thought I would at one time, too, Dario."

"You said it was over. What happened?" It was a straightforward question that couldn't possibly be answered simply, if at all.

"I don't know," she exclaimed. "Who can say what

goes wrong in relationships sometimes? It's never just one thing that can be described in a word or two, but a whole composite of factors that all too often come out sounding like fabrications when you try to analyze them," she began.

"I suppose that's true in most cases," he agreed melancholically. "But you're wrong. Sometimes it is just one thing that can be described in a single word. Try infidelity."

Her throat went dry and she reached for the glass of water on the table. "That's an awfully big word."

"Yes," he said sadly. "It sure as hell was big enough to destroy our relationship, wasn't it?"

Eliza opened her mouth to tell him she had been rash in leaving him fifteen years ago because of his transgression, but she realized she couldn't. She valued fidelity in a marriage as much now as she did all those years ago, although a part of her had always wondered whether or not they could have worked things out and had a successful marriage in spite of what he'd done. His age and emotional immaturity certainly put his behavior in a different perspective to her now that she'd had years to try to understand, but still, he was her first love and he'd betrayed her, wounded her in a way no man had ever done, and she susupected no one ever could again. "Yes, it was. Have you ever considered how you would have reacted had the tables been reversed?"

"Many times. I would have killed the son of a bitch who slept with my wife."

"That's not what I'm asking, Dario. Would you have forgiven me?"

"Not for a long time, but I wouldn't have walked out on you either. Have you regretted leaving Rome without talking to me?"

"Many, many times," she admitted.

"I can't believe what a goddamn fool I was. You know, I didn't even realize what that woman had in mind when she suggested I'd be more comfortable in her villa instead of staying at the hotel." He shook his head in self-disgust. "Liza, there were several other people staying there, too. It may sound like an odd lifestyle to you, but we did those things when we were making a film. It was like one long party that went on for months, and people treated me differently there than they had back in California. I wasn't the odd man out anymore, the sensitive adolescent genius who no one understood and few people wanted to know. I was just part of the gang, and the rest of the gang whored around so I had to do it, too. I hated myself while I did it, but I did it anyway..."

"Dario, please stop. You can't go on blaming yourself for something you did so long ago. It's over and done with." The conversation was becoming too emotionally charged for her to handle. "I don't want to discuss this anymore. Can we drop it, please?"

Feeling the way he did, halfway in love with her all over again, Dario couldn't deny her anything and was ashamed of his impassioned outburst. "Of course. I'm sorry. Do you mind if we talk a little more about Leonard?"

"What's there to say, Dario? We went together off and on for years, discussed marriage a few times, and the bottom line was that neither of us was committed enough to take the final step." She thanked him when he refilled her coffee cup. "We blamed our reluctance to get married on absorption with our careers, and for a long time I believed that, but I don't anymore."

"I overheard his statement about children last night. I guess that must have been a big disagreement between the two of you, right?"

"Yes, that was another of our major differences, but

I think had I really loved him, it wouldn't have mattered. I could have accepted his feelings.'' Funny thing, Eliza thought. She found it as easy to confide in this man as it was to pour out her soul to Barbara, which was exactly what the two friends did on many a long evening.

''Well, I can certainly understand why a devoted career woman such as yourself wouldn't want to drop everything after she's been so successful and raise children, Liza,'' he said.

She shook her head and laughed. ''You have it all wrong, Dario. I've always wanted to have a family. My fondest dream was to build my career to a point where I could step back for a while by the time I was thirty and have a few children.''

Dario was astonished, and her words were music to his ears. With each passing moment he felt more certain of his love for Eliza. Nothing would make him happier than settling down with her and fathering their children, but he knew in his heart it was too much to hope for. She'd never fully forgiven him in spite of what she said.

''Why do you look so surprised?''

''Because I thought you were totally dedicated to your production company.''

''Oh, I am! I wouldn't have to give it up, just cut back on my involvement for a while. I could write the scripts from home and do a great many of the other things that need to be done from there as well. After the mortgage is paid off next year, I could even afford someone to help with the house and baby when I had to go into work.'' Her eyes glowed as she spoke.

Dario wanted that light to stay there forever, kindled anew each moment by their love. Could she ever trust him and love him again? ''You have everything worked out, don't you?'' he asked with a languid smile.

The brightness in her eyes dimmed. "Not exactly," she confessed. "You see, my master plan in life never worked out due to the lack of one single ingredient."

"And what's that?"

"The right man."

"Don't be so sure about that, Liza. Sometimes the right man pops up in the most unexpected places." He leaned toward her, took the coffee from her hand and raised her palm to his lips.

Their knees were touching beneath the table. Eliza felt the heat through the sheer fabric of her stockings. She extended one leg, which was quickly caught between Dario's thighs. "Like where?" she challenged flirtatiously.

"Like in closed Italian restaurants. Liza, let's get married and make babies," he suggested with a sexy smile. Maybe she meant what she said, had fully forgiven him, and could fall in love with him all over. The physical attraction was certainly there between them. He'd felt it last night when she'd clung to him in that good night kiss, and he experienced it now as she stared at him with her impossibly dark eyes.

She flung back her head and laughed. "You're crazy! Why, we're not even having an affair!"

"That can be remedied fast enough," he returned, reaching under the table for her knee and stroking it with a velvet touch. "There's an unoccupied apartment upstairs."

"Is it furnished?"

"With the essentials."

She didn't trust herself to speak. Could all of this be happening so suddenly? She knew, of course, he hadn't been serious about the proposal, but last night Dario did say he was falling in love with her. Had he meant what he said then? And moreover, did she want him to mean it? "I think we'd both better hop the nearest subway and get to work."

Eliza was surprised by his ready acceptance of her suggestion. Dario removed his hand from her knee after a tantalizing run to the hollow behind and then along the gentle curve of her calf. He stood. "I can think of something I'd rather hop into than a Manhattan subway, but let's go, Liza."

Eliza had never thought she'd be thankful for a transit system that frequently forced her into close body contact with other people until she took the ride with Dario standing behind her, one arm on her shoulder and one on the overhead bar for support.

"You know," she commented as they walked into the Brooklyn studio, "I think you were deliberately bumping into me on that subway, Dario." She spoke with a giggle bubbling to her lips.

They were in full view of everyone walking into the building, but Dario kissed the laughter from her mouth anyway. "Yes, but not as much as I wanted to."

"You lech!"

"Only when I'm near you. Can we meet for lunch?"

"I can't. I'm eating with Barbara. We have to make arrangements for our trip in a few weeks."

"Oh? Where are you going?"

"We're driving to this wonderful old farm her grandparents own upstate, and I want to get the details straight with her. We were supposed to go sooner, but she couldn't get away."

"Sounds like fun. What about dinner then?"

"I'd...uh, oh," she stammered. The building entrance was in her direct line of vision as she stood facing Dario, and Eliza was stunned to see Leonard walk through the door. He was freshly shaven and impeccably attired in a gray wool suit, bearing little resemblance to the drunk who had passed out in her guest room the previous evening. His debonair and restful appearance wasn't what shocked Eliza so much as his presence at the studio. She'd never known him to digress from his daily schedule of taking patients in the midtown Manhattan office he shared with three other physicians.

"I'm not sure if I understand what 'I'd uh oh' means, Liza. Is that a yes or a no?" Dario queried. He noticed her eyes were riveted on the entrance and glanced over his shoulder. "On second thought, I suppose I do," he grumbled. "The good doctor made a hell of a recovery, didn't he?"

"Morning, everyone!" Leonard boomed out cheerfully. Dario's dark Italian looks clued him in as to who he was, and he extended his hand in a friendly gesture. "Dario Napoli, I believe? Eliza mentioned you were in New York last night."

Eliza made hasty introductions between the two men, certain they could both hear the loud thud of her heart over the street traffic outside and see the agitated throbs of her temporal arteries as she watched them exchange greetings more like two sparring partners entering the ring than anything else.

Dario took the other man's hand and shook it while appraising him from head to toe. This poised, confident individual certainly wasn't the bleary-eyed drunk he would have expected to see bright and early in the morning if Eliza's account of last night's events was at all accurate. The thought she had lied to him and slept with Leonard crossed his mind and made his blood boil. Dario glanced from Leonard to Eliza, and what he saw in her eyes made him hate himself for doubting her. Eliza had meant it when she said she was finished with Leonard, but obviously Leonard wasn't through with Eliza.

"Nice meeting you, Dr. James," Dario said, and

then turning to Eliza, "I'd better get on the set now and discuss the cast changes with your people, Liza."

Leonard's mouth twitched in an effort to keep the smile plastered on his face. "Do you work here?"

"Just temporarily," Dario said as he walked away.

"Not temporarily enough for me," Leonard muttered. "What did you hire him for, Eliza? Stud in residence?" he demanded.

"Be quiet, Leonard. You have no right speaking like that about me or anyone else," she said sharply. "What are you doing here?"

"Let's go to your office and talk, okay?"

"All right," she agreed wearily, "but I don't have much time. I have a very hectic schedule."

"I can imagine."

Beverly beamed and greeted them effusively as they passed through the outer office. The charming Dr. James had always been one of her favorite people, and Leonard paused to inquire about her grandchildren before following Eliza into the next room.

His opening statement nearly floored her. "I'm taking a six-month leave of absence, Eliza. I want you to do the same and go on a long trip with me. What do you think about touring Europe? It's something we've always talked about and never had time to do. I've been thinking a great deal about our relationship lately. We never gave it the time it deserved. I've suddenly realized I'm going to be fifty years old on my next birthday, and all I've ever done in my life is work. The time has come to reevaluate my goals in life, and that means spending more time with you above anything else. I want to get married as—"

"Oh, Leonard no," she interrupted. "It's over between us. It just won't work anymore. Can't you see that? Why, I couldn't leave my job right now even if I wanted to. HEI is attacking from the left and right, and I have a show to do for a studio in Hollywood."

"Put everything on hold for a while, please. If I'm willing to do it for you, you can at least meet me halfway, Eliza. That's all I'm asking for at this point," he pleaded.

"I can't," she repeated emphatically. "I don't want to. Leonard, please, don't make this any more difficult than it has to be. We had a good relationship in many respects, but it's over now."

"Thanks to that gigolo of yours out there," he interjected bitterly.

"No, it was over long before he came back. We hadn't even seen each other for six months before last night," she reasoned. "Doesn't that mean anything to you?"

"Yes, it meant we both had to think about the relationship. I did that and I want to marry you. I'm even willing to father children now. I'll even stay home and diaper them if that's what you want from me. What more can I say, Eliza? I'll do anything you want."

"I don't want anything from you," she said sadly, wondering how to make him understand.

"Well, then I'll just have to be patient and wait for you to change your mind. Putting off our trip for a while has the advantage of giving me more time to work with my group."

Eliza sighed. "Leonard, I'm not going to change my mind. It took me a long time to, to...realize the relationship was finally over, and I'm not going back on that." She hesitated, at a loss as to how to proceed. "What group are you talking about anyway?"

"I joined a therapy group for doctors with drinking problems this morning. It's something I should have done a few years ago, along with marrying you, but you know what they say, Eliza. Better late than never, right?"

"Oh, Leonard! I think that's wonderful! I'm proud of you. You're too fine a physician to waste it all by getting into a serious problem with alcohol. Tell me more about the group.''

They chatted until Eliza had to excuse herself to get to work. Leonard never faltered in his optimism that she'd take him back, even when she refused his dinner invitation. Reluctantly, Eliza agreed to meet him one day the following week for lunch. They had, after all, been friends for a long time, and Eliza wouldn't mind his occasional company if he could refrain from pressuring her about resuming the romantic relationship, and she wanted to do everything she could to encourage his participation in the new group.

She worked diligently for the remainder of the morning, overseeing a multitude of tasks that constituted the daily routine of running a production company involved in daily drama. Eliza was looking forward to her luncheon date with Barbara. The demands of their work for the last few weeks had kept the two women from the heart-to-heart sessions they both treasured so greatly, and today they'd have a chance to catch up. Eliza still didn't know who the new man in Barbara's life was, but then it practically took a mathematician to tabulate the number of men her friend went through in a year. She had to smile when she thought of the phone call from Barbara a few weeks ago at her Hollywood hotel.

"Oh, Eliza! I've finally found the one!" she'd said with all the enthusiasm of a teenage girl getting ready for her first date.

Eliza had laughed. "That certainly sounds familiar. I think you must have found a dozen of them in the last year, Babs."

"Well, it sure as hell beats sticking with tried and true Leonard for as long as you have, Eliza. I admit he's a nice guy, but don't you find him a little dull at times?"

"We're not together anymore, Babs, remember? Tell me more about this new man of yours. Where did you meet him?"

"Jared introduced us. Oh, Eliza! It's true love at last!"

"You mean true lust!"

"That, too! Wait until you see this hunk of male flesh! I haven't been able to get him to bed yet, but I think tonight's the big night! If all goes well, I think I'm going to spirit him away to some tropical island and keep him there forever!"

"Oh, Babs, you'd be tired of him in less than a month. You always are. I've never known you to keep anyone around for much longer than that."

Barbara fell into her Cleopatra role. "Ah, my salad days when I was green in judgment to think as I did then, to...."

Eliza giggled again. "So, Cleopatra, you've found your Mark Antony?"

"Yes," she'd replied with a languorous sigh. "And never has Rome produced a finer god."

"He's Italian?" Eliza had asked.

"Uh, huh, and so dark and so gorgeous. I could just eat him up! But no more questions now. You're going to have to see this one to believe him!"

Barbara had failed to mention her new beau again, and Eliza assumed it was over already, but perhaps not. They could still be involved. The two women hadn't really talked to each other for a while, except briefly on set. She felt a twinge of guilt now for ignoring her best friend for nearly three weeks, but Eliza knew Barbara would understand. She always did.

Eliza reached for the phone to page Barbara on set and remind her of their plans to have lunch together. She answered the page after an unusually long wait, and it wasn't what Barbara said but how she said it that worried Eliza. She wanted to cancel lunch, something the women had been forced to do many times throughout the course of their friendship for one reason or another, but something was different this time. Eliza detected a uncharacteristic mixture of emotions in Barbara's voice as she begged out of the date. There was embarrassment, resentment, and even some anger.

"Barbara? What's going on?" Eliza asked quietly. So far, she hadn't even offered an explanation for the change in plans.

"I just don't feel like eating with you, that's why, Eliza. Look, I have to go now. I'm running through my lines with Fred. We're on in less than an hour." She hung up without waiting for Eliza's response.

Eliza felt as if someone had just kicked her in the stomach. What could she have possibly done to offend Barbara? She had acquiesced to her friend's every need so far as the job went, and if Barbara had a professional problem, it wasn't like her to beat around the bush about it. She was as straightforward as they came, and Eliza knew Barbara wouldn't lie to her if she could meet her face to face.

She left her desk and joined the cast out in the studio. Dario was operating the boom and directing at the same time. He waved down at her. Eliza smiled and returned the wave, scanning around the set for Barbara. She found her sitting at a table beyond the stage, going over her lines with another member of the company. Barbara looked up and frowned as Eliza approached them, confirming her suspicions something dreadful had happened. Well, it had to be a misunderstanding. Eliza was determined to get the whole thing out into the open and clear it up as soon as possible.

The man rehearsing lines with Barbara greeted Eliza with affection. "Nice to see you around the studio again. I understand you've been working at home these days."

"I have. I've been concentrating on the scripts for the new show."

"I heard about that. Congratulations."

"Thank you," Eliza murmured. Beyond the initial frown, Barbara had yet to acknowledge her presence. "Freddie, would you mind if I take Barbara away from you for a while?"

"No problem. We have the lines down pat now, right, Babs?"

Eliza sat down and asked her friend what was going on.

Barbara fiddled with her script briefly with downcast eyes before looking directly at Eliza. "Do you mean to say you have no idea whatsoever?" she asked with a brittle laugh. "Don't make a bad situation worse by lying about it, Eliza."

Eliza shook her head, stunned by the accusatory tone with which Barbara spoke.

"Think hard."

The woman before her was an entirely different person from the gentle individual Eliza had known and loved for five years. "I'm sorry, Babs, I just don't know what's going on. I've been so busy lately that I've lost touch with a lot of things around here. Please tell me what I did to make you act this way."

Barbara pulled a cigarette from her purse, and Eliza didn't bother to remind her of the no smoking rule. "Let me give you a little hint then. You see, it's an old but true cliché. One we've used many times on the show. Remember the storyline between Jill and Carol last year?"

Eliza recalled the particular subplot at once, and it nearly forced the wind from her lungs. It was a story about two best friends who became bitter enemies when they fell in love with the same man. "Oh, no, Babs," was all she could say at first, adding, "You are talking about Dario, aren't you?"

Barbara shot her a withering look. "Of course, I am! It's sure as hell not Leonard!"

"Oh, Babs," she repeated. It all made sense now. The time Barbara had phoned her in Hollywood and mentioned the new man in her life coincided with Dario's employment at the studio. Barbara had even told her the man was a dark-skinned person of Italian descent, and though she had no idea Dario was in Manhattan at the time, she should have figured it out later. Eliza understood now why Barbara had seemed so ill at ease in her office the first day she returned from the West Coast, and she also understood why Dario knew her little girl. "I don't know if I'm in love with him," she tried. It was the truth.

"Well, a hell of a lot of good that does me, Eliza. He practically dumped me the minute you gave him the go-ahead. Why didn't either of you tell me you'd been married and were still carrying the torch for each other? At least then I would have been able to put myself on guard against Dario instead of being used to fill his social calendar until you were ready to jump back into bed with him."

Eliza gasped. "I don't think you realize what you're saying, Babs. And I did tell you I was married once to an Italian-American film director."

"How in the hell was I supposed to know it was Dario?" Barbara was on the verge of tears.

Eliza felt much the same way. "How in the hell was I supposed to know he'd come here and you'd fall in love with him?" She struggled to keep her voice down in the crowded studio. "And I must have told you his name sometime."

"But you never told me he was your ex-husband when he came back! You could have told me then!"

"I didn't find out Jared had hired him until I returned from California, Babs, honest, and you never gave me the name of the new man you'd met when you phoned me in Hollywood. I would have told you then had I known."

"Sure you would have," she said bitterly. "And why didn't Dario ever say anything to me?"

"I can't answer for Dario," Eliza explained calmly, wondering why in the hell he'd never told her of his involvement with her best friend. "He never mentioned you to me, in this context, I mean. We only discussed your work on the show. He has a tremendous amount of respect for you as an actress."

"And none whatsoever as a woman. I think he had me pegged for an easy woman the minute he met me."

The thought of Dario sleeping with another woman while he expressed an interest in her sent a crippling pain across Eliza's midsection. What kind of game was he playing? "Oh, Babs, don't say these things, please. If Dario…dated you, I'm sure it's because he respects you as a person. He's not that kind of a man," she attempted feebly, wondering just what kind of man would have an affair with her best friend, not even tell her, and then try to make love to her. It was the type of man she didn't care to know.

"The hell he's not. He used me, Eliza. I thought we had a good thing going, but when I invited him up to the farm for the weekend, he told me he couldn't come and he couldn't date me anymore because of his feelings for you." Barbara halted her tirade long enough to blow her nose. "I wonder where all this man's scruples come from, Eliza. If he didn't mind sleeping with other women while you were married, why should he care now?"

Eliza flinched at the unkind remark. "Babs, come on, you don't mean that. I'm sorry about all this, really. I'm actually not very involved with Dario right now, but had I known you were seeing him, I never would have let anything happen at all."

One of the assistant directors called for Barbara over the loudspeaker. Eliza reached for her arm as she stood to leave. "Babs, we have to talk about this later."

The other woman jerked her arm free. "I have nothing to say to you. Leave me alone."

Eliza watched in silence while Barbara joined the cast on set three. In the short time it took to walk from where they had sat to the stage, she'd managed to thoroughly compose herself. Her melodic laughter called for in the scene drifted to Eliza, who for some strange reason was drawn to the set. She sat on a stool behind the vacant director's chair to observe the unfolding drama and saw something that probably wasn't apparent to anyone else present except the parties involved.

Eliza saw the pain in her friend's eyes whenever she was off camera, saw the anxious way she looked at Dario who continued to direct from up on the mobile boom, and she even imagined that Dario was aware of a certain undercurrent of tension. She was positive of that when he noticed her near his vacant chair and asked the assistant director to take over. Eliza didn't think she'd ever forget the expression on Barbara's face when Dario joined her for as long as she lived.

She tried to evade Dario by leaving the set before he could get to her, but she wasn't fast enough.

He spun her around by the shoulder as she turned to leave. "You're not running away from me this time, Liza."

"I don't know what you're talking about, Dario," she fabricated, her eyes on Barbara who was doing a love scene with Freddie now. "I merely came down to observe a few scenes, and now I have to get back to work." Eliza still hadn't had time to assimilate everything her friend had told her, and she certainly didn't want to get into a dialogue with the woman standing less than twenty feet away.

"I saw you talking to Barbara Hesse a little while ago."

"So? Barbara's one of my most popular leading ladies. We always talk in the studio," she returned evasively.

"I see. And are all your conversations so emotionally charged?"

"Sometimes."

"We have to talk, Liza."

"Not now. I have work to do, Dario."

"How about dinner, then?"

"I don't think so."

"Okay, Liza, if you're going to be difficult, then you name the time and place. I'm at your disposal," he said affably enough, but the tight lines framing his mouth belied the congenial request.

She hesitated, choosing her words carefully. "I think it'd be better if I got back to you later, Dario."

He grabbed her around the wrist and propelled her to the rear of the studio. Not wanting to make a scene, Eliza allowed him to usher her to the same restaurant half-set they'd occupied before.

Dario didn't speak until they were both seated. "The last time I waited for you to get back to me it took fifteen years for us to get together again. I'm not letting you leave now while there's any possibility at all of a misunderstanding between us."

"There's no misunderstanding, Dario. You simply had an affair with my best friend while you were seeing me and neglected to say anything about it."

He muttered a three-syllable expletive in Italian, and

she could guess the meaning without speaking the language. "Is that what you think?"

"Of course, it's what I think!" She paused to collect herself when she heard the rise in her voice. "But don't get me wrong, Dario. You and I don't really have anything going, so what you do with other people is your own business."

"We don't? You sure could have fooled me. Then what's your complaint, Eliza?" he said gruffly.

"I'm mad as hell about the awkward position you put me in with Barbara, that's what! You knew she was my best friend, and you never said a word about her! She thinks the two of us were in some kind of a conspiracy against her!"

"I'm not responsible for Barbara Hesse's paranoia," he said dryly.

Eliza leaped to her feet. "Oh, Dario! You haven't changed at all! You're the same unfaithful, egocentric, immature person you were fifteen years ago! You take whatever you want with no consideration whatsoever for other people's feelings!" That wasn't what she meant to say at all, to hurl the past into his face to account for what had happened now, but Eliza was too emotionally wrought to separate the recent sequence of events from those that transpired years ago. And maybe they were connected, she rationalized. Only this time he couldn't use the tenderness of his age as rationale for his lack of judgment. Some men were born womanizers, totally incapable of fidelity to any one woman, and she was beginning to think Dario was such a man.

She was convinced of this when he made no effort to refute her attack. He remained seated, and she looked down at him before walking away. "Well, don't you have anything to say?"

"No, Eliza, I think you've said it all," he conceded slowly. "See you later."

Dario remained in the booth for a long time after Eliza left, staring down at the carved initials on the table. He certainly seemed to have a talent for upsetting this woman's life. A month back in town and already her best friend hated her because of him, and perhaps he was damaging her chances for working it out with that doctor. Not that he wanted any other man to have her, but at least Leonard had been steady and there for her over the years when he himself had abandoned her a long time ago. Maybe now that Leonard realized what he had in Eliza, he'd shape up, marry her, and give her the stability and family she wanted. It was becoming increasingly obvious he couldn't give her what she needed.

The time had come to stop pursuing Eliza, to hope it wouldn't take as long this time to fall out of love with her as it had before. Maybe it'd be easier the second time around, he mused, returning to the set.

Chapter Six

"Well, this just goes to prove what my mother told me, Eliza. Two women should never fight over a man. Men come and go, but the friendship remains," Barbara said. The sun was unusually warm for a fall day in upstate New York, and she unbuttoned her coat. "Did I ever tell you about the time when I was fifteen and my best friend and I got into this long, drawn-out fight over a boy in our geometry class? He'd expressed a slight interest in both of us, and then wound up with some snobby prom-queen type. Neither one of us got him!"

Eliza shook her head and laughed. "Do you suppose Dario is off with some snobby prom-queen type?" The bright midafternoon sun continued to beat down on the two women, and Eliza soon followed Barbara's example and removed her coat.

"No, he's probably off somewhere with one of those groupies who keep chasing him around because A, he's adorable, and B, they want a part in the next movie he directs."

"It wouldn't surprise me. I've followed his antics for years in the fan magazines and gossip columns. Even if you discount ninety-nine percent of it, Dario certainly has his share of female admirers. When we were in college at UCLA, every girl in the class was crazy about him," she confided.

Two weeks ago it had seemed as if she and Barbara would never be able to discuss anything again, much less Dario, and Eliza felt immeasurable relief to see their friendship restored. Barbara had called her the very night following their conversation about Dario in the studio and pleaded for Eliza's forgiveness, which was readily granted. Since then, they had been too busy to share their feelings about Dario in depth and how it had briefly affected the friendship between the two women, but their encounters around the studio were warm and affectionate.

"And you were the only woman he ever loved enough to marry, Eliza. That must mean something. I tried to get him to talk about the marriage one night, but he was pretty mum on the subject, almost as though it still hurts him to think about it after all these years. Were you and Dario able to discuss the past at all?" she asked.

"Some, not much. There wasn't really much to say when you get right down to it, Babs. Dario got caught up in a situation he was too immature to handle, became involved with another woman, and that was it for our marriage. God, if I live to be a hundred and fifty, nothing could ever possibly hurt me as much as that did!" she asserted passionately. "When I look back on my emotional state at the time, it's a miracle I was able to get to the airport and return home. I really felt like I was half-dead, in some sort of a trance, and would never be the same again."

"Maybe you never were the same again, Eliza," Barbara suggested. "Of all the women I've ever known, you're the coolest and most emotionally aloof when it comes to men. You've never fully committed yourself to anyone. Have you ever thought that perhaps Dario hurt you so much that you're afraid to love again?"

Eliza dismissed her friend's speculation with a breezy

wave of both hands. "Goodness no, Babs! I'm not afraid to fall in love. I admit I'm more career-oriented than a lot of women are, but then I was like that even before I married Dario. Our great dream was to work together, as a matter of fact, to conquer the world of film side by side. We were going to have our own production company. Dario was going to direct the films, and I was going to produce them. We were going to be rich and famous and live happily ever after," she recalled with a bittersweet smile.

"Well, part of that dream came true," Barbara reminded her. "You have your own production company and Dario has directed several major films."

"Yes, but it didn't happen according to the game plan, Babs. We were supposed to work together, not on opposite sides of the Atlantic Ocean."

"The game's not over yet, kid. I know Dario's avoided you for the last few weeks, but I have the distinct impression he still cares a great deal for you."

"No, I don't think so. He gave Jared his resignation yesterday."

"I heard about that. Oh, maybe I'm wrong then, but he definitely turned down my invitation to come here because of you. I still can't believe we got into that big scene two weeks ago. I know you've forgiven me, but I'm still ashamed for the things I said."

"Don't worry about it. I can understand how odd it must have made you feel to realize Dario was my ex-husband and that we were involved, in the loosest sense of the word, of course." Eliza wanted to change the subject from Dario. "God, it's good to get away from the studio for a while and come up here! I've been thinking about buying a small farm nearby when I pay off the mortgage on my house in Manhattan. I only have a year left to go on it, you know."

"Yes, I know. Eliza, you've got to be the worst work-

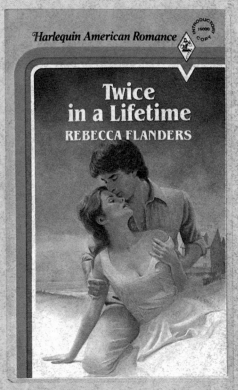

Enter a uniquely American world of romance with
Harlequin American Romance.™

Harlequin American Romance novels are the first romances to explore today's new love relationships. These compelling romance novels reach into the hearts and minds of women across America... probing into the most intimate moments of romance, love and desire.

You'll follow romantic heroines and irresistible men as they boldly face confusing choices. Career first, love later? Love without marriage? Long-distance relationships? All the experiences that make love real are captured in the tender, loving pages of *Harlequin American Romance* novels.

What makes American women so different when it comes to love? Find out with this special *Harlequin American Romance* offer!

Send for your FREE introductory book and tote bag now.

Get this Book and Tote Bag
FREE!

MAIL TO:
Harlequin Reader Service
2504 West Southern Avenue
Tempe, Arizona 85282

YES! I want to discover *Harlequin American Romance*.
Send me FREE and without obligation, "Twice in a Life-time" and my FREE tote bag. If you do not hear from me after I have examined my FREE book, please send me the 4 new *Harlequin American Romance* novels each month as soon as they come off the presses. I understand that I will be billed only $2.25 per book (total $9.00). There are no shipping or handling charges. There is no minimum number of books that I have to purchase. In fact, I may cancel this arrangement at any time. "Twice in a Life-time" and the tote bag are mine to keep as FREE gifts even if I do not buy any additional books.

154 CIA NAYA

Name	(Please Print)	
Address		Apt. No.
City	State/Prov.	Zip/Postal Code

Signature (If under 18, parent or guardian must sign.)

ARLPT384

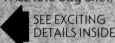

aholic I've ever known in my life!" Barbara chided gently. "I still say you're using work as an excuse to limit your personal involvements with men."

Eliza laughed and picked up a handful of crimson leaves. She playfully tossed them on Barbara's lap. "Oh, come on! You work as hard as I do." They were sitting on a pair of portable canvas chairs near the pond on Barbara's grandparents' farm in the small upstate town of Cortland, watching the children skip stones across the water. Maple and dogwood trees were ablaze in fiery reds and oranges as far as the eye could see, and the air smelled crisp and clean. Manhattan seemed a million miles away instead of less than three hundred.

"Sure, I work hard, but I play hard too. I haven't spent a fraction of the time you have moping over Dario! Where do you suppose he's headed from here?" Barbara asked.

"I'm not certain, Babs. Jared would know. At one time he mentioned directing one of Fanucchi's pictures in Hollywood, but he wasn't terribly keen on the project. I think he was waiting for something else to come through, but I never knew exactly what it was."

"Oh, that's right. I remember now; he told me about it. He wanted to do another film in Rome. Some kind of spy thriller." Barbara stood and shouted when her children began to remove their shoes. "Hey, you two! I said no wading! It's too cold, and both of you are just getting over sore throats!"

Her ten-year-old turned and glared at her mother. "The doctor said hydrotherapy is good for my leg!" Pammie disagreed, continuing to take off her shoes. Her eight-year-old brother was more obedient. Peter retied his shoelaces and headed out to the barn.

"I'm sure he didn't mean ice water!" Barbara replied. She stood and draped her coat over her shoulder.

Eliza followed her to the shore. The little girl's straw-blond hair was a mess since she'd refused to either comb it herself that morning or allow anyone else to braid it for her, and two large tears were running down her face. "Come on, honey, I'll help you with your shoes," she said. Eliza dropped to her knees next to the child.

Barbara placed a restraining hand on her shoulder. "Please, don't, Eliza. Pammie is old enough to put her own shoes on."

"I'm not having any fun at all here! I want to go home! You promised us Dario would come and ride horses with us, and he's not even here!" Pammie shouted.

Barbara paled at her daughter's words and glanced anxiously at Eliza. "Pammie, get your shoes on right this minute! I told you a long time ago Dario couldn't come with us. He's a very busy man, and he's getting ready to move away."

Pammie picked up her shoes and ran into the house in her stocking feet.

"I didn't realize your children were so fond of Dario," Eliza commented. She'd never seen either Pammie or Peter form much of an attachment to any of their mother's numerous suitors.

Barbara settled into the canvas-backed chair with a heavy sigh. "It's just Pammie. Peter liked Dario well enough, but he hasn't even asked about him since I stopped seeing him. I think my daughter must be in the throes of her first preadolescent crush. She's been impossible lately. Sorry if I snapped at you for offering to help her with her shoes, Eliza, but everyone has been babying that girl so much since the accident that I'm worried it's beginning to have an adverse effect on her. Sometimes she gets in these moods when she won't do anything for herself. All she has is a slight limp that is bound to get better with time, not a major disability, and even if she did, I'd still insist she put her own shoes on, if at all possible."

"I should have known better than to offer," Eliza admitted. "I guess I'm guiltier than anyone when it comes to spoiling her. She's such an adorable little girl. I can still remember when she was a tiny five-year-old!" Every year Eliza hosted elaborate birthday parties for Barbara's children and for the children who worked for her. No matter how hectic her schedule was, she never forgot a child's birthday party.

"You can have her!" Barbara offered with a belabored sigh.

"Sold! I'll take her."

"Sold?" Barbara returned with a laugh. "You can have her for nothing! In fact, there are days when I'd pay someone to haul her away!"

Barbara's grandfather came out to say he was taking the children into town to do some shopping. "Do either of you want to come?"

"No, Gramps, all I want to do is sit and look at this pond."

"Can I pick up anything for you?" the old man asked Barbara.

"No, I can't think of anything I need. How about you, Eliza?"

Eliza shook her head. "No, thank you, Mr. Philips. Have a nice ride into the city." She smiled to herself as he walked away with one grandchild clinging to each hand. "Your grandparents are so nice, Babs," she said after the elderly man left with the two children.

"I know. They're so active for people in their late seventies, too."

"So I've seen." Barbara's grandparents had purchased the hundred-and-fifty-year-old colonial-style clapboard house when they retired, and restoring it to the original condition had become a full-time occupation. Eliza followed their progress with great interest, since she loved working on her own home in Manhattan. Many of the skills that went into remodeling the four-story structure in Gramercy Park had been learned at the farm in Cortland, where the two older people were eager to teach Eliza everything they knew. "Babs, put your hat back on. You're starting to get a sunburn, and you're supposed to look pale and sickly on set next week."

"So, I'll put white shoe polish on my face," Barbara said with a deadpan expression.

Eliza laughed. "I said sickly, not dead."

The two women sat by the pond and chatted until it was time to go inside and help with dinner. "What can we do?" Eliza asked Mrs. Philips.

The petite, white-haired woman was kneading bread dough at one of the free-standing cupboards that flanked the kitchen walls. In their quest for authenticity, the couple had torn down all of the installed cabinets that were added to the kitchen around the turn of the century and replaced them with the type of units used over a hundred years ago. "Not a thing. You two girls go into the living room and sit by the fire. Everything is ready for when Paw and the kids get here."

"Oh, Grams, you're doing too much! You should have let me and Eliza help!" Barbara exclaimed. "At least let us set the table."

"Already been done. Now run along, girls," Mrs. Philips said.

"Okay, you win, Grams, but we're going to beat you to the dishes."

Barbara poked around in the fire and added a few more logs to it. "Eliza, do you think if we're ever old and married someday, we'll call our husbands 'Paw'?" she asked with an infectious giggle.

"I don't know. Do you think we'll call mature

women such as ourselves 'girls'?" she countered with a smile as broad as Barbara's.

"Good question! But I can't say as I mind, Eliza. Every time I look into the mirror I'm getting older and older. Pretty soon I'll be playing the part of a grandmother on *Beyond Tomorrow*. And I'm not even forty! Why did you have to cast me as someone who used to be a teenage mother who now has a promiscuous teenage daughter?" she asked with an exaggerated stage sigh.

"Every good show needs its good girl gone wrong, Babs, you know that. By the way, how's your leg?" Barbara had played the role of a villain for five years on the show, and the previous week she was accosted by an angry fan on the subway who had been unable to separate Sabra and her wicked deeds from the real-life Barbara Hesse. After recognizing her, the irate fan had proceeded to kick her in the shin.

Barbara rolled up her jeans. "Still black and blue! Lucky for me that cop was nearby or that woman would have murdered me! I swear, Eliza, she was out for blood! There I was, sitting innocently by myself, and she started accusing me of kidnapping a baby. I was so absorbed in reading a book that I didn't catch on at first what she was talking about, and the next thing I knew there was this searing pain in my lower leg!" Barbara paused to laugh. "The police officer was adorable, but he didn't recognize me and thought I might have actually tried to steal the other woman's baby! I think that was the funniest part!"

Eliza giggled while she kicked off her shoes to warm her feet on the hearth. "And I bet you explained the whole thing to him over cocktails at five, right?"

"I wanted to, but it turned out he was married. Not only married but into fidelity. He said his wife likes soaps and maybe I could meet with her sometime!"

"Too bad," Eliza consoled. "Maybe the next knight in blue who rescues you will be single. Did I ever tell you about the time Jared and I were in a restaurant talking about the best way to kill off one of the characters who was quitting the show, and the next table was filled with FBI men? They overheard everything and thought we were serious!"

"Jared told me about that. I swear, Eliza, sometimes I wouldn't trade working on *Beyond Tomorrow* for anything in the world!"

"Even if it means black-and-blue legs?" she teased.

"Even so! Oh, well, at least I'm getting recognized nearly everywhere I go now. Some lady in Bloomingdale's wanted to know if Pammie was another one of my illegitimate daughters the other day!" she said, laughing so hard she could barely get the story out.

"And to think all I ever get is nasty letters and phone calls," Eliza returned.

They were summoned to dinner a few minutes later. It proved to be a long, leisurely affair. Pammie seemed to have forgotten her request to return home as soon as possible and spent the remaining of her waking hours that day trying to persuade Eliza to give her a part on *Beyond Tomorrow.*

"You're talking to the wrong person, honey," Eliza said for the tenth time as she tucked the child into bed. "We can't even audition a child without parental consent. You have to get your mother's permission first."

"She'll never give it to me!" Pammie wailed. "I want to work with exciting men like Dario and be a star, and she won't let me!"

Eliza stifled a smile. Exciting men like Dario? Wherever did a ten-year-old pick up such phrases? Undoubtedly from her mother she concluded. "Dario isn't an actor, Pammie. He directs."

"I know that! I could still work with him, couldn't I?"

"Not on *Beyond Tomorrow*. He's going away to direct a movie," Eliza explained patiently. Barbara had entered the room and was standing near the door with a frown.

"So, I could still work with him," the little girl insisted.

"I've never seen a child in any of his movies, Pammie. Maybe if you study acting when you grow up, you can work with him then. Good night now." Eliza kissed her cheek and went downstairs. Barbara's grandparents had already retired for the evening, and Peter was sound asleep in one of the attic bedrooms. Eliza and her friend decided to stay up for a while longer and sip wine in front of the massive stone fireplace in the parlor. "I didn't know Pammie wanted to be an actress, Babs," she said after Barbara poured the first glasses. "Is this something new? Last time I heard, she wanted to be a physician."

"Yes, this is something new. You know how kids are. She wanted to be a doctor right after the accident because she was so impressed with Dr. Goodmen at the hospital, and now she wants to act because of her infatuation with Dario Napoli. Would you like another glass of wine, Eliza?"

"I'm still working on this one, thanks. Well, if you'd like, I'm sure we can work something out for her. You know, a small walk-on part at first to see how she does on camera," Eliza suggested. "Joannie's parents are talking about moving to Hollywood in the summer, so I'll need a kid who can play a nine-year-old."

Barbara shook her head. "No way! I don't want any kid of mine going into show business at her age! It's rough, Eliza. I went through it all myself, beginning when I was five. I missed a lot of growing up and had to learn to live with rejections no one under the age of twenty-one should know about.''

Eliza knew about her friend's long career in front of cameras. Barbara had worked in daytime since she was fifteen and often joked about having had twelve husbands and twenty-four lovers in the last twenty years. Before that, she'd worked in nighttime and had roles in a few movies. "I know, Babs, but you're so different from the way your mother was. You'd never try to manage Pammie's career and push her continuously to succeed the way Michelle did with you.''

"Oh, I suppose,'' Barbara conceded. "Michelle is really something else. She called me from Paris last week to ask if I'm still doing daytime! Can you imagine? I've been in it for two decades, and she's still waiting for my adult-movie debut!''

Eliza had never heard Barbara call her mother by anything other than her first name. "Well, you've certainly had your share of offers, Babs. It's always amazed me that you've never accepted any, but I understand your position with the children. I really admire you for it.''

"Thanks, I'm glad someone does! How about some more wine?'' A few glasses later, Barbara lowered her voice and moved her chair closer to Eliza's. "Eliza, do you mind if I ask you a personal question?''

Eliza shook her head and giggled. "Since when did you begin asking if you could ask, Babs? Sure. Shoot.''

"What was Dario like in bed?''

Eliza took the question in stride; however, she assumed the question was asked about the distant past. "Pretty lousy, to tell you the truth. He was almost as inexperienced as I was, but I was too naive to know any better at the time.''

Barbara was flabbergasted and sprang forward to the end of her chair. "Dario lousy? Inexperienced with women? He's not a homosexual, is he?'' she ventured at length.

Eliza's mouth dropped open in surprise. "Dario? Never! He's as heterosexual as they come, my friend. You have to remember that when we were married he was barely past his twenty-first birthday. We were each other's first lover.''

"Oh, I see what you mean!" She collapsed back into the seat with a raucous giggle. "I thought you were referring to his expertise now, not fifteen years ago!''

"Now?" she asked in amazement. "How would I know what he's like now? Babs, I haven't slept with that man for over fifteen years! Why don't you tell me what he's like? You were the one having the affair with him, not me!''

"Me? I never went to bed with him, Eliza! Whatever gave you that idea?''

Eliza was momentarily speechless. Was it possible she had misunderstood Barbara? "You did! And come to think of it, so did Dario,'' she added, remembering how he had reacted when she accused him of sleeping with her best friend while pursuing her.

It was Barara's turn to be shocked. "He said he slept with me? What a macho creep, Eliza! We hardly got to first base as they used to say.''

"But, Babs, you said yourself he used you, that he wanted you because you were—were—''

"Easy?" Barbara suggested.

"Yes, but remember those were your words, not mine.''

"Well, that's what I thought." Barbara shrugged her shoulders and closed her eyes tightly for a moment. "I mean at first. That's what most men want, isn't it?''

"A great many, I suppose." Her friend still hadn't explained why she'd led her to believe she'd had an

affair with Dario. "I definitely got the impression you
and Dario were well past the first-base stage."

Barbara left her chair, put a few logs on the fire, and
then remained sitting near the hearth. "Maybe that's
because I wanted to give you that impression, Eliza,"
she admitted at length.

"Wanted to? Why, Babs? I don't understand."

Her friend laughed. "Oh, Eliza, for a businesswoman who can outsmart any twenty people I know and for
an ace writer of gut-wrenching drama, you sure can be
naive about your own personal life!"

"I'm not following you, Babs," Eliza said slowly.
The sun had long since set, and the large room was
decidedly chilly. The fire was the only source of heat,
and she joined Barbara near the fireplace.

"I wanted to hurt you because you'd hurt me. It's as
simple as that. I can't tell you how ashamed I am about
it now. I was angry because neither you nor Dario told
me you and he had once been married, and I was furious with the two of you when he said it was over between us. I knew if you thought Dario was sleeping
with me, you'd probably stop seeing him, at least for a
while."

"And you thought he'd be interested in you again?"
Eliza probed cautiously.

"More or less, and that was certainly fallacious
thinking from A to Z because he was never very interested in me. Per usual, the minute I laid eyes on that
man I chased him around the studio until he got tired
of running and agreed to go out with me. I asked him
for the first date, you know, Eliza. And after that, I
think he came by mainly because Pammie begged him
to. One night she cooked an entire dinner for him, all
by herself, and he's just too sweet of a man to turn
down a child."

Barbara seemed terribly distraught, and Eliza hastened to reassure her. "Babs, all that is over and done with now. You don't owe me any explanations. My only major concern was that you thought I'd deliberately deceived you about my past and present relationship with Dario and interfered with whatever you had with him. Now that I know you don't feel that way anymore, we don't have to talk about it. Come on, let's change the subject. Tell me about the new man in your life. I saw him on set last week. He looks familiar. Didn't he do a bit part on one of NBC's soaps once?"

"Yes, he did, but I don't want to talk about him now. I'm not through with Dario. I think if it weren't for me and my big mouth, the two of you would still be together. I really feel bad now about not clearing the air sooner, I mean so far as letting you know I never had much going with Dario at all, except in my imagination. But I was certain he'd let you know what was going on. I think he cares a great deal for you, Eliza."

"No, I sincerely doubt that. It's been two weeks since he's said more than five words to me."

"I know, but there's a reason for that. He's hopelessly in love with you, and you broke up with him out of loyalty to your friend. I bet you didn't even give him a chance to explain what was really going on between us after the conversation you and I had on set that day, did you?"

Eliza shook her head. "But it's more complicated than that. I wouldn't say I broke up with him though, because we were never really together."

"So you were never sleeping with him at all?" Barbara reiterated, ignoring the slow flush that colored Eliza's bronze cheekbones.

"No, I wanted to get to know him again first."

"Well, that's a good way to get to know someone," Barbara mused. "In fact, I'm hard pressed to think of a better way!"

Eliza laughed. "You're impossible, Babs!"

"So I've been told. Speaking of the men in your life, how's Leonard these days? You know, I really envy you. You have one gorgeous knockout of a guy in love with you and one steady, dull guy in love with you. Between the two you should be able to come up with something that makes you happy!"

"Things aren't quite so simple, my friend. Even if Dario and I hadn't had this misunderstanding, he's still leaving New York soon. As for Leonard, he's doing fine. He joined a self-help group for physicians with drinking problems, and I've done my best to encourage him. He's a brilliant psychiatrist, you know, but I've seen him too hung over to work at least once every other month for the last year."

"That's too bad, but joining the group is probably the best thing for him. I've noticed he's spent a lot of time around the studio lately," Barbara commented as she refilled her wineglass. "Dario has made the same observation. I bet he thinks the two of you are back together."

"I told him it was over," Eliza explained with a yawn. "It's getting late. I think we should turn in now, Babs. We have a long ride back to the city tomorrow. Your schedule is particularly heavy next week."

"I know. I have to cry every single day."

Eliza giggled. "You can turn on the waterworks better than any actress I ever knew. If they ever give out an award for tears, you'll get it."

"Thanks, that's some distinction, Eliza." The two women were sharing a room next to the one the children slept in. Barbara checked on them before climbing into the twin bed. "Were you warm enough last night?"

"Yes, thank you. Good night, Babs." Eliza remained awake long after Barbara fell asleep. Her thoughts were of Dario and the look in his eyes when she'd accused him of having an affair with her best friend. She now understood that expression, which was indelibly etched upon her mind, to be one of profound disillusionment to learn she'd confirmed his fears as to her basic lack of trust in him. Before, she'd credited his emotions to something entirely different, embarrassment perhaps, maybe disappointment to realize he couldn't have both her and Barbara. Eliza continued to ponder her predicament until the roosters crowed in the barnyard at dawn. No action of hers could undo the past. All she could do was tell Dario how sorry she was.

But he made it extremely difficult for Eliza to apologize, not so much because he was unavailable around the studio, since she saw him there every day, but there just seemed to be an emotional impasse between them now, and she didn't know how to bridge that gap. Before, on the farm in Cortland and all during the return trip to Manhattan, Eliza had thought all that needed to be done could be accomplished with a few lines of heartfelt apology. She realized how hopelessly inadequate her logic was the first time Dario said hello to her as they walked past each other on the set. The look in his eyes went beyond passive disinterest in her without quite reaching the threshold of active dislike. It was as though he'd dismissed her from his thoughts forever, and all the apologies in the world wouldn't matter at all. How could they when she'd told Dario she forgave him and trusted him, only to fail the crucial test of demonstrating her faith when he needed her to do so?

Eliza allowed herself to be the recipient of his impersonal greetings for the remainder of the week and then decided to do something about the situation in the middle of the following week. Dario was scheduled to leave for Rome five days later. She didn't know if she'd ever see him again and was not going to let him go without understanding her feelings. Not that she expected her apology to compensate for the damage she'd done to whatever they had shared previously, but perhaps they could part as friends this time around.

She found him on set with the new director Jared had just hired. As Jared had been at first, the young woman was too overawed by the presence of a film legend such as Dario to concentrate on the task at hand. Eliza approached the trio cautiously and stood aside until she had Jared's attention.

"Eliza! You've met Paula, haven't you?" Jared asked, pushing the woman toward her.

Eliza extended her hand. "No, I haven't, but I've certainly heard well of her. I'm very pleased to have you here, Paula."

"Thank you! I'm more than pleased to be here, Ms. Rothcart. I've wanted to work in daytime since I was old enough to turn on a television set!" she enthused.

"Then this is your golden opportunity. All we do around here is work, work, and more work," Eliza said. So far, she'd avoided looking directly at Dario, and he'd done nothing to acknowledge her presence. She turned sharply toward him when he spoke.

"Well, if everyone will excuse me now, I have to get back to the set. It's time to begin the final taping," Dario said. He glanced at his watch. "It's nearly eight P.M. We're running three hours overtime today."

"Dario, would you mind if Paula took over for a while? I'd like to speak to you," Eliza said.

"Fine. Shall I come to your office?" he asked politely in a tone that emphasized the employee-employer relationship between them.

That wasn't the relationship she would have had stressed at the present time. Eliza didn't want to explain herself to Dario from opposite sides of the large walnut desk that dominated her small office. She looked at the large clock on the wall. "Have you eaten dinner yet?"

"Yes, but I wouldn't mind another cup of coffee."

"Good. Let's go to O'Leary's." Eliza wished he'd give her a break and say something, anything, during the five-minute walk around the corner to the delicatessen, but Dario chose to remain silent until they sat down.

"I'm going to miss working with your company, Eliza," he began. "I've gained a great deal of respect for daytime drama and the people who do it in the last few months. It's given me an entirely new perspective for the book I'm writing. I can't thank you enough for giving me the opportunity."

She wondered just how much sarcasm was implicit in the seemingly innocuous statement and was forced to conclude the ridicule she heard was her own creation when she looked up at him. "You're very welcome, Dario. Our ratings went back up during the last six weeks. They're higher than ever, and I'm convinced a major reason why is your input. You've been a source of inspiration to my entire company," she said sincerely. "So, it's Rome from here?"

The waitress came to take their orders. Eliza ordered a ham-and-Swiss-cheese sandwich on rye and a cup of coffee for Dario. "Are you sure you won't have anything else?" she asked.

"Yes, coffee is fine. Thank you, Eliza."

Every time he said her name, she thought of how he'd been unable to refrain from calling her Liza before. The elongated form now came as naturally to his lips as had the diminutive at one time. "You're welcome. Tell me about the project in Rome."

"It's my usual forte. Another suspense film. This one is a little different from what I've done previously because it's set in the future, but it's basically the same old formula."

"With flying saucers instead of fancy sports cars?"

Dario smiled. "That's about it. I understand things have worked out well for your new show too."

"They have. I'm almost finished with the ten scripts they wanted." She paused briefly. "Dario, I didn't want to meet with you to discuss our careers."

"I didn't think so," he replied. Dario had on a fawn-colored turtleneck sweater that accentuated his swarthy complexion, which appeared even darker than usual because he needed a shave.

While she sat there struggling for the right thing to say, Eliza found her attention drawn to his unruly black-and-white hair. Apparently he hadn't cut it since arriving in Manhattan nearly two months earlier, and the heavy waves touched his shoulder on the side where he tilted his head. "You need a shave and a haircut, Dario," she said at last.

He chuckled and reached for her hand. "Eliza, it's been longer than I can remember since any employer of mine called me on my long hair and beard."

The warmth of his touch brought a soft glow to her cheeks. She laughed, a husky deep sound in the noisy room. "Really? I can't imagine anyone ever citing you for that. I thought you artist types were supposed to have long hair and beards."

"So did I, but apparently the feeling's not universal." As he spoke, the pressure on her fingers increased, transmitting the tingling warmth throughout her entire body.

"Mind if I ask who objected?" Eliza cooed in a blatantly flirtatious tone that nearly brough a flush to her olive-colored cheeks, but the flush never spread past her intellectualizations. A part of her psyche dictated that it was out of character for her to flirt so openly with a man, but the diametrically opposed element told her she was a mature, single woman in her thirties who could enjoy whatever man she chose to, and she chose Dario. Her hands were beginning to perspire from the heat of his, and she loosened the grip. Dario's face fell as she did so, but the glow was kindled anew from the use she made of her fingers.

They initiated a sensuous assault of the bronze skin of his inner wrist. Dario felt his blood pressure rising and did his best to keep his volatile libido in check. He'd realized two months ago, the first time he'd seen Eliza cross the studio on her way to the office, that he had very little self-restraint where she was concerned. He'd just as soon make love to her as look at her and considered it a miracle, a tribute to his finest powers of discipline, that he hadn't barged into her bedroom weeks ago, hadn't even called her during the last two weeks. Yes, he'd maintained his distance simply because he loved her all over again and would sooner see himself dead than ever hurt her. He wasn't sure how loving her just now would hurt her, but he was still afraid. Maybe it was just the basic lack of trust that would wound her over and over again, he reflected, as her fingers inched along his forearm. His business demanded repeated contact with desirable women, many of whom would sleep with him at the drop of a hat to further their careers. It would be enough to try any relationship, much less one that had been savagely wounded in the past by his own foolishness.

Eliza regarded Dario's introspective frown with a dual sense of embarrassment and foreboding, thinking she'd made a fool of herself by flirting with a man to whom she didn't appeal, a man who no longer cared whether she trusted him or not. She eased her fingers from between his. "I wanted very much to tell you something, Dario. It loomed as a highly important subject in my mind for the last ten days, but somehow, it doesn't seem like all that big of a deal now."

Just as Eliza was about to put her hand, palm down, on the table after freeing it from his own large fingers, Dario deftly inserted both thumbs under her wrist and manacled it in a circle completed on top by his forefingers. "Why don't you let me be the judge of that?" he asked persuasively.

All the time, the sensation of his flesh against hers played havoc with Eliza's emotions. "I really made a fool out of myself a few weeks ago, didn't I, Dario?" There, she'd gotten it all out at once, no longer groping for the right words to assuage the injustice she had done by not trusting him originally, not allowing him to explain.

Dario smiled and raised her palm to his mouth. The kindness in the golden brown eyes was almost enough to bring tears to her own. "Go on."

"You're not making this very easy," she chided lightly and with great fondness. Eliza had a very strong premonition that Dario knew exactly what she wanted to say and was going to force it from her syllable by syllable.

She was correct. "No, Liza, I've waited nearly half a lifetime to hear you say I finally behaved in a trustworthy manner toward you. And I want you to say it now."

She took a deep breath. "Okay, I will. I was an idiot to think you were sleeping with Barbara at the same time, we... we were...."

He finally came to her aid. "Thinking about sleeping together?" he suggested with a slow smile that drew her eyes to the pearly white luster of his teeth that seemed blindingly bright beneath the growth of black hair on his naturally dark-complected skin. "Oh, boy," he added with a sigh, "was I ever thinking about it, Liza. I thought about it night and day, practically to the exclusion of everything else. And I still think about it."

"I noticed the torrid touch you added to all these love scenes," she murmured.

"Well, I can assure you, my dear Eliza, that wasn't where I wanted to place my torrid touch."

"Dario," was all she could say, and the word was spoken with reverence.

"Go on," he repeated.

"I should have given you a chance to explain instead of jumping to the wrong conclusion. I'm sorry. Am I forgiven?"

"A hundred times over. I have to admit I was at fault too. I should have told you your friend thought there was something between us that didn't really exist outside of her own mind. To tell you the truth, it took me a while to realize how Barbara felt about me," he confessed almost awkwardly as though it embarrassed him to discuss the female admiration he aroused nearly everywhere. "I thought the whole thing was pretty casual, strictly platonic, if you know what I mean."

"I know what you mean."

"Eliza, do you mind if I ask you the status of your relationship with Leonard? I've seen him around the studio nearly every day for the last few weeks."

"No, I don't mind. I'm trying to be friends with him, but he wants more than that now. If I've spent more time with him than I should, it's mainly because I want to encourage his participation in the group he's joined. Did I tell you about that?"

"No, I don't believe you did."

"It's a self-help group for physicians with drinking problems. Leonard hasn't had a single drink since he started attending their meetings," she said.

"That's good, but you can only do so much for a person with that sort of problem. Basically he has to do it for himself, not stop to impress you," he advised. Dario held on tightly to her hand while he spoke about a friend of his in Rome who had been a heavy drinker for years and was presently a recovered alcoholic.

"You're right, Dario," Eliza said fifteen minutes later. "I get your point, but I disagree. Leonard isn't doing this just for me. He's very concerned about his career."

"I hope so. Eliza, I'm getting tired of this Brooklyn diner. Mind if we move on?"

She stood. "Not at all. I should probably be getting home now. I have work to do. It's time to write up the new six-month story projection for *Beyond Tomorrow*."

"I have some ideas too. Take me home with you and I'll explain."

"Ideas for new plots?" she asked while he helped her into her coat.

He rested his arm on her waist as they exited the restaurant. "Will it improve my chances of getting an invitation to your home if I lie and say yes?"

Eliza laughed. "No, I've always felt honesty is the best policy."

He hailed a passing cab. "I have three days and two nights left in Manhattan before I have to go to Rome. What's the probability of spending at least one of those nights with you?" He opened the cab door for her.

"Extremely high." Eliza grabbed his hand and slid into the back seat, pulling him in with her. She told the driver where she lived.

Chapter Seven

The dog greeted Dario like a long-lost friend when they entered the house, wagging his tail profusely and jumping up to rest huge paws on the man's chest. "Eli must think I have food in my pocket," he quipped.

The dog's behavior amazed Eliza. Eli seldom took to people he barely knew the way he had to Dario. "They say that children and animals are good judges of character, Dario. I've heard how fond Pammie is of you, and it's obvious Eli loves you, too."

"I'm very fond of Pammie, Eliza. I'm sorry I haven't had the opportunity to see more of her, but I find it awkward to be around her mother for very long."

"Poor Dario," she consoled with a smile. "It must be difficult to be the object of so much affection."

"It's a tough life all right. How is Pammie these days?"

"Not too well. The progress on her leg isn't what it should be, and she's scheduled for surgery in a few weeks. Can I get you anything?" Eliza asked, motioning for him to sit down on the sofa.

"I'm sorry to hear that. Why don't the two of us take her somewhere before I have to leave Manhattan?" he suggested. "By the way, I'd like a glass of brandy."

"I'll get it for you. I'd love to spend some time with Pammie, but I have too much work to do between now and the end of the week. Just give Barbara a call and tell her you want to take Pammie out for a while. There's a new man in her life. I don't think she's interested in you anymore."

"Ah, how soon they forget," he drawled in a stage whisper. "I'll do that." He thanked her for the glass she passed to him. Dario heard a loud scurrying sound from the upper level and glanced at the staircase. "Do you have mice up there?"

"That's Tim, my rabbit. It would take a hell of a big mouse to make a sound like that," she said with a giggle.

"Let's go see him. Take me upstairs."

"Are you sure this isn't just an excuse to get near my bedroom?" she teased.

"Nope, I'm not sure."

"And don't forget that rabbit bites."

"I won't." He stood and extended his hand, and they climbed the stairs together. "So, where's the territorial rabbit?" Dario asked when they reached the top.

"Coming straight toward us," she said. The animal ran down the hall, stopping a few feet short of them.

"He doesn't look all that ferocious to me." Dario bent over and stroked the white ear.

"Not at the present, but he's very tempermental. Apparently rabbits are skitterish, nervous creatures. Once in a while, he even bites me for no discernible reason."

"How long have you had him?"

"Since June. I found him eating my petunias in the yard and brought him in. I tried to find his owner, but with no luck."

Dario stood and looked over the balcony railing to the floor below. "This is an awfully big house for one person, Eliza. Whatever possessed you to buy it?"

"My accountant persuaded me to invest in real estate when my yearly earnings became so large nearly half of it went to taxes. I considered several others but fell in love with this one at first sight. There goes my phone. I bet it's going to ring all night. Excuse me."

She answered the telephone in her bedroom. Dario followed her into the room, sitting at the foot of the bed briefly, before standing to gaze through the window. Like all the others in the house, it was covered with a latticed grille.

Eliza didn't speak long, and when she hung up, Dario was still staring out the window.

"Business?" he asked, turning toward her. The moon shining through the wrought iron cast uneven shadows on his face, making him appear older than he was and either very tired or very worried about something. He only halfway heard Eliza as she began to answer his question. Dario's thoughts were of the consummation of his deep love for her, and he found it odd that anxiety should seize him when he considered making love to her.

She nodded. "That was Beverly. She said she needs me to go into the studio tomorrow. A lot of things are happening. Have you heard that HEI's pilot soap has turned out to be a major disaster? They tested it on several sample audiences this week, and everyone hated it."

"I know. I saw Gene Stone the other day. Apparently he and the rest of the HEI people have decided to let you have your way with *Beyond Tomorrow*, at least for a while."

"A while is the operative word, Dario, but I'll enjoy it while I can, especially the extra money they've allotted us. We're going to do some major scenes on location."

"I've heard about that, too. Don Kennedy has already asked me to set up something with the person I know who owns an island in the Lesser Antilles. I mentioned it to you a while back, remember?'' he said vaguely, wondering how they could possibly discuss business at a time like this. Dario wondered if her behavior signified a basic disinterest in what was the most precious thing in the world to him at the present moment.

"Very well," she replied, recalling in particular that Dario had once suggested that the two of them visit the island together, and her thoughts ran parallel to his. She had taken him to her room, and he'd yet to kiss her, to touch her, to take her in his arms. "It sounds super! I had a tropical island storyline once. We decided to shelve it though because the best we could do was to throw a pile of sand onto one of the sets and use file clippings for the outdoor scenes." Eliza paused. "Would you be going there with us? I mean to the island?"

"That depends."

"On what?" she urged.

"On several things I don't care to think about now," he said evasively, and she had to leave it at that.

He seemed uncomfortable in her bedroom, and Eliza wished she'd answered the phone in some other room. "What's the matter, Dario?"

He was about to speak when the phone rang again.

Eliza picked up the receiver, her eyes never leaving Dario's face. "Hello?"

It was one of the actresses who wanted out of her contract. A better offer had come through from HEI. "I'm sorry, Joan, I can't do that now," Eliza replied.

"But I only have six months left," she said. "Please, Eliza? The new show is nighttime, and I need the exposure."

"I can't, Joan," Eliza repeated. "I'm losing at least two people this month. I'm going to have enough problems writing you off the show if you decide not to renew your contract in six months, much less now."

The conversation continued in the same vein for another five minutes until Eliza excused herself. The phone rang immediately afterward, and she flicked a switch on the underside to turn off the bell. At the same time, she activated the message recorder. "So much for that. All night long I'd probably have people wanting to get out of their contracts and other people wanting their jobs." She flung her legs onto the bed and lay back into the pile of pillows. "I tell you, Dario, sometimes I really feel between a rock and a hard place."

He smiled a slow wistful smile. That was the way he felt, and it had nothing to do with business. He had no desire to complicate this woman's life further, and some inner sense told him she'd not agreed casually to take him to her bed. True, he loved her, but Dario felt in his heart it would never work because Eliza would never be able to free herself of the deep-rooted lack of faith she had in him, even though she now understood about Barbara. Other problems were certain to arise. "Yes, I know the feeling," he said. Dario remained at the window, leaning into the dark walnut sill.

"Sit down on the bed and tell me what you're thinking, Dario. It's obviously not about my professional woes."

He came to the bed and took her hand. "Don't forget I have to leave Manhattan in a few days, Liza." Dario had too much insight into his emotions not to know he was thinking of his own vulnerability as much as hers. He couldn't bear the thought of making love to her only to be sent from her bed the next day.

She traced her thumb across the fine black hairs on his knuckles and then raised her hand to his face. "Is that your way of telling me this is a dead-end affair?"

"Those aren't the words I would have used, but I suppose you can say that."

"Why say anything at all?" she demanded. "I have no expectations. I'm not seventeen years old anymore. I'm not about to burst into tears this time and ask you to set a wedding date."

He had to smile at the memory she'd evoked. "Yes, baby, I know. I just thought something needed to be said."

"Are you always so considerate of your prospective lovers?" she asked. "So upfront?"

"No, I'm not. You're special, Liza. You always have been and always will be."

"So are you."

"Thank you." Dario loosened the silk tie on her blouse and undid the upper buttons, revealing the full slope of her breasts.

Eliza put her arms around his neck, drawing him to her body while he continued to unbutton the blouse. When it was completely undone, he pushed it past her shoulders, grasping one breast in each of his hands.

His eyes lingered there briefly, illuminated by the mounting desire, until Eliza tilted his chin upward and covered his mouth with hers. Pushing her backward on the bed, he came to lie halfway atop her, their lips still joined and his hands fastened to her breasts.

She sighed contentedly as one by one Dario's fingers slid beneath the thin fabric of her underclothing, moving toward the dusky-rose nipples. Eliza's outstretched hands ran down his back, but when she tried to insert them under his collar, all the things he had on prevented it. She withdrew from the prolonged kiss, and instantly his mouth found the hollow between her breasts, while his hands glided along her thigh, exposed where the skirt had ridden past her knees. Dario's hair was thick and full beneath her fingertips, his unshaven

beard coarse on her thumbs and against her breasts.
Eliza sighed again and then swore mildly when a phone
rang. "Damn!" she repeated, gently pushing him
away. "I have to get that."

His eyes had been closed, and he blinked in the
brightly lit room as he sat up straight. "I thought you
turned off the ringer. I can't believe this happened! It's
just like on your soap opera. The phone either rings or
someone knocks on the door the second a couple is
getting ready to make love!"

She giggled, a response to the sheer frustration of it
all. "We try to prolong the dramatic moment for as
long as possible. I have two phone lines here. I turned
off the regular line," she explained, jumping from the
bed. "That's my red line. Only a few people know the
number," Eliza called over her shoulder as she raced
downstairs to the study.

He dashed from the bed to follow her. "Your red
line? Well, give my regards to the White House, okay?
Tell the President to do something about inflation and
lower the interest rates."

Eliza smiled weakly as she picked up the receiver.
Usually the red line meant bad news, though that
wasn't always the case. Sometimes a close friend used it
just to say hello, knowing the regular line would not be
answered at certain times, and lately she'd received
several wrong numbers on the unlisted line. Apparently a new restaurant in town was recently issued a
number just a digit off from hers.

It was Jared again, and Eliza's smile in response to
Dario's light comment faded as she listened to his message. Her senior cameraman, Bobby Marquez, and one
of her leading men, Dolph Peterson, had been struck
by a drunken truck driver while taking a cab across
town. "My God!" she said grimly. "When did this happen, Jared?"

"Less than an hour ago, Eliza. Bobby's wife Rita just phoned me. She tried to get in touch with you, but apparently you had your other lines unplugged."

"That's right, I did. The phone hasn't stopped ringing since I came home. How bad are their injuries?"

"Not as bad as they could be. Neither man is on the critical list, but we can't expect to see either at work for a while."

"Damn," she interjected, mentally chastising herself for thinking as much about the repercussions for the show as about the poor men. "Any idea how long? What exactly happened?"

"Like I said, the truck driver apparently stopped at a bar for dinner and had one too many. He hit the cab broadside on Fifth Avenue...."

"That's not what I meant, Jared. What is the extent of their injuries?" she asked impatiently.

"Oh. Bobby has a mild concussion, two broken ribs, and a fractured femur. Dolph is a little better off and should be released from the hospital in the morning. His right shoulder is badly bruised, and he has several abrasions on his chest and face. Best guess is he'll be out for a week or so, and Bobby for at least a month."

This wasn't the first time unexpected injury or illness had struck a member of the company. They had managed in the past and would get along now. "I'll just have to make the best of it. Where are they staying? I'll give them a call in the morning."

Jared gave her the name of the hospital. "Dolph is scheduled to do several important scenes tomorrow," he reminded her. "I feel awful about walking out on you now."

"Don't worry about it. I'll think of something. Thanks for calling." She hung up and turned to Dario who had made himself comfortable on the couch.

"Bobby Marquez and Dolph Peterson were in an automobile accident this evening."

"I assumed as much. What are you going to do?" The upcoming fate of her show was the last thing on his mind as she stood there with her breasts exposed.

"I'm not sure yet." Eliza realized for the first time since leaving the bedroom upstairs that her blouse was half unbuttoned in front, and she turned away from Dario long enough to readjust her clothing.

"Don't stand on propriety on my account. I liked your blouse undone."

"Dario..."

"Okay, have it your way, spoilsport," he said fondly. "I know my way around a camera pretty well, Liza, if I do say so myself. Like I said before, some of the films we did in Rome were virtually one-man shows. I can handle one of the cameras and direct at the same time, so don't worry about Marquez being out, at least not for the next few days. Dolph is another problem though," he said, rising from the couch and taking her into his arms. Dario kissed the top of her head just as she pulled away from him, too distracted by the recent turn in events to respond to his affectionate gesture.

"Is he ever! Tomorrow was the day he was doing the big scene with Dora! You know, the one where he confronts her for having an affair with Dr. Parker. We could have another actor play the role, but I hate to do that in a major scene. What do you think, Dario?" She removed a copy of the script from her briefcase and began to review Dolph's part, sitting at the desk with lips pursed in concentration.

Dario placed his hands on her shoulders. "Do you really want to know what I think?" he asked.

"Of course, I do," she said, thumbing through the fifty pages until she reached the critical scene.

"I think both of our fathers were onto something when they married domestic women," he said flatly, dropping his hands and returning to the couch. "A few minutes ago I was in bed undressing you, and now you're trying to rewrite a scene."

Eliza didn't need that. She slammed the script down and stood. "What kind of a statement is that?" she demanded.

"The kind a desperate man makes when he's about to make love to a lady who decides to get out of bed and burn the midnight oil instead," he explained simply and with a smile in the gold-brown eyes.

"Fine, then I suggest you walk out the front door now, go ten blocks east, and then three blocks south."

"Now why would I want to do a thing like that?" A playful grin tugged at the corners of his mouth.

"Because there's a singles bar over there where you'd be more than likely to find the type of wind-up Barbie doll you're looking for," she informed him, returning to her desk.

He laughed, the laughter deep and rich in the quiet room. "How is it that a busy career lady such as yourself happens to know of a place like that?" he teased.

"I get around," she shot back. Actually Eliza knew of the place only from gossip on the set.

"I wonder when you find time."

"You'd be surprised." Eliza glanced at the grandfather clock in the corner. "You'd better hurry, Dario. Happy hour is starting."

"Not for me it isn't. I'm going to hang around here and help you work on revising the script. I already have an idea."

"I can manage on my own," she said sharply, still annoyed by his crack about domestic women.

"Oh, stop being so damn self-sufficient! It's only becoming up to a certain point, and then it turns into a liability. Come sit down on my lap and hear what I have to say about revising Dolph's scene."

"I can hear you just fine from here. How do you suggest we revise the scene?" she asked him, spinning the swivel chair around.

"First of all, I agree with you about not having someone stand in for Dolph. It would alienate the viewers, especially since the scene is so important, and secondly because Dolph is such a popular character."

"So what do you suggest?"

"That Dolph's character, whatever his name is... I still can't get them all straight... telephones Dora and tells her he's found out about the affair and has left town for a while to sort out his feelings."

She had to admit her immediate idea was identical to his. "You know, the same thing occurred to me the instant I hung up the phone, but I'm worried the action would seem terribly out of character for Judge Goldberg."

"Judge Goldberg?"

"The character Dolph plays. I have difficulty imagining the ever-steady judge running off, leaving his job and family because he's found out his wife is having an affair. It just doesn't jive, Dario." Eliza twirled a tendril of her disheveled hair around her forefinger and looked up at him. There was a look of incredible warmth in his eyes as he gazed at her, and her annoyance with him quickly ebbed away.

He sensed the change in her mood and left the sofa, placing his hands on her shoulders and massaging her neck, gently forcing her head back so that it rested on his chest. "It's not so farfetched, Lisa. People sometimes act out of character when confronted with extreme stress like that, and I'm certain Dolph would prefer to see things handled this way." His fingers were combed through the tangled waves, and Dario stooped to kiss her neck, exposed where he'd lifted her hair. "I think you'd be more comfortable on the couch," he suggested.

Eliza sighed, caught up in the rhapsody of his touch. "That's what I'm afraid of, Dario. I have to work out that scene tonight."

He pulled back the chair and eased her into a standing position. "We are, baby. So what do you think about having the good judge go off for a while?"

Eliza allowed him to lead her to the sofa. "You know, Dario, the more I think about it, the better it sounds. And you're right about one thing. Dolph would love it. He's been after me for a long time now to change his character from an all-around nice guy. He's actually a very talented actor with a fantastic range, and we've never allowed him to display anything other than kindly understanding, tempered by a little bit of righteous indignation once in a while. Maybe the viewers would like to see his role expanded, too."

He linked his fingers through hers. "I think so. Maybe we can turn him into a real bad guy. He could return from wherever he's going and sentence his wife's lover to life in a prison camp for a traffic violation."

Eliza giggled. "I think that's carrying things a bit far, but we don't have to work out all the subtleties tonight, just deal with the major problems at hand."

He raised her palm to his mouth, tantalizing the sensitive inner wrist with little tingling kisses. "Let's do that," he said, his eyes sparkling.

The warmth of his lips against her skin radiated throughout her body. "Dario," she said in a breathless tone, "why is it that I get the definite impression we're thinking about different major problems at hand?"

He paused long enough to kiss her hand again before speaking. "Because you're a very perceptive woman, Liza, and you know that the major problem I'm referring to is whether or not we turn back the clock and start something over again."

She felt her heart lurch against her ribcage. "Turn back the clock? What on earth are you suggesting?"

"That we go back to half an hour ago when your hotline, or whatever you call it, rang. Remember where we were?"

Eliza expelled a sigh of relief. "I remember well."

"Well?"

She found his directness to be a tad disconcerting and laughed nervously. "Well, I always thought Italian men were a bit more subtle when it came to seducing women."

"I'm not Italian, and I'm not trying to seduce you, Liza," he contradicted. Still holding her hand, Dario drew her into his arms, covering her mouth with a prolonged kiss.

"I meant of Italian descent," she explained when he moved his lips from hers.

"I know what you meant. Let's go upstairs. You lead the way in case the rabbit decides to turn on us." He pulled her to her feet.

"How gallant of you! But really, Dario, I have to rewrite the scene."

"We'll do it over breakfast. I can work pretty fast."

"So I see."

He laughed into her ebony hair, removing the pins one by one and loosening the coil on her head. "The hell you do. Fast in this respect would have been taking you weeks ago instead of waiting until now." Let tomorrow and the prospect of losing her be damned, Dario had concluded. The fire he felt inside would never be quelled until he knew her one more time, took her as he had so many years ago when she was barely a woman, a trembling girl in his arms.

Eliza drew back and looked up at him, both hands

resting on his chest. "What's so special about now? The fact that you're leaving at the end of the week?" she ventured boldly.

Cupping her face in one hand, Dario brushed his thumb across her mouth. "Shush now, Liza. Please don't ask questions like that. You said you had no expectations, remember?"

She began to unbutton his shirt. "Oh, perhaps you misunderstood me. I have very great ones, but they're short-term expectations. Come here." She led him up to her bed. "We're overdressed for the occasion, my dear," she murmured. "Get rid of this sweater and shirt and everything else you have on."

Her boldness both surprised him and ignited his volatile desire. To his way of thinking, a woman didn't speak like that to a man unless she knew her way around a bed fairly well. He supposed that Eliza had had many lovers over the years, and the notion made him downright miserable, no matter how he tried to rationalize it to himself. After all, she was a beautiful, dynamic woman, a successful, unmarried career woman. He couldn't imagine any man in his right mind not wanting her, and he forced away the unbearably painful thought that had he not been such an adolescent fool, no man save him would ever have had her.

She didn't understand why he looked so unhappy. "Dario, have you changed your mind about making love to me?"

"Never. Why do you ask?"

"You don't look particularly happy. What are you thinking?"

"I wish no one had ever touched you but me," he admitted.

"Funny thing, I've had the same thought a few times over the years, but I don't want to think about it now. I said take off your clothes."

"Help me," he whispered.

"With pleasure." She undid the remaining buttons on his shirt, pausing to run her lips over each nipple in turn. Unaccustomed to the type of belt he wore, her fingers fumbled with the clasp as her mouth descended along his midriff.

Dario's passion was too great for the delay. "Let me do this." He retreated from her embrace to finish undressing, well aware Eliza's eyes never left his body. All the lights in the room were on, an overhead chandelier with twelve small bulbs and a floral print hurricane lamp by the side of the bed, and neither bothered to dim them.

His unclothed body was heart-stoppingly beautiful to her. Eliza raised her hand to his chest just as he sat on the edge of the bed and brushed it across the hair that grew in marvelous fluffs here and there, coursing wildly down his abdomen, circling the nipples and gracing the bronze shoulders that didn't need the sun to make them darker than honey and twice as sweet. "Nice, Dario, very nice. I've always wondered what you'd look like when you grew up." Her voice was husky with emotion.

And Dario was too intent upon undressing her to say anything immediately. It nearly took his breath away to see her breasts tumble from the sheer fabric of her underclothing into his waiting hands. "I hope you're not disappointed," he finally managed to say, the words slurred from the way he spoke with his lips buried in her abdomen as his hands struggled with the delightful task of removing the rest of her clothing, which came to rest on the floor next to the bed.

Eliza lay back on the bed, and he crouched down to the floor, his hand intimately affixed to her body. She placed her hand over the larger one on her right breast. "No. On the contrary. You're beautiful."

"So are you. More beautiful than I ever remembered. I thought about you all the time." Dario drank in the sight of her unclothed body briefly, then he joined her on the bed and covered both of them with a quilt from the bottom. Pulling her to his chest, he kissed her again, pausing first to look into her eyes. When his mouth moved from her lips to her neck, Dario placed one hand over her lower abdomen.

She reached for the Saint Christopher medal around his neck and held it in her hand. Eliza was about to rotate it and read the inscription but dropped it instead. She couldn't. Not just now.

Dario undid the silver chain. "I shouldn't be wearing this, Liza. It appears to have upset you." He placed the medal on her nightstand.

She looked away from him, unnerved by the intensity in his eyes. "No, it doesn't bother me. You didn't have to do that. I...."

Dario's other hand strayed to her waist, and he drew Eliza closer to him in the bed. "Shush, baby. We'll talk about it later, okay? I want to make you very happy right now. Nothing else is important to me."

"I am happy, Dario." Because something is happening to me that hasn't happened since I was a girl, she reflected. I'm falling in love. Getting there was just as exhilarating as it had been before, but she felt a small stab of pain in her midriff when she thought of the reverse process, of falling out of love. No, she wouldn't think about that. Not now.

"Good. You keep it that way." He stared into her eyes and then kissed her, very softly at first, until the passion erupted between them. Dario groaned and eased her from the sitting position to one partially beneath his body. His hands moved slowly over her inflamed skin, taking great delight in the urgency of her response to his caresses. The quilt came to rest in a rumpled heap at the foot of the bed as they sought more intimate knowledge of each other.

All the lights in the room were still on, and whenever Eliza opened her eyes, she was blinded by both the glare and his beauty, potent and alive against her flesh. His actions were slow and sensuous, heightening her need for him with every touch, and Eliza returned his warmth twofold, reveling in the sleek and downed places in the planes and hollows of his body.

There was no going back to their point of departure when he took full possession of her, and Eliza wasn't surprised. For her there had been no return to the way she was before he reentered her life since the first time she spoke to him.

Dario raised his head from her shoulder and blinked in the brightly lit room. He kissed her forehead and closed his eyes again. "Let's try a few candles next time," he suggested.

She smiled, too content to say anything for a while, cradling his head between her arms. "You've got it," she said at length, overcome by the beauty of what they had shared.

He was uninclined to move from his position atop her. "Oh, Liza, it was so good."

"Yes, I know. Dario, do you remember the first time?" Lovingly, she caressed his firm buttocks.

"Do I have to?" He chuckled softly against her neck, his hand reaching between their bodies for her breast. "I wasn't very good, was I?"

"Well, I wasn't a sensual banquet of earthly delights either."

"Let me make my shortcomings up to you, no pun intended."

"I bet."

They made love once more, and Dario was stunned when she made a motion to leave the bed.

"Aren't we going to sleep now?"

She sighed, ruffling his tousled hair with her expelled breath. "Sleep before nine o'clock? Don't I wish! I have too much work to do now."

"Right now? You're going to get up and work?" He played with her earlobe while he spoke.

"Not right this very minute, but soon."

"And leave me all alone?" he teased.

"I'll send the dog in to keep you warm. Move now, honey."

Dario shifted onto his side with a leg straddled over her hips. "I thought we had agreed to work on the revisions in the morning."

"We did, but I have something else to do. I probably won't get any sleep until Christmas." Eliza petted the silvery sideburn on the right side of his face. "I should get up now, but somehow, I find it very difficult."

He smiled and turned his head to kiss her hand. "I'm not exactly dying to get up and work on my lecture, but if you're going to work, maybe I will, too."

"What are you going to talk about?"

"Some films made by American directors in Paris in the late twenties."

"I didn't know there were any American directors in Paris in the late twenties."

"They did some obscure but very interesting work, Eliza. Would you like to come and hear the lecture? It's the last one in the series."

"I'd love to, but I'm too busy right now. How about a private lecture some time?" Eliza yawned and left the bed.

"Sounds good." Dario watched her put on a red silk kimono-style bathrobe.

"I'm going to make a pot of coffee. Want any?" she asked.

"Please." Dario slipped into his jeans and took Eliza

in his arms as she turned to leave the room. "Okay, I'm ready to go downstairs now," he said after holding her for a while.

"How can you write a lecture without any reference material?" she asked Dario after returning from the kitchen with the coffee. He sat cross-legged on the floor in front of the coffee table, writing on a yellow pad.

"I've given this one several times before, Liza." He sipped from the cup. "How did you remember I like it black?"

"I saw how you drank it around the studio."

"Really? I thought you were completely ignoring me."

"Yes, I was, but I could hardly keep my eyes off you," she admitted with a grin.

"Same here, baby." He leaned over and kissed her knee, exposed by the short robe.

"Where did you give the lectures?"

"Oh, here, there, everywhere. I get invitations to speak all the time. I've been back to our old alma mater several times. I even bumped into your parents once."

"Oh? When was this? They never told me anything about it."

"I don't suppose they would. I was never one of their favorite people. It was three years after our separation. I came back to the drama department to give a guest lecture and ran into both of them in the cafeteria afterward, you know, the big one with the center courtyard."

"Hmm. I wonder what they were doing. My mother never went on campus much."

"I know. From what I saw, your father kept her in the kitchen whenever possible, but apparently she got involved in some kind of Mexican-American event on campus. I saw posters for it around the university. Her mother was a poet in Mexico, wasn't she?" he asked. Dario refilled his coffee cup, pouring some for Eliza.

"Yes, she still is, as a matter of fact. I remember the event now. Mother wrote me about it. You're right, my father did resent her involvement with anything outside the house. Did they talk to you?"

"No. I think your mother wanted to, but your father wouldn't let her. I swear, Liza, if looks could kill, I wouldn't be sitting here right now. How is the old man these days? Still head of the physics department?"

Eliza put down her cup. "As far as I know. He was offered another position, but I don't know the status of it. My father and I don't communicate much. I've rarely seen him since my mother's death."

Dario left the floor where he sat cross-legged and joined her on the sofa. "You sound awfully bitter," he remarked, running his hand down the length of her arm.

"That's because I am. I love my father, but I don't like him very much. He did everything possible to stop our marriage, has been entirely unsupportive of my career in television, and as I told you, kept your letters from me. He completely dominated my mother and made her life miserable half the time."

"Well, maybe it wasn't as bad as you think. Sometimes children aren't the best judges of their parents' marriage, and he only did what he thought was best for you. You were so young at the time."

Dario surprised her by coming to her father's defense. "You sound like you're making apologies for him," she accused.

"In a sense, perhaps. He was right about one thing: I did wind up hurting you. It was just as he said. I was too young and emotionally immature to get married."

She remained intractable to his logic. "I don't see how you can defend him, Dario! Remember when he threatened to bring criminal charges against you for sleeping with his virgin daughter?" She shook her head in disgust at the memory.

"How can I forget? He went to the dean of the graduate department. I nearly lost my teaching position and my scholarship."

"You never told me that!" Eliza found herself indignant over all those things in the past once more.

Dario saw her agitation and tried to console her. "I saw no reason to upset you. It was pretty unpleasant all the way around. Josh, the dean, was a nice guy, and it put him in an awkward position. Technically your father was right. You were a minor when we first made love. I could have been prosecuted for statutory rape."

She brushed his hands from his arms. "You sound like you condone his actions." Eliza left the couch and began pacing the length of the room.

Dario asked her to sit down, going to her when she refused. "You know I don't, baby. Stop getting so upset about it, okay? Those things didn't happen yesterday. As much as I resented your father at the time, I think I've made my peace with him over the years. If I had a young teenaged daughter, the last thing in the world I would want her to do is run off and elope with the adolescent jerk I was then."

Eliza knew he was right. "Oh, I know, but some things are hard to forget."

"And unforgivable?"

"Just about, and my father's done more than one over the years."

Dario frowned. So had he to her, and he wondered if Eliza could ever completely forgive him. He opened his mouth to come to her father's defense, then decided against it, knowing it was his own cause as much as the old man's he wanted to address. "Yes, I know, Liza."

"Oh, it all happened so long ago. I suppose I'm just being silly. What did the dean say?" Dario's chest was bare, and she raised her hand to the white mark where the sun had tanned around the medal and stroked the base of his neck.

"I explained to him you were nearly eighteen, and we were going to get married on your birthday. He promised your father he would follow through on the matter, but let it drag out with no intentions of doing anything under the circumstances. After the marriage even your father realized there was no point in pursuing it," he said, not telling Eliza that Professor Rothcart quickly figured out how the dean wanted to handle the matter and went over his head to the chancellor. Dario slipped her silk kimono past her shoulders and kissed the slope near her neck. "At least you're of age this time around," he murmured against her skin.

"Yes, you have a point there." She rested her head on his chest. Eliza noticed his skin felt cool beneath her cheek, and the hair stood erect in the follicles. "Are you cold, honey? Should I turn up the heat?"

He lowered the robe to her waist, running both hands down her back to the full rise of her buttocks. "Umm, you're doing it, Liza," he whispered. Dario initiated a sensuous assault of her neck, running little kisses along the length.

"Honey, we have to get back to work," she reminded him.

"Do we?" Dario opened his mouth over her earlobe.

"Afraid so." She summoned up the willpower to leave his arms and sat back down on the couch with her notepad, resting with her back against the arm and her feet extended in front.

Dario sat on the opposite end and placed her legs on his lap. "Do you always write in longhand?" he asked.

"Only for outlines. I do dialogue on the typewriter, or sometimes dictate it for Beverly to type. How's the lecture going?"

"Fine. Your coffee is probably cold by now. Can I refill your cup?"

"No, thank you, I'm fine."

They worked quietly for the next hour. Eliza found herself somewhat distracted by Dario's light caresses on her feet and legs, but it was a pleasant distraction and didn't greatly impede her work.

"That should do it," he said, placing his notes on the table. He noticed the lengthy outline for her proposed show there and asked to read it.

"If you promise not to laugh," she said, without looking up from her work.

Dario chuckled. "Not even an occasional snicker?"

"Okay, but just a few."

"One per page?" Dario leaned over and kissed her cheek.

"If it makes you happy." She kissed him back and returned to the outline.

"This script surprises me," Dario said after reading for half an hour. "It's so much more sensational than what you do for *Beyond Tomorrow*."

She put her pad aside and stretched her arms overhead. "I know it is, but we may only have a week to grab our viewers."

He seemed confused. "A week? Right, I remember now. You'll be running opposite that sporting event for a week. Nice timing."

"Yes, but it needed more planning," she agreed with a yawn. "Ten one-hour scripts was an awful lot for me to come up with in less than a month, but I'm nearly finished." It was midnight; Eliza was exhausted and couldn't see getting to bed before two or three. "Damn! I wish Jared weren't leaving! He's a big help when it comes to writing up long-term projections."

"Can't you get someone to help, Liza? What about your two cowriters for the HEI show?" he suggested.

"I lost my good writer last month, Dario. The two I have are pretty green. I can't depend on either of them, and besides I need the money."

"Need the money? What for, Eliza? Isn't four stories in Gramercy Park enough for you?"

She laughed. "It belongs to me and the bank. I purchased it on an eight-year mortgage and the payments are enormous."

"An eight-year mortgage?" he asked in astonishment. "I thought mortgages these days were more likely to be eighty years, passed down from father to son. Why did you get an eight-year one?"

"It's complicated, Dario. I don't want to get into the details right now. Basically I did it for tax reasons upon the advice of my lawyer and accountant. It seemed like a good idea at the time, but now I'm committed to all the work I'm doing to make the payments."

"Can't you refinance?"

"Very unlikely. I'd probably have to sell the house if I can't make the payments. And I don't want to do that. I love this big old place."

"Yes, I can see that, Liza. What would you sell first? The house or rights to *Beyond Tomorrow*?" Dario's legs were getting stiff from remaining in one position so long. He gently moved her feet from his lap and stood.

"I don't know. That's a tough one. Hopefully neither." She covered her mouth and yawned again, sitting up erect on the sofa.

Dario crouched down on his haunches on the floor before her, taking Eliza's hands in his own. He knew she was exhausted and had been working since six in the morning. "You can't keep up this pace, baby."

She rested her head on his and yawned into the black-and-white waves. "I know, Dario. It's only for a little while, another month or so."

"Okay, but try to find time for me in that schedule of yours, Liza. Don't forget I have to leave Saturday."

"As if I could." She kissed his mouth briefly. "What do you think of the new show?"

He rose to his feet and returned to the sofa, once again sitting at the end opposite Eliza. "It's pretty good."

She saw right through him and laughed. "You liar! You hate daytime drama. Admit it, Dario."

Dario grinned. "I wouldn't say that, Liza. I just can't get into it like all you other people. But, as I said earlier, I do have more respect for the form now. Did you like it before you began working in daytime?"

"Oh, yes. I was hooked a long time ago. That's why I proposed it to HEI. I worked in Burbank on several shows before I did my own, too."

"That's right, so you did. Well, hurry up and finish whatever you're doing so we can get to bed, okay?"

"You don't have to stay up with me, Dario. Go to bed now if you're tired," she told him. It was nearly one now.

"No, I seldom get to bed before two myself. I think I'm going to finish reading your outline for the new show."

Around two, Eliza suggested that they watch a videotape of the latest segment of *Beyond Tomorrow*.

Dario agreed with her. "I haven't had time to see them all at the studio. Where's the video recorder?"

"In the bedroom."

His smile widened. "Let's go." He extended his hands and pulled Eliza to her feet. "Oh, hold on. I forgot to bring that leftover salad to Tim." He ran down the stairs and returned a few minutes later with the bowl.

"That was nice of you, Dario," she said.

"Just fattening him up for Sunday dinner," he teased.

She knew he wasn't serious and laughed, watching Dario as he dropped to one knee and put the bowl on the floor at the top of the stairs.

"I'm going to take a quick shower before I get into bed. Set up the tape for me, will you? Please?"

"Sure." He picked up a cartridge from her dresser. "Is this it?"

"Yes, it should be sixty counts back from wherever it is now." Eliza stepped into the adjoining bathroom and turned on the water.

She didn't hear him come into the room over the sound of running water and jumped when he entered the shower almost immediately after she did.

"Easy, baby," he said, steadying her with a warm hand on her shoulder.

"You startled me!"

"I did? Who in the hell were you expecting?" He lifted the wet mat of hair from her neck and kissed the moist skin.

She leaned backward into his chest, the spray running down her body. "Well, not you. I don't recall inviting you into my shower, Dario."

"It's part of the package for inviting me to your bed, Liza. Hand me the soap."

"Lucky me," she said flirtatiously, passing the bar over her shoulder.

"Luckier me," Dario countered. He began to wash her back.

She expected him to linger in the shower, but he didn't, suggesting they return to the next room and watch the tape. "I want to have you asleep as soon as possible," he explained.

It had been a long time since anyone took care of

Eliza the way Dario was doing. And she liked it. "You're spoiling me."

"My pleasure."

Dario flicked on the video machine, and he and Eliza settled into the bed. "Do you watch the tapes every day?" he asked.

"Yes, shush."

"Hey, look, my name's on the opening credits. Can't I use a pseudonym in case anyone I know watches the show?"

Eliza nudged him in the ribs. "Shut up, Dario." Both his arms were around her waist, and she lay in the bed with her head on his shoulder. "I don't want to miss this part."

"Are you sure?" he said as the scene began. It was one filmed in Central Park with the children cast members. "The cinematography isn't bad, considering everything," he said after a few minutes.

"Oh, come on. Stop being such a snob. The crew did a damn good job and you know it."

"Adequate. Merely adequate," he contradicted.

"Well, on our budget, that's close enough. Oh, Dario. Look at little Tommy on the slide. Isn't that cute?"

"If it were any cuter, I'd put the blanket over my head. Whose kid is he, anyway? I mean on the show. I know he actually belongs to the Oriental woman in wardrobe."

"He could belong to Brad or Paul or Jerry, and it's not clear yet who his mother is. Stay tuned," she advised.

Dario laughed. "Isn't anyone of known parentage on these shows?" His hands moved along her body, and Eliza found it almost impossible to concentrate on the tape.

"A few are."

"I see. Liza, do we really have to lie here in bed and watch that kid go up and down the slide in slow motion for the next half hour? This has got to be the longest scene I've ever seen done for that show," he asked after a few minutes. Dario lowered the blanket and began to kiss her.

She gave in to him because it was what she wanted more than anything in the world at the moment. "Oh, all right. Turn it off and do what you want."

He answered with an indolent grin, kissed the palm of her hand, and flicked off the video equipment. When Dario returned to the bed, Eliza greeted him with open arms.

Chapter Eight

Eliza disentangled herself from Dario's arms when the alarm went off at four in the morning. She had set the one on her wristwatch rather than the clock radio so as not to awaken him, and he continued to sleep quietly as she crept from the bed. She paused to kiss his forehead before reaching for her robe.

It proved to be a mistake. He opened one eye and grabbed her hand, pulling Eliza back down to the bed. "Babe, it's pitch dark outside. Where do you think you're going?" Holding her against his chest, he sat up enough to see the digital readout on her clock. "Four A.M.? You've got to be kidding, Liza! Be a good girl and get back in bed."

She nuzzled briefly against the warmth of his chest before escaping the embrace. "I wish I were. I have to get some work done, honey. Sorry I woke you up. Go back to sleep, okay?"

He reached for her arm again. "Sleep with me," he murmured in a thick voice.

"I can't now, honey. Let go."

He groaned. "Lord, save me from the working woman." Dario drew her elbow to his mouth, kissed it, then released her. "Want me to get up with you?" he asked with a yawn, sitting up in the bed.

Eliza raked her fingers through his sleep-tousled

hair. "Of course not. Stop giving me a bad time now, and get back to sleep, okay?" She pushed him downward in the bed, tucking the bedding around his neck.

"Will do. What time are you going in to the studio?"

"Around nine."

"Wake me up at seven thirty. I'll go home, shower, change, and then come back here and go in with you, okay?"

"All right, honey." She kissed his cheek and went downstairs to put a pot of coffee on.

Eli let out with a short woof when she passed by the third floor study where he slept on a sofa and, recognizing his mistress's footsteps, immediately fell back to sleep.

Eliza worked quietly and efficiently for a few hours and was then surprised to hear Dario up and about by six. She set her work aside when he came into the study. "What are you doing here?" she asked, caressing his neck when he bent to kiss her.

Dario yawned, ruffling the long dark hair that tumbled down her back. "I spent the night, remember?"

She laughed. "Somehow, my dear, I'd find that damn difficult to forget. What are you doing up so early?"

"Oh, I woke up a few minutes ago and couldn't get back to sleep." He took a sip of her coffee. "Too sweet," he said, returning it to the desk.

"There's more over there," Eliza replied, pointing to an automatic coffeemaker near the window. She stood from her chair. "I'll go to the kitchen and get another cup."

He poured the coffee into the previous night's wineglass. "Don't bother. I'll drink it out of this."

Eliza flung back her head and giggled. "Very classy." She'd never seen anyone drink coffee from a wineglass before.

"Thank you. I did manage to acquire a fair amount of continental charm when I lived abroad, Liza. How's the work going?" He settled into the sofa, next to the dog.

"Actually very well."

"What are you doing?"

Eliza turned off the electric typewriter. She'd been at it for nearly two straight hours now and could use a break, and she couldn't think of a finer break from her work than an early morning cup of coffee with Dario. The sun hadn't risen yet, and the same streetlight that shone through the iron grating on the window last night was still on. She joined Dario on the couch. "The new show."

He put his arm around her shoulder. "What's it called?"

"To tell you the truth, I don't know, Dario. I named it *Pleasure Point*, which is a beach area where all the wealthy characters live, but the producer they hired didn't like it. He changed the name to something else, but the head of daytime for the network didn't like his title. Everytime I talk to them, they have another one."

"Do you care what they call it?"

"No, not at all. It's all the same to me."

"Will you be flying out to the West Coast much once the new show premieres?" he asked.

"At least once a month. Dario, have you completely ruled out doing the film with Fanucchi? Is there any possibility you'd go to California after you finish the film in Rome?"

"Some." When he stood to refill the long-stemmed glass with coffee, he paused and stroked her face with his hand. "What I'd really like to do after I finish in Rome is work in New York again. Maybe we could see each other some more," he suggested in a tone that struck her as rather casual. Dario took her empty mug. "Can I get you another?"

"Maybe we could get together if you return to New York," she replied in the same noncommittal vein. "And, yes, please, I'd like some more coffee. Thank you."

He returned to the window and stared out at the deserted streets after handing her the coffee. Everything with Eliza was getting far more complicated than he'd ever bargained for, but at least her underlying lack of trust in him wasn't so important anymore. How in the hell could it be, since she didn't seem to return his love anyway?

Dario was dressed in the same clothes he had worn the previous evening, a little worse for a night on the bedroom chair where he'd tossed them before joining her in the shower, and he needed a shave. He hadn't even bothered to run a brush through his untamable hair. Disheveled as he was, Eliza found him overwhelmingly attractive. She watched how the sun coming through the latticed window made shadows on his face. His skin was a warm bronze color as he stood in the early morning light. With a monumental effort she returned to the desk when he handed her the mug. "Back to work."

Dario looked at her unlikely costume and smiled. "That first day I saw you at the studio I never would have guessed you work at home in army surplus clothes and combat boots."

She laughed at his comment. "I'll have you know, my dear, these aren't army surplus clothes. The jungle look was in last year, and I paid a fortune for this outfit."

"Well, thank God it's out this year. You look like an extra for a war epic. Do you have a copy of today's script around here? I have to block it. Have you written in any of the revisions yet?"

"No, I haven't. We should do that now."

"Why don't you let me take a stab at it on my own?" he suggested generously. "You seem to have your hands full with other things."

"Dario, you're a lifesaver," she said with appreciation. "I'd like that." She handed him a copy of the script and got back to her own work, which went amazingly well. By seven thirty Eliza was finished with the last one-hour script. "And thus the scene fades with a smoking gun held by an unidentified gloved hand," she said, filing the pages in an oak cabinet next to the desk.

Dario looked up and smiled. "Done already? That was fast."

"I know. It doesn't usually go so well though."

"Must be you have a good muse in residence."

Eliza walked over to the couch and placed her arms around his neck. "Must be. Dario, can you stay here again tonight?"

"I don't know, babe. I have that class at Columbia tonight. It runs until ten, and I usually stay around afterward and talk to the students."

"That's fine. Come when you can. I'll be up working late again. I feel like a walk after sitting at that typewriter all morning. Can I go down to your place with you? We can catch a subway to work from there."

"Sure, if you're not offended by the sight of actors and dancers sleeping around the living room in various stages of undress."

"Is that what goes on there?" she asked.

"Sometimes."

"How do you stand it? I would hate living with a bunch of people."

"It's not so bad. Are you going to work like that?"

Eliza looked at her outfit and laughed. "No, I have an image to maintain. Give me a few minutes to change." She was ready to leave a little while later.

"I've always liked you in blue," Dario said when she came down the stairs in a dark blue crepe dress. "But then I like you in just about every color I can think of," he added.

"Except army green."

He agreed. "Except army green. Are you going to be okay walking in those high-heeled shoes?"

"For the distance, I'll be fine."

Dario took her hand as they cut over to Third Avenue, walking toward the neighborhood where he lived. It was an invigorating fall morning, and the wind whipped through his hair and brought color to Eliza's cheeks. They walked without speaking, exchanging smiles along the way. "We're turning right on Tenth," he said as they neared the intersection.

"Well, this is it. What do you think?" he asked three blocks later.

Eliza was a little out of breath from the long walk. "Not much," she said, looking at the old brownstone that had seen better days, a long time ago.

"Come on, Liza, don't be too hard on my humble abode. It's not without charm. When I'm up high, I can see the Brooklyn Bridge from here." He ushered her up the stairs with one hand on her elbow.

Eliza laughed. "Up high on what, Dario? A bottle of cheap Chianti from Little Italy? Come on, you can't see the Brooklyn Bridge from a building down here that's only six stories tall."

Dario chuckled and made a playful motion to pat her bottom, stopping abruptly when he saw another tenant exit a nearby flat. "No, Liza, when I'm up that high I can see all the way to California."

"And what do you see then, Dario?"

He took her into his arms. "Sometimes I see a beautiful girl in a white organdy dress and a big white hat that's blowing so hard she can barely keep it on," he said in a low tone.

For some reason it hurt to be reminded of their wedding day. Eliza tried unsuccessfully to hide her feelings from Dario. "Can you really see the Brooklyn Bridge?" she asked, turning her face from his, staring down at the worn carpet.

Dario knew she was upset and figured he ran the risk of upsetting her further by apologizing. "Only the towers, but that's okay. I can live without the traffic below."

She still didn't believe him. "And I suppose you can see the Statue of Liberty too, right?

He laughed. "Don't I wish. I like that big green thing." He inserted his key into the knob. "We have to be quiet. Anyone here is sure to be asleep."

"I hadn't planned on striking up the band," she said with a soft laugh.

He led her to his room, tiptoeing quietly past a man sound asleep on the sofa. Eliza looked around. It was just like something he would have lived in sixteen years ago, with scripts and books everywhere and an open suitcase at the foot of the bed.

"I won't take long. I've found a little time to work on some storylines I'd like to see for the show. You can look at them while I shower, if you'd like."

"Where is it?" she asked as he stepped into the adjoining bathroom.

"In the desk drawer, the upper right."

When she opened the drawer, her attention was drawn to something else. It was a lengthy movie script, written by Dario. The name of the film was *Eliza*. She removed the manuscript from the drawer and sat down on the bed with it. Thumbing randomly through the pages, her eyes picked up lines of dialogue that were very familiar to her. Eliza quickly realized they were familiar because they were things she and Dario had said to each other a long time ago, statements she had forgotten until today when she saw parts of their lives spread out on the pages before her. She found herself highly offended by what she perceived as his willingness to put their intimate moments on public display. Eliza flung the script onto the floor in disgust when she reached the passage about the night when the seventeen-year-old woman in the movie made love for the first time.

Dario emerged from the bathroom just as it hit the floor. "That bad, huh?" he said. He was freshly shaven and dressed in a pair of gray wool slacks and a corduroy jacket with leather patches on the elbows.

"Oh, Dario, how could you?" she besought sadly.

"What's wrong? They're only a few ideas for your soap. If you don't like them, don't use them. I never claimed to be Agnes Nixon."

Eliza jumped from the bed as if it was on fire when Dario sat down to put on his shoes. "Damn it, I'd be embarrassed to death if any of this was filmed!"

"So, don't use it, honey! Frankly I don't think my ideas are half bad. Jared liked most of them."

"You showed this script to Jared? How could you!" she repeated in the same betrayed tone.

Dario was thoroughly baffled by her reaction. "Hey, what's the big deal? Liza, I don't understand. All..." he began, halting abruptly when he bent over and saw the script on the floor. "Take that back, I think I do understand." He picked up his manuscript and returned it to the drawer, slammed it shut, and then whirled toward her with a tightly clamped jaw. "You had no right to go through my desk."

"You gave me permission to take your story proposals out of the upper right drawer," she reminded him.

"That's not where the screenplay was."

"Yes, it was."

Dario thought for a few seconds. That certainly wasn't where he had left it, but then he'd given one of his roommates, a young director who worked at an off-Broadway theater, permission to read the script. "I guess Ted put it there."

"Who in the hell is Ted?" she demanded.

"A friend of mine."

"Oh, great. Just wonderful. Did you show him the letters I wrote you while you were at it?" she said bitterly.

"Of course not. I've never shown anyone those. I wouldn't do a thing like that."

"Why not? You're so willing to put our entire marriage on display for the world, what's a few letters?" She heard well the childish element in her words, but they came out anyway, goaded by the outrage she felt at his decision to write about their courtship and the eventual dissolution of the marriage.

"Liza, try to understand, please. I know you didn't have time to read the entire script because I wasn't in the bathroom that long."

"I've read enough to know it's about us."

"It's less autobiographical than it might appear on the surface," he argued.

Eliza wasn't convinced. "I read the scene about when they made love for the first time. Damn if it doesn't sound familiar to me. You even had the boy kissing away the girl's tears!"

"So how many different ways do you think there are for a young couple to make love for the first time? I truly doubt that we wrote the original script back then."

"That's not what I mean, and you know it! I don't want you to ever have this movie produced, Dario," she said with a sense of urgency in her voice.

He took a deep breath. "I don't think you realize

what you're asking me to do. I invested an entire year of my life in that screenplay, and it's good. I know it is."

"I don't care how long it took you to write! I won't have my personal life put on public display like that!"

He saw the pain in her eyes and decided to do what she wanted. He had hurt her enough in the past and had vowed to never knowingly wound her again. "Okay, Liza. Take the script with you. It's yours now. Just promise me one thing, will you? Read it sometime." He went to the desk, opened the drawer, and gave it to her.

She didn't know whether to believe him or not. "You probably have more than one copy."

"Of course, I do. Three, as a matter of fact. I'm keeping the original."

"How do I know you won't go ahead and produce it someday?" she challenged.

"I don't know. I guess you just have to trust me."

"Trust you? That's a joke! When could I ever trust you?" she blurted out unthinkingly, gasping as soon as the words were said. "Dario, I take that back. I didn't mean it."

She had admitted once again to what he feared the most, to her mistrust of him, that slow inevitable poison that was sure to destroy whatever they had between them now. "I suppose never, Liza. But, here. I'll give you something you can trust." He returned to his desk and took out a contract. "This is a standard screenplay contract that I show the kids in my class." He signed the twenty-page document. "I'm assigning all rights to the movie to you."

She thought he was bluffing and decided to play along with him. "How do I know it's legally binding?"

"Call your damn attorney," he said flatly.

"I will," she shot back.

"Good, you go ahead and do that. There's a phone in the next room."

"No, I'll wait until I get to my office. I wouldn't want to awaken sleeping beauty in there." Eliza put both the script and the contract in her briefcase. She had the definite impression Dario was relying upon her integrity and belief in artistic freedom to return it to him, along with the script. And she wasn't about to comply. "I suppose you know what it means if you go ahead and try to have someone produce this screenplay," she said.

"Eliza, I've been in this business too long not to know what it means. Don't worry."

Once again she was Eliza to him, after a long night of endearments and listening to him call her by his pet name. Oh, well, she hadn't expected it to last long anyway. "Good. Don't you forget it." The thought of walking to the earliest BMT line and going to work with Dario seemed ridiculous under the present circumstances. Eliza was about to suggest she take a cab instead.

Dario saw the expression on her face and knew what she wanted. His bedroom fronted on the street. He walked to the window and hailed a cab driver on the opposite side. "That's for you," he said to Eliza. "I remembered some work I had to do here. I'll be in later."

She nodded mutely and left his room. Eliza's thoughts were a hundred miles from the papers on her lap as the cab crossed over the bridge to Brooklyn, and when she arrived at the studio, the demands of her job pushed Dario to the back of her mind. But he was never far removed from her thoughts. All morning long she anxiously awaited his arrival. When he didn't show up by noon, she asked about him.

"Mr. Napoli?" Beverly said in response to Eliza's

inquiry. "He's upstairs auditioning replacements for Sam and Elliot."

"Already?" she replied. "He certainly got on that fast. Well, that's good. It needed to be done." Eliza asked Beverly to bring a lunch from the local deli to her office. She ate while reading Dario's screenplay.

The decision to return it had been made earlier in the morning before the cab even reached the Brooklyn Bridge. If Dario had indeed gambled upon her good faith not to keep it, then he had won. Though it would widen the chasm between them and embarrass her personally to see the film produced, Eliza knew she had no right to seize control of his work. It belonged to Dario, not to her, and she would return it at the earliest opportunity.

There were tears in her eyes by the time she finished reading. Dario had written a beautiful, moving script, and though it was evocative of so many things Eliza wanted to forget, she saw the beauty of it and knew she couldn't keep the screenplay from the public if Dario chose to produce it. And he had been right about one thing. The script wasn't as directly autobiographical as it had appeared on the surface. It was drawn far more from emotions engendered by events not described in the script than from the events themselves as they had actually happened years ago. And only she and Dario knew how they had felt then, and Eliza realized their feelings weren't all that unique. Any couple experiencing the joy and discovery of love for the first time would have felt the same ecstasy, only to know the same hell when the dream shattered. Dario had told a very old story and told it well.

Eliza set the script aside and asked her secretary to get Dario on the phone once more after lunch. "I see," she said when Beverly told her he was unavailable. "Try to get him later, okay?"

Jared entered the office unannounced and undoubtedly over Beverly's protests. Eliza hastily shoved the script into her desk, motioning for him to sit down.

He noticed the moisture in her eyes and smiled. "Writing more gut-wrenching melodrama, Eliza? You must be working on a good one. I've never seen you moved to tears by your own scripts yet." He handed her a handkerchief from his pocket.

Eliza declined it. "That won't be necessary, Jared, but thanks anyway. Actually I was reading something else. What brings you here? I heard you were starting in immediately with HEI."

"I changed my mind and turned them down, Eliza. I tried calling you several times last night, but apparently you weren't answering your phone. Didn't you listen to your messages on the recorder?"

"No, I never got around to it. I figured I would only be bombarded with business calls, and they can usually wait until the morning. I don't understand why you've changed your mind. Why would you turn down a chance to do nighttime with HEI? Especially after just accepting the position?"

"Loyalty," he explained in a single word.

Eliza leaned back into her chair and smiled at him. "Are you sure it's not stupidity? Sometimes there's a fine line between the two."

"Quite certain. They only offered me the job to put pressure on you, and I owe you a lot. I know they've come around and expanded the budget because the pilot on their new show was so disastrous, but Donald Kennedy still wants to gain more creative control of *Beyond Tomorrow*, I can't just defect to the enemy camp the minute they wave a few big bills under my nose. The more I thought about it, the more I realized it was a lousy thing to do. And besides, who's to say how long they'd keep me on and how much freedom

I'd have with the new show? If HEI really wants me, they can make another offer. Maybe I'll take it and maybe I won't. But if and when I do, it will be after I've given you sufficient notice and trained a replacement for you and definitely not when you're working on another show," he said.

"I appreciate what you're saying more than you'll ever know. But are you sure? I'd hate to see you miss a good opportunity."

"Yes, I'm sure." He opened the notepad on his lap. "I've made a chart of who's leaving the cast and when. I thought it might help you in rewriting the storylines. And here's something else you're sure to like." He gave her a blue box, the kind that was used for typing paper.

She recognized it at once as the one from Dario's desk, the story proposals he had wanted her to read before she stumbled upon the screenplay. "Did Dario give you that?" she asked.

"Yes. How did you know?"

"Oh, he mentioned it to me," she replied evasively. "Have you had a chance to read over any?"

"Yes, I have. Most of it anyway. They're quite good. I think you'll be impressed. Dario can really write. Did you know that?"

"Yes. I recently read something he wrote."

"More story proposals for *Beyond Tomorrow*?"

"No, something entirely different. Any major problems on the set this morning?" Eliza asked, changing the subject from Dario. "I had a long talk with Elliot before lunch. He's dead set against doing the duel scene in the park."

"I know. Dario and I talked to him, too. I don't see what it is to him. He's quitting our show anyway. Why should he care how he exits?" Jared asked. "Is it okay if I smoke? I'll sit on the fire escape."

"If you must," Eliza said. She left her desk near the window and sat where Jared had been.

He opened the window, climbed out, and sat on the sill. "What are we going to do about Elliot?"

"I'm not sure. You know how recalcitrant he can be when he wants to. The last time we forced him to do a scene he objected to, he turned my tragedy into camp humor. I think he just wants to leave an opening for himself in our show in case his new one bombs. I'd prefer to simply kill his character off, but maybe we'd better have him go into a coma or something like that and be shipped off to never-never land until such time when we decide to resurrect him or have him die there. What do you think?" Eliza coughed and waved her hands in front of her face when a gust of wind blew the cigar smoke into her office. "Jared, try to be careful, okay?"

"I'm sorry." He stood and exhaled over the balcony. "What you've suggested is so predictable and almost the same thing we did when Terry Barnes left the show three years ago. I really hate to do it."

"Well, so do I, but I can't make a life's work out of writing a scene that would please Elliot. He only has a matter of days left on his contract. We're going to have to come up with something soon, real soon."

"I know, I know. I'll continue to mull a better way to get rid of him through my mind. Maybe Dario can come up with something. He seems to have a flair for this kind of thing. Well, onward." Jared ground out his cigar butt on the railing outside the window and climbed back into the office. "Where can I get a good buy on a wedding gown for a pregnant woman?"

She smiled. "Is your girl friend in trouble?"

"No, I meant for one of the people on the show. I've scheduled the wedding scene for next week, remember?" he reminded her.

Eliza snapped her fingers together. "That's right. We're really hard up in the wardrobe department right now. Sally is actually seven months' pregnant herself, and she always dresses so nicely. Ask her if she has something of her own to wear for the scene, okay?"

"Good idea. I should have thought of that myself. Do you think she'd have a wedding gown?"

Eliza giggled. "Don't be so dense, Jared! I wasn't referring to a white gown with a lace veil. Sally's been married for fifteen years, and her character is over forty, working on her fourth husband, and ready to deliver any minute. You can't expect her to walk down the aisle in virginal white. Any nice dress will do."

"I'll talk to her right now. She's on set doing the scene with Sam." He excused himself and left the office.

Eliza returned to her work after asking Beverly to try to get Dario again. He was still unavailable, and they failed to touch bases for the remainder of the day. The thought that Dario was intentionally avoiding her crossed Eliza's mind more than once. Though she had little desire to impose her company where it was unwanted, she felt she should return his screenplay personally, along with an apology for taking it from him in the first place. She worked at her desk until around nine thirty and then took a cab to Columbia University, planning to meet Dario when he finished with his class.

Eliza found the room location from a class schedule that was posted on a bulletin board in the building that housed the drama department. It was ten fifteen. The class would be over, but Dario had mentioned lingering afterward with his students. Eliza had no idea how long that might be but not wanting to risk missing him went directly to the room. The door was open. Dario sat on a desk, surrounded by several students. He had changed his clothes since the morning and looked very professo-

rial in his gray slacks and dark blue pullover sweater
that he wore with a shirt and tie.

The questions the students asked of him were audible where she stood, and Eliza smiled when she realized his class seemed to be far more interested in
Beyond Tomorrow than in American film directors in
Paris. He answered their questions patiently until he
looked up and saw Eliza standing in the doorway.

"You'll have to excuse me now," he said. "My lady
came down to meet me and I have to go."

A leggy blonde groaned as several other heads
whirled toward the door, appraising Eliza with undis-
guised curiosity. "But, Mr. Napoli, I wanted a few minutes alone with you! It's very important!" the girl
complained loudly.

"I'm sorry, Laura. It will have to wait. My lady's a
very busy woman, and we have to go now. Good night
now, everyone, and I hope you'll have time to see the
film I mentioned. It's considered a classic in the
genre." He packed up his briefcase and joined Eliza at
the door, taking her by the elbow and ushering her
down the corridor.

She was amazed that he had greeted her as though
nothing were wrong. "I tried to get hold of you all
day," she said.

"I'm sorry we missed each other. It's been a hell of a
day. Thanks for rescuing me from those kids. You'll
never guess what that one wants, the blonde named
Laura."

Eliza laughed and linked her arm through his. "I
think I have a damn good idea. You're a very attractive
man, and I certainly remember what I wanted when I
took a class from you at her age."

He appeared slightly embarrassed by her comment
and dismissed it with a shrug. "Well, thanks, but that
wasn't it. She's been bugging me all week about getting

a part on your show. Most of the kids in the class have seen my name on the credits, and it's all they can talk about. They all watch it when they can.''

"That doesn't surprise me. The soaps are very popular with college-age people. We get letters from them all the time.''

"Well, it sure surprised me. I didn't think those damn things were so popular among younger people.''

"Hey, watch how you refer to my show!'' she said with a light laugh. "What did you tell the girl?''

"To call you at work.''

"She might as well. Everyone else does. Can she act?''

"How in the hell am I supposed to know? Not if she acts the way she writes. Her first paper was atrocious. She has a lot of nerve though. It should serve her well in getting a break somewhere.''

"Oh? What did she do?''

"She manages to appear on my doorstep at predictable intervals.''

"And what does a handsome director-professor do when an attractive young woman appears on his doorstep?'' Eliza asked with a note of jealousy in her voice.

"I tell the nearest available person to say I'm not home,'' he said reassuringly.

"Good boy. You keep on doing that.''

He chuckled, squeezed her arm with affection, and then held open the door for her. "Don't worry, Liza. Coeds haven't been my style for fifteen years. Where are we going?''

"I have to talk to you,'' she said soberly. Eliza opened her briefcase. "I have something that belongs to you. I'd like to be able to say I came by it accidentally, but unfortunately, I can't.''

He put his hand over hers. "Don't. Keep the script. I have no plans of ever using it. Shall I get a cab?''

"Please. Will you come back home with me? We have to talk more about your screenplay."

It was starting to rain, and Dario drew her into the shelter of the building. "Forget the screenplay. Liza, I don't think I should spend the evening with you, not for a while anyway. It's just not going to work for either of us. I think it would be best if we didn't see each other, except professionally, until I have to leave on Saturday."

His suggestion that they discontinue the personal relationship sent a cold chill throughout her body, but Eliza chose not to think about it, not just now. "I think you should go ahead and try to produce the movie you wrote. It's good. It's damn good. I don't know what went through my head this morning when I took it from you and made you sign over the rights. Here, take everything back, please?"

"I don't want them. They're of no use to me anymore. When I saw the look in your eyes after you read a few scenes, I knew I could never use that material. I wrote the screenplay five years ago. I had no idea then we would meet again, had no idea about..." he paused briefly. "About a lot of things that I don't care to discuss now."

"I feel awful about this, Dario. Your script is so good. Don't let me be the one who keeps it from the public," she pleaded.

"Dario pressed his lips against her forehead. "Don't feel bad, babe. There's plenty more good ones where that came from."

"At least let me return the contract," she insisted.

"No, that's not necessary, Liza." He placed his hand over hers to prevent her from opening the briefcase.

"But what if you have a change of heart five years from now and want to sell it?"

"I won't. And if I were to do so, the contract wouldn't matter anyway. You see, you've released me from it verbally, and I trust you because you've never violated any trust I ever had in you. I know you never will. That's the big difference between us. A relationship on any level can't survive long without trust, and I don't think you'll ever fully trust me again. I don't blame you, but I can't live with it, either."

She could barely see his face against the shadows of the old building, but Eliza knew he stared down fondly at her. She heard a few cabs beyond the pavement and turned to leave him, her heart tight with emotion. "Thank you for trusting me. I hope you change your mind someday and make the movie. I'd better go now." Dario was right. It just wouldn't work between them and for more reasons than the one he had verbalized, one she couldn't in good faith deny. Already he was restless to leave New York, and she sensed he'd never want to settle down in any one area. He'd been on his own too long for that.

She turned to leave, but Dario held on to her arm, preventing her departure. It was obvious he didn't want her to go. He embraced her, holding her tightly against his chest, kissing the side of her face. "Shakespeare had the gender all wrong when he talked about fickleness in women. I've changed my mind already."

She pulled back, her face lit up with happiness. "You're going to let someone make your movie?"

He kissed her upturned nose. "No, I'm going home with you. If you and I aren't going to work, then we can do it tomorrow as well as tonight. What do you think? Are you willing to take that chance?"

"That's one chance I'm willing to take. But I'll up the ante. What the hell! You only live once. I'm willing to give us a whole two days instead of a night not to work," she said in a light tone that belied her uncertainties about their relationship. "Come on."

Dario smiled. "I'll see that bet and up you a day."

"You're on." She took his hand and they walked to the waiting cab.

Chapter Nine

Eliza rested her head on Dario's shoulder and tried to persuade him to change his mind about the screenplay while the cab made its way from the Upper West Side to Gramercy Park.

Holding tightly on to her hand with all his fingers entwined through Eliza's, he listened with a tender smile and then silenced her with a kiss after ten minutes. "Stop it now. I've made my decision, and I don't intend to change my mind."

"You have to," she pleaded. "Do it for me."

"No, shush now. To tell you the truth, I had second thoughts about the script shortly after we met again. I phoned my agent in Hollywood and asked him not to show it to anyone else until he heard further from me."

"Didn't you say MGM was reading it?"

"They were, but it's not uncommon for an agent to pull a client's script back for whatever reasons may be. They have no rights to it until the contract is signed."

"So your agent's just sitting on it?"

"More or less," he replied. "And that's been the status since I met you again. You've put everything into an entirely different perspective."

"Why?" she persisted, undaunted by his weary tone that begged to have the subject dismissed.

Dario frowned once more and glanced at her sideways as though to reassert his reluctance to pursue the matter any further, but he figured he owed her some kind of an explanation, if only to persuade Eliza to forget the screenplay. "It's difficult to explain. At the time I wrote it, I had no idea we'd ever meet again, so I tended to view the script more objectively. Once we met, it became a more personal issue. I never expected to be so attracted to you again, and that forced me to take your feelings into account about the script. Also I realized that even if I didn't feel the way I do about you, that you had every right to privacy about your personal life. I had planned on discussing the script with you at some time, but each and every time I remembered it seemed like the wrong time to dredge up the past. Understand?"

"I'm beginning to, but just be warned I'm not giving up on encouraging you to have it produced."

He kissed her hand. "Good enough. I stand warned, but unless you plan on using carnal encouragement, can you do it some other time?"

"I didn't have carnal encouragement in mind. I've thought of something much better."

"I wasn't aware anything better existed. What did you have in mind?"

"A business proposition."

Dario groaned in an exaggerated fashion. "I should have known better than to hope for the other kind with you, Liza."

"I'll take that as a backhanded compliment. But seriously, I wasn't joking last night when I said I had a producer friend in Hollywood. I could have her read the script the next time I'm out there, and maybe she and I could come up with enough investors to begin the project. We could collaborate on it."

"Who's we?"

"You, me, and Joyce Jordan. She and I could coproduce, and you'd direct, of course. I'd also like to rewrite a few scenes. The characters lack depth in certain respects," she said hesitantly, wondering if he'd take offense at her criticism.

Dario chuckled. "So did the young man the boy is patterned after. By and large, he was a pretty shallow character. Seriously, Liza, I don't know if I have time to work on that particular film anyway, not for quite a while. The project in Rome will take at least six months, and I'm under contract to complete my book on the history of television in America by the end of summer."

"It would take at least that long to get the project off the ground. Give me your consent to get started." There were few things in life Eliza enjoyed more than producing something new. She thrived on every aspect of the business from inception of the original idea to the premiere of the completed film, be it a feature-length movie or a thirty-minute tape for a daily drama. Her near-black eyes glowed like polished jet as she continued to elaborate on her plans for the film.

Dario saw that shine in her impossibly dark eyes and smiled contentedly. "You really love all the wheeling and dealing that goes into making a film, don't you, Liza? Frankly I can't stand it," he said after she nodded. "I'd just as soon sit back and consider the artistic components."

"Good! That's exactly what I want you to do! What do you say, Dario? Is it a deal?" she asked excitedly.

He extended his hand, pulling it back slightly as she was about to grasp it in a shake to seal their new business alliance. "Under one condition."

"Oh? What's that?"

"I get to sleep with the producer whenever I'm in Hollywood."

"That can be arranged. Joyce saw you on a talk show once and said she'd give anything to take you home for the night," she answered with an impish grin. Eliza grabbed his hand before he could retract it.

"That isn't the arrangement I had in mind," he muttered.

"Oh?" she murmured provocatively, nuzzling against him. "What did you have in mind?"

"Stay tuned." The incendiary warmth of her breasts on his arm fired his every sense. Dario cleared his throat and forced Eliza upward from her reclined position against his side. "Lovemaking in the backseat of cabs makes me uneasy," he explained in a hushed tone.

She laughed. "Who's making love?"

"You are, you hopeless flirt."

"I'm just trying to get you to work with me on the film. So is it a deal?"

He was still ambivalent to the idea. "I don't know."

"Just give me your permission to have Joyce read it. I promise not to take any further steps without your consent."

"I will if you drop the subject for now," he agreed wearily, as though he didn't really care one way or the other what became of the screenplay.

"Done! Dario, wouldn't it be fun to collaborate on a film project together?" she said enthusiastically.

"I thought we weren't going to discuss it?"

"Sorry."

"You're forgiven. So how was your day, babe?"

"Not too unreasonably hectic, considering everything. I just wish I could go back in time and undo the events of this morning," she repeated. Shame over her hasty act in leaving Dario's flat so indignantly lingered on.

"Sorry, but no one can go back in time. It's over and

done with now. Stop harping about it, please?'' Dario raised her hand to his lips, halfway wishing himself it were possible to move backward in time, to undo the past and redo it once more. There wasn't a great deal he would have had changed, but he certainly knew what he wouldn't do if he were twenty-one again. He would not allow himself to be absorbed by the group he wanted to belong to at the risk of forsaking his own values and losing everything sacred to him, and maybe the woman at his side might still be his wife. None of the things he'd aspired to as a young man had ever tasted as sweet since he'd lost Eliza, though Dario had never been in want of any of them over the years. Success and wealth had always been his, but more than once they'd rung hollowly in his ears.

"Yes, I suppose,'' she replied wistfully. Her thoughts ran parallel to his. She had been rash in leaving Rome without even speaking to Dario fifteen years ago, but as he said, one couldn't go back in time. It was over and done with now.

He opened his briefcase. "I have something in here that you should like.''

She took the video cassette from his hand. "What's this?''

"Read the label.''

She held it up to the window. "Final shoot-out scene with Elliot and Sam? How did you get him to agree? And why did you film it today?'' she asked excitedly. "When I spoke to Elliot earlier, he was adamant about not doing the scene our way.''

"He still is. He doesn't know about this,'' Dario said mysteriously.

Eliza was dying with curiosity. "So what did you do? Hypnotize him and film the scene while he was in a trance?''

Dario laughed his deep resonant laugh, the one that

made her pulses race. "Better yet. I used clippings from the old tapes. We'll have to do it a little differently than originally planned, but I think the scene will still work. Remember the episode four years ago when Elliot tracked down the gangsters in the Bowery and got shot?"

"Yes, quite well. Mobster stories were big that year on all the soaps."

"I spliced together some scenes from that and a few other shows. We'll need a double to make certain parts convincing, but that's no problem."

"This is great! We've done similar things in the past, but I didn't think of it this time around. Elliot is going to be furious," she speculated, knowing of the actor's vanity and stubbornness to see things done his way.

"Let him. I went round and round for two hours with him this afternoon and couldn't get anywhere. I'm glad we're getting rid of him once and for all."

"So am I, but he has a fairly large following with the viewers. Beverly tells me you auditioned his replacement this afternoon. Any luck?" Eliza was still exhausted from the hectic pace she had maintained for the last few weeks. She shifted down lower in the seat, resting her head on his chest. The wool sweater was comfortably coarse beneath her cheek, and she stroked his midriff with a feather-light touch that made Dario's blood pressure rise.

"I'm not sure yet. I'd like to do more auditions tomorrow. Here we are." He paid the driver and then took the briefcase from her lap, carrying it under his arm along with his own as they climbed the stairs.

"Woof! Woof!" Dario said to the dog who greeted him with a loud bark when Eliza unlocked the door. Eli jumped up, placing both paws on Dario's chest.

"Down, Eli. He sheds all over the place," she told Dario. "Can I fix you anything to eat?"

"No, thank you. I had dinner right before class. I wouldn't mind a cup of coffee though."

"Neither would I." Eliza put the water on to boil and joined Dario at the kitchen table. She flipped open her briefcase and handed him a copy of the next day's script. "You haven't blocked this, have you?"

"No, I haven't. I used all my free time to splice together tapes for Elliot's last scene."

"Good, you can do it while I work on the new show."

He shook his head and frowned. "Are you saying you invited me over here to work? You really know how to show a man a good time, don't you?" The humor in his eyes erased the censure implicit in his words.

"Sure. I'm going to prove you wrong when you said we couldn't work together," Eliza stated with a broad grin. She took his hand and led him to the study. After depositing Dario on the sofa, she pushed back the desk chair with one foot and settled in at the typewriter.

"This wasn't the kind of work I meant," he complained with a good-natured wink. "But I'll do it anyway if it means sitting here watching you at your desk. How long do you plan to work?"

"At least a few hours."

"Have you ever heard the story about the lovely lady who burned the candle at both ends?"

"Have you ever heard the story about the lady who lost her house because she couldn't come up with the mortgage payments?" she countered with a grin.

"Yes, that's an old one, too," he agreed. "You can always come and live at my old place. Over there no one would notice an extra person, and I can show you that view of the Brooklyn Bridge before I leave."

"Ah, huh. If you can get me high enough." She inserted a blank sheet of paper into the typewriter and began to write dialogue, using the detailed outline as a guide. "Damn! I forgot to tell Jared what we decided to do with Elliot's demise. Does he know about the tapes you've spliced together yet?"

"I didn't see any reason to tell him."

"I'd better let him know then. He's probably home, racking his brains for an alternative solution."

"Jared? Good. I was pleased to hear he'd reconsidered the job with HEI. You need him now. What made him change his mind so suddenly?" Dario had a pretty good idea what had motivated the younger man. It was impossible to be around Eliza and Jared for more than five minutes without picking up on the way they related to each other.

"Loyalty," she replied. "Jared felt it was lousy to leave me without notice after all the things we've been through."

Dario quirked one eyebrow. "Such as?"

She heard the insinuation in his question and found herself mildly flattered by his jealousy. "Oh, there was the madcap trip to Rio one summer, the time we ran off to a tropical island for the winter and got stranded until the following summer, and then the romantic holiday in the Swiss Alps one year," she teased, dialing the number. "Not to mention all those wild weekends in Paris."

"Sounds exciting," he said, wondering if she had exaggerated as an evasive tactic.

She explained the decided course of action to Jared briefly, instructing him to get in touch with the rest of the cast members who were involved, and then returned to Dario on the sofa. "Well, it wasn't because I made the whole thing up," she confessed, kissing his forehead.

Dario smiled and pulled her onto his lap "Were you trying to make me jealous by any chance?"

"No, just having a little fun with you."

He smiled, lowered his mouth to hers and kissed her. His hands tightened over the full rise of her breasts under the thin crepe fabric. "And is it all right if I have a little fun with you?"

"Depends on what kind," Eliza whispered against his neck, "and when."

"This kind." He kissed her again. "And whenever you say."

The phone rang while their mouths were joined, and they muttered a mild obscenity, both at the same time.

Dario slid down on the sofa and rested his head on her breast. "Is that the red line or the other one that can wait?"

"The one that can't wait. Move, baby."

He shifted upward and groaned. "Next time remind me to get involved with a lady plumber instead of a businesswoman, okay?"

"I'll do no such thing!"

Eliza prepared herself for bad news when the caller proved to be the executive vice-president from HEI. Mr. Talbort seldom called unless he had a complaint to voice about something.

"I understand a few of your people were involved in an accident recently," he began.

Eliza was certain he hadn't called solely to offer his condolences. "Yes, that's right. Fortunately, the injuries weren't serious, and both men will be back at work soon."

"Well, I'm glad to hear that, Eliza. I've been meaning to call you for the last few days and apologize for not making the monthly meeting at 21 a few weeks back. Got tied up in some last minute negotiations. You know how it is, Eliza."

She made a face and sat down on the sofa, looking at Dario who had decided to build a fire. "Yes, I know how it is.'' Eliza wished she had never given Bud Talbort the private number in the first place.

He made small talk for a while longer before getting to the point. ''So I understand you're against the spinoff.''

''You understand correctly. I'm totally opposed to the way you want to handle the show, Bud.''

''Are you sure?''

''Yes, quite.'' At least he was ready to talk business now, although Eliza was fairly certain it would be the kind of business she didn't like.

She was pleasantly surprised when he informed her of his purpose in calling. ''Well, Eliza, since you won't give us rights to create a spinoff, how about if you do it? You'll have complete creative control over the new show, of course, and the option of working at either our New York or Hollywood studio. What do you say?''

''I say it sounds good, Bud. What kind of budget are we talking about?''

''That's up in the air right now, Eliza, but we're open to something more ambitious than the present scale of *Beyond Tomorrow*,'' he said.

Eliza would have preferred to channel all of the additional funding into her existing show, but knew it wasn't a feasible alternative to suggest to HEI. They stood to gain more by having two daily dramas instead of one done more elaborately. ''How about a weekly nighttime series that leads into a daily drama?'' she proposed.

''That's a definite possibility, Eliza. It's always a good way to hook viewers who wouldn't normally tune into daytime. How soon can you have the treatments ready?'' he asked, referring to the short outlines that would summarize the new story ideas.

She was about to say by the end of the week when

she remembered Dario was leaving for Rome then, and she had no idea when they would be together again. Clearly he was lukewarm at best about the prospect of collaborating with her and Joyce Jordan on the production of his screenplay, and Eliza didn't know if his reluctance signified more of a desire not to work with her than a wish to keep the film on the shelves.

"Well?" Bud Talbort demanded impatiently when Eliza failed to respond to his question. "I know you already have some proposals down on paper because we've considered this possibility in the past, Eliza. Can you get back to me by Saturday? I'm anxious to get the ball rolling on this one because our own pilot turned out to be a miserable flop, and we've been promising the viewers something new by way of a daily drama for the last four weeks in the commercials. Did you hear about the pilot?"

"Yes, I heard," she replied. "How about if I get back to you by the middle of next week, Bud? I have a pretty full schedule for the remainder of this week."

"Good enough," he agreed. "Is the trip down to the islands still on for the end of the month?"

"Oh, yes! I've waited a long time for that kind of funding."

"Great! I hate to push you into moving so quickly on that one, Eliza, but I'm afraid the ratings on *Beyond Tomorrow* may suffer from the departure of some of your actors. Even though we won't be going through with our soap, we're keeping Marath and some others for a new nighttime show that's under development at the Hollywood studio. Eliza, my other line is ringing. Get back to me as soon as you can, all right?"

She hung up the phone with a victorious smile and rushed to Dario's side. He was lying flat on his back in front of the fire. "Guess what?" she said, leaning down over him.

"Do I have to?" Methodically, he began to remove the pins from her hair until it was free, and the black waves tumbled across his chest.

"Have to."

"All right, HEI offered you another show to do. It's going to be a spinoff of *Beyond Tomorrow*, and you'll have full creative control. You can even introduce it as a weekly drama if you prefer." His fingers closed over the base of her neck while the thumb caressed the underside of her chin.

"Right. Dario, you either have a crystal ball or you're an eavesdropper."

He smiled and pulled her down to his chest. "If I had a crystal ball at my disposal, I'd ask it what plans you were referring to when you told Bud Talbort you'd be too busy to work on the new show for the rest of the week."

She stared silently into the golden brown eyes, reveling in the candent glow there and delighting in the flutter of his breath against her face. Like hers, his breathing was labored, short and shallow, and she could feel the rapidity of his heartbeat beneath her breast. Never in a hundred years of dreaming up the most dramatic scenarios possible for the characters she created, sometimes interposing her own fantasies there-in, would she have ever imagined this would happen to her, that she'd fall in love with her first love once more, after all the years and all the heartbreak she'd known because of his youthful indiscretions. Funny thing, she reflected, continuing to gaze down at Dario, that she'd never once considered the possibility of loving him again. At the present moment it was impossible to imagine not loving him, as though the entire sequence of events for the last few months was preordained, almost as though she were destined to love her first love again, to love him always.

"Do you really want to know what I plan to do for the next few days?" she said in a hushed tone.

"More than anything in the world." He unzipped her dress in back and eased it past her shoulders.

"I'll give you a hint. It's going to shock everyone down at Rothcart Productions, Incorporated."

Dario spoke with his lips parted over the hollow on her throat. "Go on."

"I'm taking a vacation. I'm not even going to think about the show."

He showered a downpour of kisses along her shoulder and arm. "Going any place in particular?"

"Wherever you go for the next few days, Dario. I'll even drive you to the airport on Saturday."

"Hum, I like that. I like it a lot, but I have a better idea." He rolled her onto her back, his mouth still buried in the crook of her arm.

She clasped his head to her breast. "What? I can't imagine anything better than spending the rest of your time in Manhattan together."

He kissed her elbow and then took her face in his hands. "Get on the plane and go to Rome with me, Liza. Put everything here on hold and give our relationship a chance to work this time around."

"I can't." Dario had never once said he loved her, and she was amazed that he'd ask her to jeopardize a career she worked so hard for and had done so well at for a romantic fling. "I just can't," she replied in a hoarse whisper, adding, "but it's a nice thought."

Dario winced at her choice of words. A nice thought? That was almost as meaningless a phrase as when the teller at the bank told him to have a nice day, but then what right did he have to ever think she'd give more serious attention to his suggestion? Obviously Eliza didn't love him, would never love him again, and her career in New York meant everything to her.

Eliza sensed his shift in mood. She kissed his forehead and then stroked the side of his face where less than a day's growth of beard ran deliciously rough beneath her fingertips. "You do understand why I can't just leave everything and go with you, don't you?"

"Yes, I understand."

"Any chance of your getting down to the island? Jared and I went over the topographical maps this morning. The trails seemed impossible to follow. We could certainly use someone who knows the area."

Dario pressed his mouth against her hand and laughed. "You little witch. And to think I actually thought you wanted me down there so you could avail yourself of my luscious body on a moonlit beach at night, and all you want is someone to keep you and your crew from getting lost on the island."

"That was my ulterior motive, you fool. I was just trying to be subtle," she confessed.

"I don't like you when you're subtle. It makes me feel insecure."

"Liar," she laughed, "you knew all along why I wanted you there!"

"Show me," he cajoled with an intimate caress that nearly took her breath away.

"My, you certainly take liberties with a lady," she said coyly as his hands slid beneath her clothing.

"Like it?" Dario murmured, parting the blouse in front and taking her breast into his mouth with a suckling motion that was felt in the depths of her.

"Oh, love it." They undressed each other before the fire, and Eliza marveled at the beatific glow that transfixed his gaze whenever he looked at her. It's almost as though he loves me, she thought, nearly despairing because he hadn't said those words to her for over fifteen years. Her despair soon took the form of rapture as he led her from the brink of ecstasy to a sublime place she had never visited before, save in his arms the previous time they were together.

Chapter Ten

"Breakfast in bed?" Eliza asked when presented with a lap tray. "You're much too kind, sir. To what do I owe this honor?" She could almost taste the freshly ground coffee, the croissant was divine, and no cut rose from her garden had ever seemed lovelier. Every sight, scent, and sound that bombarded her senses that morning did so with a beauty and serenity that bedazzled her, and it all came from loving Dario.

"Let's just say I want you to conserve your strength." He snapped the white linen napkin into the air to unfold it. "Hum, can't figure out how to tuck this in," Dario murmured afterward, rubbing his chin with one hand. He finally settled for tying it loosely around her neck.

"I knew you'd think of something," Eliza said, congratulating him with a kiss on his cheek. "Aren't you eating?"

Dario pulled up a chair and sat at the edge of the bed. "I already did. It's nearly noon."

"Oh, my God! I've never slept this late in my life! And on a weekday, too!" she exclaimed. Some internal biological clock dictated that she rise from the bed now. Eliza pushed the tray away, only to have it shoved back.

"Relax! The sky isn't going to fall simply because Eliza Rothcart slept in one fine fall morning. And with good reason, I might add."

"Hmm, the best of all possible reasons. How long have you been up?" She smothered a croissant with butter and strawberry jam.

"A few hours. The doorbell woke me up around ten."

Eliza was surprised she hadn't heard the ring. "Did you answer?"

"Yes, the bell rang more than once, and I didn't want it to wake you up. Also, I couldn't get the dog to stop barking. You've been working hard lately, and I wanted you to get some rest."

"I can't imagine sleeping through all that racket. Who was it?"

"Leonard James."

Eliza found herself mildly disturbed by the thought of an old companion dropping in on her when she was with her new love. "I'm sorry, Dario. Did he say what he wanted?"

He tugged at a tendril of her disheveled hair. "Don't let it bother you. These things happen. He didn't elaborate, but he wanted to talk to you about your father. He said it was quite important and for you to call him as soon as you're up. Maybe you should do it after you eat. He said he'd be at his Manhattan office."

Her contented smile faded, and she sat idly stirring the coffee with a silver spoon for a while before Dario eased her face upward with his palm.

"Why so glum?"

She shrugged her shoulders. "Oh, I don't know."

"Yes, you do. You're still at odds with the old man and don't want to hear anything about him," he guessed.

"Just how much did Leonard tell you?" she asked suspiciously.

"Nothing other than what I told you. I assumed as much from what you yourself said about him a few weeks ago. Maybe you should give Leonard a call anyway and see what's up. As I said, it sounded important.''

"I will," she agreed reluctantly. "One of Leonard's great missions in life was to reconcile me with my father," she confided after a few more sips of coffee. "Whenever he visits the East Coast for a seminar or something, Leonard always tries to arrange for us to get together. I'm sure he heard father is in town and wants me to see him."

"Perhaps you should," he suggested. "How long has it been since you've seen him?"

"Last Christmas. It was very awkward. He kept holding my mother up as a shining example and asking why I wasn't married with six kids yet, and of course, he managed to tell my seventeen-year-old cousin the unfortunate story of our marriage as an incentive to encourage her to drop her steady boyfriend."

Dario chuckled. "Sounds like the old man hasn't changed much. But he's still your father and you're really all he has now that your mother is no longer alive." Eliza was finished, and he removed her tray. "Here, call him now."

"I'll do it later," she replied, springing from the bed. "Oh, Dario, you should have made me get up earlier! There's so many things I wanted to do with you before you have to go to Rome!"

He caught her in his arms as she made a dash for the shower. "Like what?"

"We're going to pretend we're tourists in the Big Apple for the first time in our lives. We're going to take a ferry to the Statue of Liberty, elevators to the tops of the Empire State Building and the World Trade Center, and ride through Central Park in a horse-drawn carriage! After that, we're...."

"Whoa! Slow down, Liza. The only thing I want to

see in the Big Apple is right here in these four walls. You'll never turn me into a New Yorkophile that way." He saw her downcast expression and relented. "Oh, all right. We'll make like tourists. But do me a favor, please? Call your father."

"If you insist." Dario handed her the phone and she called Leonard's office. Eliza was disappointed when the secretary put her through immediately.

"Eliza, how are you?" he asked.

"Fine, Leonard, and you?"

"Not too well. Dear, I have some bad news," he said bluntly. "It's about your father."

"Is he all right?" Eliza asked. It wasn't like Leonard to call news bad unless it really was. Dario caught the frantic note in her voice and jerked his head toward her.

"I'm afraid not. I flew out to L.A. last week for a conference at the medical school and ran into Sheila Polasky. Remember her? You met once at a party in Hollywood."

Eliza recalled the name well. The woman was a physician who specialized in chemotherapy and had been very helpful to her once in providing background information for a storyline on *Beyond Tomorrow* dealing with cancer. "Does my father have cancer?"

"Yes. He's been her patient for nearly a year, Eliza."

"A year! And he never told me!" She leaned into the bed for support. Dario sat down on it and took her hand.

"I don't think he's told anyone. That's not uncommon in these types of things. Sheila knows she's breaking a patient-doctor confidentiality by telling me, but she feels strongly that someone should know."

"How bad is it?" Eliza asked quietly. Dario's grip on her hand tightened. She began to shake, and he wrapped a warm blanket over her shoulders.

"Not too good. It's a multiple myeloma. Your father's undergoing the same treatment the character did on the show last year, remember? As I recall, Sheila consulted with you on the script, didn't she?"

Eliza saw a ray of hope. Based upon true medical cases, her character had made a full recovery. "Then a remission's possible, isn't it?"

"Anything's possible, Eliza, but don't count on it. The last remission I heard of in a case like your father's was on that soap opera of yours. You really shouldn't air things like that. It gives people false hope."

She knew he hadn't cared for the near miraculous cure at the time she aired the series, but Eliza and her writers gave in to the demands of the viewers who wrote her countless letters requesting that the character, a very popular leading man, get better and live. If only it were that easy in real life, she thought sadly. "Maybe so, but we never would have written the remission into the script if Sheila hadn't said it was possible. She knew of similar cases herself," Eliza replied, still clinging tenaciously to hope.

"It can happen, but don't forget that Sheila has been a practicing physician for over forty years. She's probably seen everything that can happen, happen at least once in all those years. Look, I think you should go and see your father. Don't let on you know anything, okay?" he advised. "Would you like me to fly out with you?"

"No, that's not necessary, but thanks, Leonard. How sick is he, and what is the prognosis?" She couldn't bring herself to ask directly how long he had to live.

And Leonard couldn't bring himself to tell her. "It would be best if you got the details from Sheila. That really isn't my field."

"Is he in the hospital?"

"No, as a matter of fact, he's still teaching at the university. Eliza, are you sure you don't want me to go with you?" he repeated.

"Yes, I'm sure, but thanks again anyway. Good-bye, Leonard." She hung up and collapsed into Dario's arms.

Wordlessly he held her until the sobs abated. Dario felt a sense of endless frustration and futility because there wasn't any more he could do for her, other than hold her against his chest as the convulsive sobs racked her body. God only knew how willingly he would take all her pain onto himself if it were at all possible. "There, there, baby," he crooned repeatedly. When Eliza withdrew and groped around for a tissue, he located one on the dresser and dried her tears for her.

"I suppose you'd think I was a terrible hypocrite if I told you how much I love that stubborn old man right now, wouldn't you?" she asked between gulps for air.

Dario smiled and kissed away a lingering tear. "Not at all, my darling. Not at all. But I think it'd be better if you told him. Are you leaving right away?"

"On the earliest flight I can get."

"I'll make the reservations while you get ready."

"Thank you." She began to pack, halting abruptly when Dario made reservations for two people. "You're going with me?"

Dario was still on the phone and motioned for her to be quiet while he inquired about flights from Los Angeles to Rome. "Very good," he said, returning the receiver to the cradle. "Of course, I'm going with you. We had an agreement to be inseparable for the next two days, remember?"

She was too moved to speak at first. "But it didn't mean this. We were going to have a good time. You don't have to go."

"Yes, I do. This isn't what I had anticipated, but for me, the agreement meant for better or for worse."

"For better or for worse?" she echoed, not daring to read more into the words than were intended by the speaker. "Sorry it's been so awful. I had all fun and games in mind until you went away."

"Fun and games, huh?" he repeated, smiling to himself. I had love and happily ever after on my mind, he mused, with the same bittersweet smile animating his mouth.

"Sure. Isn't that what you wanted?"

"Among other things, but we'll discuss it later. You know what?"

"What?" God, she prayed, let him say he loves me.

"I'm just thinking. My presence in L.A. may have a therapeutic effect on your old man. Knowing him, he probably hates me so much that he'll live just to make certain he can come up with some way to keep me out of his darling daughter's bed. Take your time in the shower. The earliest flight I could get leaves at five. It seems like heavy fog in the area is delaying all incoming flights to the West Coast. I wouldn't be surprised if we have to stay over in Denver. I couldn't get a direct route."

Dario was on the verge of telling Eliza how much he loved her when she left to shower, her face mirroring disappointment from his news about the flight to California. Quietly he finished her packing, putting the rest of the clothing she had taken from her closet and drawers into the suitcase.

The cross-country flight was long and uneventful. As they had feared, bad weather on the Coast delayed the connecting flight, and they were forced to spend a miserable twelve hours in the airport. Eliza wouldn't hear of Dario's suggestion that they spend the night in a motel nearby and leave later, so they passed the hours brooding before a window near the landing strip. He tried everything he knew short of standing on a table and tap dancing to cheer Eliza up, but she became progressively morose as the journey continued, unable to sleep once they finally left Denver.

"I guess this is where we say good-bye for a while, honey," Dario said as the cab approached her father's house in Santa Monica. "I'm going to find a hotel in Westwood, near the campus, so I can look up a few old friends while you're busy with your father. I'll give you a call tonight and let you know where I am."

She grabbed onto his hand. "Oh, Dario! I thought you were staying at the house with me!" Eliza was bitterly disappointed by his decision and the fact he hadn't informed her of it earlier. God knows they had had enough time. "That place has ten rooms, half of them bedrooms."

Dario's religious upbringing prevailed over his natural impulses, and he was shocked that she would suggest such a thing. "Liza, I can't do that," he muttered. "We're not married, and your father wouldn't like it even if we were. You know how he feels about me. Show a little respect, will you?"

"We don't have to sleep in the same room," she argued. "Besides, father is expecting both of us."

"He is? How so?"

"I called him from Denver. Didn't I tell you?"

"No. What did you say?"

"I couldn't tell him the truth."

"The truth about what? His dying or us sleeping together?" He caught her hand in his when she winced. "I'm sorry, baby. What did you say?"

She yawned, covering her face with her free hand. "It's all right. Why mince words at this point? I didn't tell him the truth about either thing, of course. I said you were working for me, and we came out to discuss a new show for ABC."

"He must have been suspicious when you said we were staying at his house."

"Well, I didn't exactly say it. I said we'd drop by when we got into town."

Dario looked at his watch. "It's not quite eight A.M. California time. What if he's still in bed?"

"He has a live-in housekeeper. She'll let us in."

It was Mrs. O'Riley, the woman who had kept house for Professor Rothcart since his wife died, who met Eliza and Dario on the porch. She'd been with the Rothcarts for years, coming in three mornings a week since Eliza was a child and switching to full-time employment as of the last five years. "Oh, Eliza, I'm so glad you came!"

Eliza embraced the rotund woman. "So am I. Is my father up?"

"Up? He got up two hours ago and went to his office at the university. You know your father and his precious physics lab! That man will work until the day he dies, Lord bless him!" she enthused, pulling Eliza into the house.

Dario had just enough time to grasp her hand before Eliza was propelled over the threshold. Apparently her father had kept his illness a secret from the housekeeper, who had begun to babble on about the professor's long-term projects at UCLA.

"You aren't staying, are you?" Mrs. O'Riley asked Dario when the cab pulled away.

The censure in her voice told Dario she knew of him from family gossip and didn't like what she'd heard. "For a while perhaps," he replied graciously.

"I must say the professor was surprised when Eliza told him she was traveling with you," she chastised sharply. "I can't say as he liked the idea one bit." Mrs. O'Riley had never placed much stock in observances of the social amenities.

"I'm sorry," Dario apologized. "How is Dr. Rothcart these days?"

She answered the question, but it was clear her comments were directed exclusively to Eliza. "Your father's not as young as he used to be. Sometimes I worry about him. I think he works too hard for a man his age. He should slow down some. Some days he looks so tired that I don't think he has the strength to get out of bed, but, of course, he does it anyway and goes off to that office or lab of his and doesn't come back until nightfall."

Eliza bit her lips to keep from crying. She had a strong hunch that many of her father's long days were spent in chemotherapy at the medical school instead of in his office on the UCLA campus.

Dario knew what she was going through and intervened on her behalf. "Mrs. O'Riley, the food on the airplane was about five times as awful as airplane food usually is. Would you mind fixing something for Eliza to eat? She hasn't had anything since we left New York."

"Will you be staying?" she demanded gruffly.

"Yes, he will," Eliza replied in a tone that didn't brook further inquiry, before Dario could say anything.

He took her into his arms the second the housekeeper disappeared into the next room. She made a valiant effort to stem the tide of tears and then wept briefly with her head resting on his shoulder. "Where's your room, baby?" They'd been in transit for the entire night, and Eliza looked dead on her feet.

She rubbed her wet face on his shirt and smiled. "Don't you remember?"

He kissed her nose and smiled. "Ah, yes, how could I have forgotten? I nearly broke my neck climbing into it one night. You still use the same room when you're here?"

"Yes, but I'm not here that much," she said in a tone of self-reproach.

He led her up the stairs. "Well, you're here now. That's all that matters, and thanks for reminding me where your room is. With the reception I'm getting around this place, I may be forced to sneak back into it if I want to see you tonight."

"Would you?"

"If need be, love." He took off her jacket and shoes and eased her into the bed. "You rest now. I'll tell Mrs. O'Riley you're tired."

"I'm too tense to sleep. Don't go. I'll ask her to serve us in the dining room. Mrs. O'Riley doesn't know anything about my father's illness, does she?"

"That's the impression I got. Didn't Leonard say he hadn't told anyone?"

"Yes. I wonder why."

"Why not?" he countered gently. "A man has a right to die the way he chooses."

"I suppose that's true. I won't let on that I know anything." She left the bed. "I'm going to take a real quick shower and change into something else. Tell Mrs. O'Riley I'll be down in ten minutes."

"Do I have to? I swear, Liza, that woman's looking at me with murder in her eyes. I guess it's good practice for gearing up to see your father after all these years," he remarked. "Now I know how Rhett Butler felt in *Gone With the Wind* when he met Scarlett's mammy for the first time."

"Mammy came around in the end. As I recall, she wound up liking Rhett better than Scarlett."

He excused himself when she began to undress. "That was because Rhett was a nicer guy than Scarlett. I thought she was a real bitch. See you in a bit."

Dario went downstairs and offered to help Mrs. O'Riley with breakfast. The more charming he tried to be, the less she seemed to like him. After fifteen min-

utes he'd exhausted his repertoire of amusing anec-
dotes and winsome smiles. Dario gave up and went into
the dining room to wait for Eliza, who took longer in
the shower than she said she would. He supposed she
was trying to regain her composure and prepare herself
for meeting her father.

The housekeeper joined him a few minutes later,
slamming the plates onto the walnut table with a ven-
geance that jerked Dario's head up. "Why don't you
like me, Mrs. O'Riley?" he asked politely, reasoning it
might be better all around for her to get her animosity
out into the open.

"Because you're the last thing that girl needs now,
that's why!" she said passionately, whirling toward him
with both hands on her hips. "A person can only take
so much at one time, and if you do what you did fifteen
years ago, it'll just be too much!"

Dario stood from the sofa, easing himself up slowly
wondering if he dared to place his hand on the
woman's shoulder. "You know, don't you?"

"Know what? What you did to her once? Of course,
I do," she asserted, but not convincingly enough.

"No, Mrs. O'Riley, that's not what I mean. I'm talking about the professor." His hand fell to her shoulder
and she didn't withdraw at first.

"I don't know what you're talking about."

"Okay, Mrs. O'Riley."

"All I know is you better love that girl or go away.
There's no in-between for her where you're concerned.
You two come here saying you're on a business trip,
but I can tell there's more than business between you
from the way Eliza looks at you." She brushed his arm
from her shoulder and left the room, nearly knocking
Eliza over on her way out.

Eliza had overheard the woman's parting shot, and

her face paled. "Don't pay any attention to her, Dario. She's almost as bad as father when it comes to trying to marry me off."

"And I suppose I'm the least unlikely candidate, huh?" he muttered, almost as though speaking to himself. Damn, if only the old lady were right, and she were in love with him.

"From their way of thinking, yes," Eliza replied. But not mine. If only you could love me as much as I love you, she added to herself.

"Well, that's neither here nor there now, Liza. We have to work this thing out with your father better. It's going to look awfully suspicious to have both of us staying here. It's too much as though we've come together to pay our final respects. Sit down and eat, and we'll decide what to do."

In the end Eliza agreed with Dario, realizing it was only the trauma of a night-long cross-country flight under such unhappy circumstances that had compelled her to plead with him to remain at the house. After breakfast they borrowed Mrs. O'Riley's car and drove to the Westwood area of Los Angeles and found him a hotel room near the university.

"I think it'd be better if you saw your father alone, at least at first," Dario suggested after tossing the few things he'd brought from New York in an old duffel bag into the standard hotel chest of drawers. "I'll be here when you need me."

She could see his reflection behind her in the mirror where she stood rearranging her hair. "Oh, Dario, I'll never be able to pull this off! Look at me! I'm a wreck. He'll know something is wrong and figure out exactly what it is in about five seconds. Maybe it was foolish of me to rush to his bedside like this. Leonard implied he wasn't in any immediate danger of ... Well, he couldn't be that ill now if he's still working, could he?" she implored hopefully, turning to him.

"No, love, I'm sure he has his good days and his bad days just like everyone else. I think you did the right thing by coming to L.A. when you did. Why wait until his condition declines? Here, take this phone and see if you can locate him on campus, okay?"

She took the receiver from his hand and dialed the physics department. Eliza learned her father was in one of the teaching labs, giving an impromptu demonstration to a group of foreign visitors to the university. "Will you drive me there?" she asked.

"Of course, I will. Let me hold you for a few minutes before we leave though." Her heartbeat was accelerated against his chest at first, but after a while she seemed to calm down. "Ready, baby?"

"As ready as I'll ever be for something like this." Eliza invited him over to the house for dinner when he dropped her off near the professor's office, where she'd decided to wait for her father.

"I think it would be rather awkward."

"He knows we flew out together. Perhaps it would be more awkward if you stayed away." she disagreed. "Please come."

"Why do I find it so damn impossible to say no to you?" He cupped her face in his hands and kissed Eliza soundly on the mouth.

"Maybe for the same reason that I've never been good at saying no to you." She rested her head on his chest briefly and then opened the car door. "We find each other totally irresistible. What are you going to do this afternoon?" she asked, leaning down into the window on the driver's side of the vehicle.

"I have to get in touch with one of my roommates at the place I was staying and arrange to have my luggage shipped to Rome. We left so hastily that I didn't have time to do it.''

She hated to think of his departure. "I wish you didn't have to go, not just now. But I know how important the new film is to you," she added quickly, thinking it was self-indulgent of her to request more of his time after all he'd done for her, flying out to California just to hold her hand with so little advance warning. Surely there were a thousand more enjoyable ways for a man like him to spend his remaining few days in New York. "By the way, it's no big deal about getting down to the island. Jared and I can manage.''

That sounded like a brush-off if he'd ever heard one, and he was reluctant to be dismissed from her life. "But I've always wanted to be stranded on a tropical island with a beautiful woman.''

"We'll hardly be alone. Jared, the technical crew, and the two new kids we hired for the added roles will be there.''

"Let them go to their own island. I want..." He stopped talking. "Liza, I think that's your father coming down the stairs.''

She whirled around. Her throat went suddenly dry. "It is. God, he looks so much older than I had remembered." For the first time she doubted the wisdom of leaving New York as soon as she learned of his illness. Eliza didn't think she had given herself sufficient time to adjust to the news and simply couldn't handle the present encounter. The thought of leaving before her father saw them occurred to her, but it was too late. The old man looked at her, and involuntarily her fist jerked and tightened against her side before reaching out for Dario's waiting hand.

Eliza's father had actually recognized his house-keeper's car before he saw who was standing next to it and walked toward the vehicle. "Good morning," he said when he realized who they were.

"Hello, father," she said softly. The greeting struck her as hopelessly inadequate after all that happened between them and preceding all that was to come. Her father's eyes strayed to her hand that was still locked in Dario's clasp, and she broke the grip, recalling his censure of years ago. She had defied him then, she would not now. "How are you?"

"Very well, thank you. What type of project brings the two of you to Los Angeles?" he inquired in a politely distant tone.

Dario left the car and extended his hand to the older man. "We're collaborating on a film together, sir," he ad libbed in a partial truth.

Professor Rothcart shook his hand. "That's nice. What's it about?"

There was no way he could ever tell the man he'd written a screenplay about his early marriage to Eliza. "It's a contemporary drama."

"You mean no story and a lot of sex? I don't like the way they do movies nowadays."

Eliza laughed, amazed that she could. "Neither do I, father. I don't think you'd like the picture we might produce." She'd told her father they were working on another soap for ABC but didn't bother to contradict Dario's explanation.

"Probably not. Can I buy the two of you a cup of coffee, or are you anxious to rush off to the studios?" he asked. "We can walk over to the faculty lounge."

Eliza and Dario both noticed that her father leaned against the car for support while he spoke, and there was a yellowish tint to his skin. "Why don't we drive somewhere?" she suggested.

"I'm not dead yet. I can walk," he snapped, leaving

Eliza and Dario to wonder at the significance of his response.

"Okay, fine."

"If the two of you will excuse me now, I think I'd better get back to my hotel," Dario said. "I have to make some arrangements for the trip to Rome."

"Don't forget dinner," Eliza reminded him.

She took her father's arm as they walked. "I invited Dario to dinner, father. I hope you don't mind."

"Since when did my opinions as far as you and Dario Napoli are concerned ever matter?"

"Oh, Dad, let's not get into that, please? It's been fifteen years, for goodness' sake!"

"How did you run into him again?" His breathing became progressively labored as they continued to walk along the path.

"I don't really want a cup of coffee. Let's just sit on that bench over there, all right? I've been up all night and could use the rest." They sat down and she explained how she came to meet Dario again.

"I never did like that man, Eliza. I still don't."

"I know. Maybe I shouldn't have invited him over for dinner. I can call and ask him not to come," she offered. Why put Dario and her father through the stress of sharing the same table simply because she'd like to see the two men make peace with each other and because she needed Dario now?

"No, he can come. I suppose you have a right to pick your own friends, even if you have a knack for picking the wrong ones. So who told you?"

"Told me what?" she asked. The words caught in her throat.

"About the myeloma."

There was no point in lying to him now. "One of the doctors at UCLA told Leonard, and he called me."

"The bastard! I wonder who he was? Doesn't a man

have a right to any privacy anymore?" he said emphatically.

"Oh, Dad, I'm so sorry!" Eliza fell into his arms crying when she wanted to be brave and say something encouraging to him.

"Don't be. I'm nearly seventy and have had a good, full life. My career at the university has been successful, I was married for over forty years to the most wonderful woman in the world, and I've even lived long enough to see my daughter fall in love with the same jerk twice. What man could ask for more?" he replied.

Eliza lifted her head from his shoulder and saw the smile in his eyes. "Dario's not a jerk, Daddy."

"You said that to me fifteen years ago."

"Well, he was a jerk then, but he's since grown up."

"He still runs off to Rome when you need him, doesn't he?" the old man pointed out.

"Business is business. That film has been under negotiations for a long time. He has to go. Besides, I'm a big girl now and don't need Dario to sit around and hold my hand," she argued back. "And I have my own work to tend to. I have a new show that's coming out on NBC in a few months, I'm doing another show for HEI, and Dario and I might do a major motion picture together."

Her father smiled fondly at her. "Eliza, did I ever tell you how proud I am of you? How proud I've always been?"

"No, I always thought you wanted a boy-scientist son and not a girl into television," she admitted with a rising lump in her throat.

"I never said any such thing! You and your mother were always putting words into my mouth! I wouldn't trade you for two dozen sons! I'm so proud of you and all the fine things you've done."

"Thank you, father," she said quietly. Eliza had waited a long time to hear those words.

Chapter Eleven

"That girl moves with all the grace of a bull in a china shop, Eliza," Jared grumbled for the tenth time in less than an hour. "I've directed quarterbacks with more finesse. What are we going to do?"

"I'm not sure yet. The obvious alternative is to shoot background scenery only this time around and return with another actress in the future." Eliza shielded her eyes from the high noon sun and scanned the horizon beyond the beach. "God, Jared, isn't this island beautiful? I've never seen anything like it in my life! The sand is so white, and look at the color of that water!" The Caribbean Sea undulated endlessly before them in half a dozen shades of blue and green. Eliza and her crew had been there for nearly a week now, taking and retaking the same scenes.

"Oh, it's all right," Jared agreed without any enthusiasm. "Wish I could say the same for the girl. It's gonna shoot the hell out of our budget to come back here with another actress for the part. Man, she tested so well." He threw the script onto the oyster-white sand and headed down to the shoreline. "I have to get away from here for a few minutes. I'm going nuts trying to come up with something."

"I'll get Barbara and we'll talk about this." Eliza raised the bullhorn to her mouth. "Take ten, every-

one," she ordered. "Wait, make that half an hour."
She waved Barbara over. Her friend had no on-camera
role in the island scenes but had been anxious to direct
a few episodes for a long time. With her typical persua-
sive tactics, Barbara had talked Eliza into taking her and
her two children down to the small isle south of the
Virgin Islands.

"Well, so much for my directing debut," Barbara
said despairingly when she joined Jared and Eliza.

Jared was hasty to reassure her. "It's not your fault,
kid. Like they say, you can't make a silk purse out of a
sow's ear."

"I've seen a good director bring a scared kid like that
out before. I bet Dario could have pulled this one off."
She was about to expand on Dario's skills as a director
when the frown on Eliza's face silenced her. Since
returning from California two weeks ago, Eliza had
been mum on the subject of Dario. It was common
knowledge on the set that he had accompanied her to
Los Angeles. Barbara assumed the relationship simply
hadn't worked out, and Eliza was trying to forget the
man.

"Maybe Dario could have pulled this one off. I really
don't think so though. Jared and I have both tried to
talk to her. The poor kid just tenses up every time the
camera rolls. Her previous credits were so impressive,
too. She's been on the stage since she was about five or
six. I know it's different playing to a camera rather than
a live audience, but I really thought Mary Kaye could
pull it off. She auditioned well."

Eliza smiled sympathetically at Barbara and patted
her shoulder. It was clear her friend felt terrible about
her failure to salvage the scenes with the young actress
and that she felt equally bad for inadvertently mentioning Dario's name. The rest of her company had treated
her the same way since she returned from California,

astutely avoiding any references to Dario and eyeing
her with the pity usually reserved for recent widows
and orphans. It was all so transparent, though they
surely meant well. As far as she could tell, she only
hurt on the inside, going about her work at the same
frenetic pace, but it must have shown on some level
that was evident to her friends and coworkers. And of
course, she was still upset over her father and hadn't
discussed her primary motivation in going to Los Angeles with anyone yet. Father and daughter were recon-
ciled at last, but both his illness and their newfound
closeness were things Eliza had been able to share with
only Dario as of yet.

Barbara took off her tennis shoes and wiggled her
toes in the sand. "I know how well the kid tested. I saw
the tapes. Shoot, it's too bad HEI wanted everything
done so fast! There should have been time to work
with this girl more before we went on location. What
are we going to do?"

"I have a few ideas," Eliza said. Unlike Barbara, she
didn't need to remove her shoes while they walked along
the beach. She hadn't worn any for nearly a week. Jared
lit up a cigarette, and she chastised him for smoking in
such an unspoiled setting before elaborating on her
thoughts. "I'm thinking about either reversing the roles
of the boy and girl or of going for background shots only
and replacing Mary Kaye at a later date."

Barbara was intrigued by the idea. "You mean the
girl would be the one fleeing from San Juan and ship-
wrecking on the island? That might work. All Mary
Kaye would have to do is lie around unconscious for
the opening episodes."

"I doubt if she could do that," Jared interjected.
"The goofy kid would probably get nervous and start to
giggle when she's supposed to be at death's door."

The temperature was climbing past the mid-eighties.

Eliza picked up a palm frond and began to fan herself. "Oh, I don't think so. Mary Kaye could pull that one off."

"And what do we do when she's supposed to wake up and run off with the boy?" Barbara asked, searching in her pockets for something to tie up her long red hair, which was redder than ever due to a change in tint.

"I guess she'll have to die, or we'll have to get someone who looks like her to play the role...unless she improves, that is," Eliza speculated.

"Well, so much for *Beyond Tomorrow*'s great bid to do the love affair of the century! The girl dies before the boy even learns her name! I don't like it one bit, Eliza," Barbara said emphatically. "I think we should go along with your first suggestion and shoot background and the boy only. It would intrigue the viewers to see this darling young hunk washing ashore on a tropical isalnd and wandering around wearing a loin cloth!" She snapped her fingers together and jumped about three feet into the air. "Hey, I got it! I know how you can film all the island scenes now and still have a great love story!"

"I'm almost afraid to ask how," Eliza giggled. She was beginning to wish she'd worn shorts instead of jeans, but what New Yorker ever thought of shorts in the middle of November?

"Let me play Mary Kaye's role!"

"That's perverted!" Jared hooted with a laugh. "Barbara, you're old enough to be his mother! Besides that, you've played the town slut on the show for five years. I don't think the viewers would be swept away by lusty old Sabra chasing after a seventeen-year-old kid!"

Barbara stuck out her tongue at Jared. "And why not? Sabra is only thirty-five. Last year we had a man nearly forty fall in love with a teenager. Wasn't Terry supposed to be eighteen?" she asked Eliza.

"Yes, but that was different," Eliza responded. Her young viewers had been clamoring for a love story between two teenagers for months, and she knew it wouldn't work to have the woman twice as old as the young man. Not that Eliza had anything against relationships involving older women and men far their junior, but now wasn't the time. Too many storylines had been already written around a pair of star-crossed young lovers.

"Different!" Barbara wailed. "You're as bad as Jared, Eliza! Talk about the old double standard! I thought you would be on my side!"

"Oh, Barbara, if you're bound and determined to have a romance with a younger man in the show, I'll find you one someday, but it wouldn't fly now. There's no way we could work it out if we wanted to. We're airing the tapes of your hiding out in Maine with the baby Sabra kidnapped. How can we show you down on an island in the Caribbean all of a sudden?"

Barbara took her lower lip into her mouth and considered Eliza's question. "Got it! We can have me selling the baby for twenty-five thousand dollars to a pair of childless millionaires and going to the island because I'm afraid of getting arrested!"

Jared and Eliza looked at each other and burst into uncontrollable laughter.

"Talk about the sympathetic heroine in an idyllic romance," Jared said dryly, "an ex-hooker turned town tramp who deals in black market babies! Our viewers won't be able to get enough of it!"

"Oh, phooey on you, Jared! I was only trying to conserve our budget. HEI is going to be mad as hell if we come back from this trip with nothing!"

"Then try coming up with some reasonable suggestions, Babs," Jared replied hastily, slapping Barbara on the bottom.

"Okay, I will. But it would stimulate the creative process greatly for you to get lost for a while, my dearest Jared. Go back and feed my kids and start filming the scenes with Greg. I don't think there's anything else we can do with Mary Kaye for a while. She nearly cried every time I looked at her today," Barbara remarked.

"I know. Poor kid. She's trying so hard, you know," Jared said. "She's such a lovely girl. If we can't use her, there's no way I'm going to break the news. I mean, that girl is really giving it her best shot!"

"She is," Eliza agreed. "That's certainly part of the problem; she's trying too hard."

"Run along now, Jared," Barbara repeated.

"Give me one good reason why I should," he asked, resting one arm on each of their shoulders. "I'm as tired as you two are of trying to work with that girl."

Barbara leaned into him with a seductive swagger. "Because Eliza and I are going to take off our clothes and sunbathe au naturel," she purred.

"Babs!" Eliza shrieked.

"All the more reason to stay," Jared crooned, drawing the two women closer to his body.

Eliza broke free of Jared's embrace. "I think the two of you are suffering from sunstroke."

Jared kissed Barbara's mouth. "Have fun, you dynamic duo!" he called out as he strolled back to the set.

"Guess who snuck into my tent last night?" Barbara said when he was out of hearing range.

"I don't think I have to. You two have been fawning over each other ever since we left San Juan. How serious is it this time?" The two women lay down on the beach.

"As serious as ever."

"That's what I was afraid of. Well, tread easily. Don't break Jared's heart. He lacks your experience in *affaires du coeur*."

"Everyone lacks my experience in affairs, Eliza."

"What happened to the other man? The one you were involved with a few weeks ago?"

"He's on location in Brazil."

"Where does this put Jared when he comes back?"

"Only time can tell. All right, out with it now. I'm sick and tired of seeing you moping. You've been acting like an abandoned puppy ever since your return from California. I thought the fact that Dario flew out with you on a business trip meant things were going well for the two of you. What happened?"

"A business trip? No, Babs, it wasn't that. I wish it had been."

"I don't understand then. What's with all the mystery? Why else do you go out there?"

Eliza rolled over onto her stomach and sifted the fine white sand through her fingers. "My father is dying. He has maybe a year to go at best."

"Oh, Eliza! I had no idea! Everyone thought you and Dario were sewing up some kind of a film deal. He mentioned to Jared that you were interested in producing a film script he'd written."

"I am, but we didn't get around to discussing it with the people we know in Hollywood."

"I can understand why. Just how sick is your dad?"

Eliza told her, her head still resting on the sun-warmed earth.

Barbara could see that her friend preferred not to talk about her father's illness just now and cautiously broached the subject of her ex-husband. "How did your father take seeing Dario after all these years?" She removed some sunscreen from her purse and rubbed it on her face and shoulders and offered the tube to Eliza, who declined it.

"He still doesn't like him, but at least he managed to be polite this time around. It was actually quite awkward. Dario was simply wonderful to go out there with me and put up with such a gloomy situation the way he did."

"And where is this wonderful man now?" Barbara asked. She rolled up her jeans legs as far as they would go and stared at her fair skin. "You're lucky to have such pretty bronze skin. Don't I look deathly pale?"

"No, you look fine. Be careful you don't get too much sun. Redheads burn so easily."

"Well, my red hair is ninety-nine percent natural dyes, so there's nothing to worry about. You still haven't answered my question. Where's Dario?"

"You know where he is, Babs. He had a film to do in Rome."

"I know, but before he told Jared he'd be here when we were. He mentioned something about being responsible for the island because his friend owns it. Obviously that was only an excuse to be with you."

"If that's the case, then his absence must signify he no longer wants to be with me," Eliza said philosophically.

"Maybe he got tied up in Rome or something," Barbara suggested.

"Or something. Let's get back to the set. It's not fair for us to loll out on the beach while everyone else works under the blazing sun."

"Tyrant. And I was just starting to tan, too."

Two people, walking hand in hand, approached them on the beach. "Well, would you look at that!" Eliza murmured as they passed by. It was Mary Kaye and her leading man, Greg Lee Ferber. "Did you see how happy she was? That young lady was all lit up!"

"Yes, too bad she can't light up when the camera rolls. I didn't know those two kids were romantically involved," Barbara commented. "They make a fine looking couple. How old are they?"

"Mary Kaye is seventeen and Greg is twenty. Of course, I've cast them to be a few years younger for the show. I didn't know they were dating either. Or in love, I guess I should say from the looks of those kids. This gives me an idea. Let's film some of the later sequences before we do the opening scenes. If we can get that girl to look at that boy the way she's doing now, we'll have something worth watching, Babs! What do you think?"

"Do you think it would work?"

"At this point, anything's worth a try."

Eliza and her ensemble were winding down an all-night beach party when an unobserved figure approached the noisy merrymakers. He could have been invisible for all that mattered to them, toasting and congratulating one another repeatedly as he sat down on the sandy bluff above the beach. Their every word drifted upward on a briny trade-wind breeze redolent with the scent of tropical blossoms. It was a cast party not unlike many he'd attended himself, and it was clear Eliza was the star of the moment, everyone's darling. Well, that was only fitting and proper. She was his darling, too. He smiled as she shifted the praise from herself to her people. A young black girl he'd never seen before was hugging her and hanging onto Eliza's every word. She was tall and beautiful, and he couldn't help but notice how the young man at her side adored her and kept following her. Even Barbara and Jared were locked in each other's arms. It was a night made for love all right, out there on that windswept beach where the trade-winds blew in humid and sweet. Obviously, the girl with her ebony-skinned boy in tow was in love, Barbara was in love again, the cameraman was trying to lead the sound engineer off into the night, and Eliza was in love, too. It was one vast celebration of love he witnessed, with the woman he loved in love with all of them. Dario wondered where in the hell he fit into this scheme of things.

If he'd ever seen a woman in her natural element before, it was Eliza when she worked with her company. Damn, he thought selfishly, why couldn't she seem just a little down, like she'd missed him just a little? God only knew how much he'd missed her, flying back to Rome, directing that film like a high school amateur because he was too distraught to concentrate, and finally resigning the job before the producer could ask him to leave. All the time he was there, he kept thinking about fifteen years ago when he'd left her for a project in Rome and how he'd spent the next decade and a half wondering what would have happened had he not left her to begin with or had he followed her back to Los Angeles and pleaded his case personally instead of relying upon letters that were destined not to reach her until it was too late. Damn, he was not going to spend the next fifteen years of his life wondering what would have happened had he stayed and loved her this time. A man couldn't go through that kind of torture twice in a lifetime.

Her melodic laughter made his blood run swift with desire, and he wished the wind would stop blowing through the palm trees so he could hear her better.

The wind died down and he heard her speak. "For the last time, Mary Kaye, I didn't do anything! You did it all! You're a very talented young lady. I predict a long and glorious future for you."

"Oh, Eliza, I was horrible until you helped me out today, and you know it! I never could have done a thing if you hadn't switched the scenes to warm me up. I was like a wooden soldier for the last three days!"

The woman he loved laughed again. "Honey, I wasn't the one who warmed you up out on the beach."

"Tell her about it, boss lady," Greg encouraged Eliza. "It was my charm that drew her out, right?"

"I rather think so," Eliza agreed.

"Speaking of inspiring young actresses, Mary Kaye, there's something else I have to show you," Greg said, pulling the slender girl away from where she sat next to Eliza.

"I can imagine," Mary Kaye said. "Good night, Eliza, and thanks again for being so patient with me the last few days. I know how close I came to being replaced."

"Our patience was well worth the wait, Mary Kaye. Our fans are going to love you. Well, good night, you two. Don't forget we're starting at eight tomorrow, I mean this morning," she corrected herself when she saw the first signs of dawn in the sky. The rest of the crew began to wander away. Jared and Barbara said good night, leaving Eliza alone on the beach. She supposed she should be leaving for the campsite herself and try to get some sleep before work began once more, but it was too beautiful a night to leave just yet.

Eliza heard Barbara let out a little yelp when she and Jared reached the top of the bluff, but when she turned around they were gone. She assumed she and Jared were playing some kind of a lover's game. It sounded like such a joyous cry.

Barbara and Jared had stumbled upon Dario on the sand dune above the beach and were quietly requested to leave without calling down to Eliza who was still sitting near the fire. He watched her for a while longer as she sat hugging her knees to her chest and then left his hiding place.

Eliza heard the sound behind her and wasn't alarmed. She assumed some member of the company had decided to stay up and enjoy the beauty of the tropical sunrise along with her.

He would never forget the expression on her face when she saw him for the rest of his life. It was an expression of unspeakable joy, one that reflected his own unbridled happiness at seeing the woman he loved. "Hi," he said softly, approaching Eliza with the wind blowing his hair in ten directions at once. The predawn glow lent it those same unreal shades of silver and black as the studio lights the first time she saw him on her set. "Is that a private party or can anyone join."

Eliza had lain awake every night since they came to the island, fantasizing this very scene, but never had she dared to believe it would come to pass. She held out her hand, and Dario dropped down to the sand next to her. "This is a very private party and only you can join," she whispered in a hushed tone. "What brings you here, Dario?"

He searched for the right words. "Would you believe I thought of a hundred great opening lines on the flight from Italy, and now I can't think of one?"

"Just say what's on your mind. Why are you here?"

"Because of you," he replied in a few words. "I love you, Liza."

That phrase said everything she yearned to hear from him. "Oh, Dario!" She fell into his arms and kissed the bare skin exposed by his unbuttoned shirt. He tasted like the salt water, and there were fine grains of sand on the coarse black-and-white hair. "I thought you just felt sorry for me."

He lifted her head from his chest. "Feel sorry for a woman who has everything? Why on earth would I do that? How could anyone?"

She would have had everything now, if only Dario loved her as much as she loved him. "Because of my father. I thought you went out to California with me as a good friend. Sort of like you owed me a favor for old time's sake; like you wanted once and for all to atone for what happened so long ago. A final act of contrition, if you will, so you could forget about me forever. I didn't think you'd come back, because I was getting too serious about the relationship."

Dario clasped her to his chest so tightly he felt he'd break her and then loosened the hold. My God, how could she think such things? "Well, you were wrong. Tell me one thing, baby, just how serious about this relationship are you?" She'd yet to say the words he longed to hear with all his soul.

"As serious as one can be. I love you. I feel more strongly for you now than I did when I was seventeen, and you know how much I loved you then." She spoke with both hands resting on his chest. Their breaths mingled in the early dawn air, and the fact that they were on one of the most beautiful places in the universe didn't matter to Eliza. She'd love this man of hers on the most god-awful corner of the earth.

"Yes, baby, I'm beginning to know, but I didn't know anything then."

"So where do we go from here?" Eliza knew life was no fairy tale. Dario would probably have to return to Rome soon and she had commitments in New York, and she didn't expect him to renege on anything for her sake. All she demanded to know was when he would return to her again. Just knowing he would be back would be enough.

He heard the unspoken question. "I'm returning to Manhattan with you. I'm not going to run out on the best relationship in my life twice."

"And the film in Rome?"

"To hell with it. It's only a film. Do you have any idea how many I'm offered each year? And how many good relationships? Just two."

"Two?" Eliza exclaimed with a giddy laugh. "And to think I thought you had eyes for only me! Care to inform me about my competition?"

"There is none where you're concerned, Liza, my love. Silly, I meant you now and fifteen years ago. No one else really ever mattered."

"And no one else ever really mattered for me. Where are you going to stay in New York? And what are you going to do?"

In an intimate gesture he clasped her left breast in his hand. "I haven't quite decided yet. The place in the Village is out of the question now. You see, I'm going to concentrate on my book for a while, and there was too much hustle and bustle in that flat, if you know what I mean."

"Absolutely." She had a premonition of his desires so far as living accommodations. "I'm getting cold sitting here. Want to walk along the beach?" she said, rising to her feet with both her hands in his.

"Love it. So what I need is something more peaceful, if you know what I mean," he said for the second time.

"I think so," she reiterated. "What exactly did you have in mind?"

"Hum, something quite exclusive. A good neighborhood. A big old house, with maybe one other person."

"Maybe Gramercy Park?"

"Perhaps. And I'd like a rose garden in the rear."

"How would you feel about a man-eating rabbit on the fourth floor?"

"I could live with it. I prefer dogs, though."

"Any particular kind?"

"Yes, great big shaggy ones that shed all over you."

"Dario, I know just the place."

"Do you?"

"Yes, live with me for as long as you're in New York."

"I want to, Liza, I really want to," he replied, when he wanted above all to ask her to marry him, but he couldn't, not just now. A long time ago, a very long time ago so it seemed now, he'd promised her happiness and forever after and failed to fulfill his promises. There was no doubt in his mind that he'd ever fail her again, but some internal sense forewarned him that deep down he had to prove himself to his lady. Maybe if he lived with her for something beyond a whirlwind courtship of a few months, she would believe in his love.

Eliza took him into her arms. "Then, welcome into my home, my love." She would give him a week to ten days to realize the past had been set aside and perhaps a few days after that for them to be man and wife once more.

He began to lead her to a secluded part of the island. "Why the secretive smile?" he demanded.

"I'll never tell. Dario, where are you taking me?"

"I'm going to take you at a place where we can have some privacy."

Hand in hand they climbed the sandy bluffs over the beach and walked until they came to an abandoned set about a quarter of a mile from the campsite Eliza's people had made. All that remained was a roofless hut that allowed moonlight to illuminate the activities of two impassioned lovers.

"I'll never be able to get enough of you, Liza," Dario murmured as his mouth sought the sweet secret places of her.

"What if I give you a lifetime to do it in?"

"Possibly, love, just possibly."

Chapter Twelve

The six-week-old baby on Dario's left knee reached out for the newspaper her father was reading and managed to rip it down the center. "Don't care for the review, huh, kid? You know, this critic could have been more generous in his praise, but coming from Wilson Dupont it's not bad. Let's see what they have to say about your Mommy and Daddy's movie in the *Times*. Maybe you'll like that one better." He tossed the review section onto the floor and located another one from the coffee table. The little girl in his arms began to wiggle, finally bursting into tears before he could find the movie section. Dario lifted the tiny child over his head and kissed her chubby cheeks. "Is Daddy's little girl hungry?" he crooned softly. The baby quieted down briefly and then resumed her whimpering. "That means yes, doesn't it, little one?" He carried the child over to her mother who sat on the sofa opposite them. "Ready to switch babies now, Liza?"

"Ready. Christopher is almost asleep. Why don't you put him to bed, darling?" She eased her nipple from the baby's mouth.

Dario wiped away a few drops of milk from his son's lips with the cloth that seemed to be over his shoulder more often than not and took the baby, depositing his sister on Eliza's lap. "I don't want to put him to bed now. I've been out all day and haven't had time to play with him." He smiled as his other child groped for her mother's breast. "All right if I sit here and hold him while you feed Angela?"

"If you promise not to wake him up, Dario." Eliza lowered her face and kissed the silky black hair on the baby's head. "Oh, Dario, did you ever see such a beautiful little girl?" She placed one tiny palm in her hand. "Look how small and perfect it is!"

He put Christopher's palm on his. "Just like this one. You must have looked like Angela when you were a baby, Liza."

"Sort of. Did you see the old pictures my father sent over before our babies were born?"

"Yes, I did. He looked so proud holding you. I'm sorry he didn't live long enough to see his grandchildren. He would have loved them."

"I know. Dad was pleased as punch at the prospect of our having twins." It had been nearly six months since her father died, and Eliza was beginning to find it possible to speak about him without that inevitable lump rising to her throat. Professor Rothcart had lived longer than anyone thought he would and had passed away painlessly in his sleep.

"I know. It was all he could talk about when we were in Italy."

"I still can't thank you enough for agreeing to let him take the trip with us," she said. The baby girl continued to suckle at her breast, and her parents continued to watch her with a sense of profound amazement and love unique to new mothers and fathers. "She eats more than Christopher, I think."

"It seems to me they both spend a lot of time there. One of my favorite places in the whole world has been usurped by a pair of greedy little cherubs," he commented. Dario nuzzled his coarse beard against his son's head. The baby stirred and randomly opened his mouth against his father's alpaca sweater. "No can do, son." Dario kissed him and swayed the boy in his arms until he fell asleep once more.

"And it seems to me you still manage to occupy plenty of time there, my love."

"All the time I can. You must feel like earth mother sometimes. Angela seems to have had her fill. She's sleeping. Let's put the two of them to bed and try for another pair," he suggested as he caressed the dark-haired baby at his wife's breast. Both her breasts were exposed, and Dario reached for the one Christopher had just nursed from. "Liza, I'm so glad the six weeks is up. It's been nearly two and a half months since we could make love right."

"We've been doing it wrong?" she teased, well aware Dario was referring to the standard abstinence from marital relations before and after the birth of a child.

He leaned over and kissed the rise of her breast, right above the baby's mouth. "I've been fairly content, but it's not the same."

"I know, darling. I was so tempted to ask the doctor for a reprieve to get back to normal earlier, but I knew you'd want to be conservative. Let's hurry and get the babies to bed, okay?"

"Fine with me. We gonna try for two more?" he repeated.

Eliza giggled. "This pair will do quite nicely for a while, my dear." She removed her breast from the perfect little mouth and passed the baby to Dario. "But I wouldn't mind doing what we did to make them."

"That's my girl. Do the babies need to be changed before I put them into their cradles?" he asked with his eyes fixated on the new fullness in his wife's breasts.

"There's only one way to find out," she reminded

him. Eliza accompanied Dario to the nursery next to their bedroom. "They should be dry though. Mrs. O'Riley bathed and changed them before she gave them to me to nurse."

"Dry as a bone." Dario secured his children in the side-by-side brass cradles. He seemed reluctant to leave, and Eliza crept up behind him, resting her head on his back. "Who do you think looks more like me, Christopher or Angela?"

"Neither, they both look like me. You don't see any beards or graying hair, do you?" She slipped her hands under his sweater, stroking the firm flesh beneath.

"Give my boy time. Did you notice how they were the prettiest babies in the hospital?"

"Oh, Dario! I'm sure every father thought his were the prettiest babies, or baby, in the hospital!" she laughed.

"Well, mine really were. Your friend's baby was all red and bald. Ours had curly black hair and beautiful olive complexions, didn't they?" he insisted.

"That they did. Come on now, let's go. I'm so anxious to make love with you. But I want to take a bath first. Come sit with me."

"Want me to read you the latest reviews while you take your bath?" Dario bent down and kissed his babies.

"Yes, I do." Eliza kissed them afterward, and together they tiptoed from the room. "But just read the good ones, okay?"

"They're all good, love. I'll go downstairs and get the papers. Jared gave me some from Boston today when I dropped by the Brooklyn studio." Eliza was already in the tub when he returned, and Dario had great difficulty in taking his eyes off his wife's body long enough to read.

"Well?" she said expectantly. "Read."

"I'd rather look at you."

"You'll have all night for that."

"Or at least until two in the morning when that little pair of monsters wake up howling for their mother's milk." Since the birth of his children six weeks earlier, it was Dario who changed their diapers and brought them to the bed he shared with Eliza for her to feed, not falling back to sleep until she did.

"You love it! Come on, Dario, read the reviews to me. I've been so busy with *Beyond Tomorrow* and the babies this week that I haven't had time to look at any."

"Kiss me first, you fool," he said, bending over the tub.

"I'm going to get you all wet," Eliza warned him. She wrapped a pair of dripping arms around his neck and brushed her lips across his.

"I've become accustomed to such things, my dear. There, now I can concentrate." He cleared his throat and began to read. "'*Broken Promises*, a new release by Rothcart-Napoli Productions, premiered in three hundred theaters coast to coast this week.' Hey, wait a minute, wasn't that supposed to be Napoli-Rothcart Productions?" he asked with a smile.

"I won the coin toss, remember?"

"The one where you said heads you win and tails I lose?"

"The very same. Go on, Dario. I want to hear about how brilliant everyone thinks we are."

"Okay." He continued reading. "'Audience reaction was mixed...'"

"Mixed? Oh, Dario, I thought you said everyone loved it!"

"Patience, my dear. 'Audience reaction was mixed between those who simply loved it and those who loved it so much they left the theater after the movie to buy a second ticket for the later showing.'"

"Oh, isn't that nice? What else do they say?"

"Let's see, there's a summary of the film here, you don't need that, then it talks about the actors. Everyone agrees that Mary Kaye and Greg did outstanding jobs in their movie debuts. Do you want to hear that part?"

"Yes, read it to me."

Dario quoted the highlights from the lengthy review and then skipped to the end of the article. "Listen to this. 'Take heart, you lovers of happy endings. Although Mr. and Mrs. Napoli have never publicly admitted that this screenplay, which has catapulted two young black actors to instant stardom, is based upon their own early marriage to each other sixteen years ago, this critic has it on the best information that the movie was indeed highly biographical. Though the film ends unhappily for the pair of young lovers, such was not the case for the characters upon whom it was based. Remarried after a long separation, the Napolis recently became the parents of a beautiful set of twins and are currently residing in Manhattan after they met again at the HEI Studio in Brooklyn.' Etcetera, blah, blah," he concluded, setting the paper aside. Eliza stood in the tub and was enveloped in a huge velour towel.

"What was the etcetera, blah, blah, part?" she demanded with a giggle.

"That, my love, is where they go on more about your great accomplishments in the exciting world of daytime drama than about the films I've made." He dried her off with slow, deliberately seductive motions.

"Jealous?" she asked sweetly, resting her palms on his shoulders while Dario crouched to his knees to dry her legs.

"Hardly. Who do you think supplied some of the information to this critic when he called the studio last week?" he returned with his mouth buried against the soft curve of her abdomen.

"Jared?" she teased as her fingers combed through his hair.

"Guess again."

"I don't have to. I know you gave an interview. When I gave mine to the reporter from Chicago, you were all I could talk about, too. Let's go to bed now, darling. I want you so much."

"I want you more," he argued.

"Impossible. Oh, Dario, what was in those little boxes you brought home with you tonight? You said it was something for the babies, didn't you?" Eliza asked just as he was about to turn off the lights and get into bed with her.

"I'll show you." He retrieved two velvet boxes from their dresser and handed them to Eliza.

"Oh, Dario, how sweet," she gasped when she opened them to see a pair of miniature Saint Christopher medals. Eliza rotated one to read the inscription on the back, the one she knew she'd find before she turned it over. "Don't ever forget the road back home," she murmured. That was what she had had engraved on the medal she had given her husband sixteen years ago. "But, of course, they can't wear these yet, you know; they'd put them into their mouths," she said practically.

"I know that, you silly. It's just something I felt like buying when I passed a jewelry shop on Fifth Avenue today." He took the boxes from her hands. "Come here, Liza, we have some very important work to do now. Millions of people are counting on us." He climbed under the blanket with her and rolled Eliza onto his chest.

"To do what?"

"Have a dozen kids in the sequel to *Broken Promises*."

"You're crazy."

"Yes, crazy about you."

She opened her mouth to thank him for the gift of his love that had transformed her life into something more glorious and full than anything she'd ever imagined, but Dario was quick to cover her lips with his. It didn't matter. They understood each other and there was no need for words. Her husband was home at last.

Get this book FREE!

Mail to:

Harlequin Reader Service

In the U.S.
2504 West Southern Ave.
Tempe, AZ 85282

In Canada
P.O. Box 2800, Postal Station A
5170 Yonge St., Willowdale, Ont. M2N 5T5

YES! I want to be one of the first to discover

Harlequin American Romance. Send me FREE and without
obligation *Twice in a Lifetime.* If you do not hear from me after I
have examined my FREE book, please send me the 4 new
Harlequin American Romances each month as soon as they
come off the presses. I understand that I will be billed only $2.25
for each book (total $9.00). There are no shipping or handling
charges. There is no minimum number of books that I have to
purchase. In fact, I may cancel this arrangement at any time.
Twice in a Lifetime is mine to keep as a FREE gift, even if I do not
buy any additional books.

154-BPA-NAXF

Name   (please print)

Address   Apt. no.

City   State/Prov.   Zip/Postal Code

Signature (If under 18, parent or guardian must sign.)

This offer is limited to one order per household and not valid to current Harlequin
American Romance subscribers. We reserve the right to exercise discretion in
granting membership. If price changes are necessary, you will be notified.

Offer expires December 31, 1984.

AMR-SUB-2